on a

WING

and a

PRAYER

Arun Sarma is a noted litterateur and playwright from Assam who has the rare distinction of being the only Assamese to have won both the Sahitya Akademi and the Sangeet Natak Akademi awards. He began his career as a journalist and went on to become Director, All India Radio, North Eastern Service—a post he held till his retirement. In 2010, he was honoured with the Padma Shri.

Maitreyee Siddhanta Chakravarty is a freelance translator, editor and Assamese language consultant. Her first translation, *The Hour Before Dawn,* was shortlisted for the Vodafone Crossword Book Award. She lives in Bangalore with her husband and daughter.

on a

WING

and a

PRAYER

*

ARUN SARMA

translated by Maitreyee Siddhanta Chakravarty

RUPA

Published by
Rupa Publications India Pvt. Ltd 2013
7/16, Ansari Road, Daryaganj
New Delhi 110002

Sales centres:
Allahabad Bengaluru Chennai
Hyderabad Jaipur Kathmandu
Kolkata Mumbai

ISBN: 978-81-291-2395-4

10 9 8 7 6 5 4 3 2 1

The moral right of the author has been asserted.

Typeset by Recto Graphics, New Delhi

Dedicated to the memory of my Mama and Mami with whom I started reading novels in my school days.

—Arun Sarma

To Arun Moha, for his unconditional faith in me, and to my family for their support and encouragement.

—Maitreyee Siddhanta Chakravarty

1

A night in July 1935. The *Misimi* floats on the Brahmaputra. Mansoor Ali, lying fast asleep on a wooden bunk, is jolted awake by the honking of the ship's horn. The cabin, allotted to engine-men Rehmat Khan and Karim Khan, is tiny, and he isn't authorized to be inside, but a sequence of events has led to a special arrangement for him to be here.

◆

A little before reaching port, an accident in the engine room all but severed the fingers on Karim Khan's right hand. The bleeding wouldn't stop in spite of the tight cloth bandage; his clothes, too, were spattered red. Sailing at full speed, the *Misimi* arrived at a port and docked to a flat called the *Lahoti*. The ship's master, serang, sukhani and lascars conferred with the flat's headman and storekeeper and agreed that Karim Khan should be sent ashore right away.

Another reason for sending Karim ashore was the availability of a car—nay, a cart, a buffalo cart with motor-car tyres. Borthakur, an estate supervisor, was travelling to his village home in Upper Assam, having timed his annual leave around his father's death anniversary. While waiting, he had announced to the port staff that his manager had asked him to ride to the ghat in his Ford; and he had to make do with the cart only because the car had to go into the district to fetch medicines for the memsahib, who had a cold. This cart was now returning empty to the estate.

The ghat headman shared a special relationship with managers of the neighbouring estates. Tea crates, which were routinely shipped to Kolkata, needed to be stacked before they were loaded, and the lack of godown space was a perennial problem. So the managers forged an 'amicable arrangement' with the ghat staffers. Now the headman wrote to the estate manager that Karim Khan was being carted to an estate hospital, and signed the letter 'Your most obedient servant'. There was no other option—the only medical assistance available in the area was at the estate hospitals, or at the district headquarters.

Two crewmen led a moaning Karim Khan to the cart. The *Misimi* unhitched itself and floated into the wide expanse of the river, its long hoots deflected by the waters and reverberating through the entire area.

Karim's colleague Rehmat took over his duties, controlling the steam engine according to signals telegraphed from the cabin-master on deck—'stop-ahead-half-full', 'stop-back-half-full'... The engine-men's double-deck cabin was empty, and that bothered Rehmat. A few months ago, in spite of people milling all around, somebody had sneaked into his empty cabin and stolen his money. So he requested the off-duty junior fireman Mansoor Ali to sleep there, and the man now lay on one of the bunks.

•

Mansoor blinked awake and raised his head to take stock of things. Apart from the horn, he heard swift telegraph signals and then the whir of anchor chains being lowered. They hadn't reached port yet, although the sounds were the same. Something must have happened again! Peeping into the moonlight through a porthole, he saw the riverbank at a distance, tall grasses masking the horizon. They must be midway between two ports, he gathered—probably near the vast grasslands by the Kuroi river.

Suddenly he realized that the ship, which had been moving upstream, was slowing down. The excited clamour of the crew added to the noises. There was no point sitting there and speculating— he might as well step outside and find out. Leaving the cabin and turning towards the engine room, he yelled, 'What's up?'

'Sandy bank,' someone replied from below.

Mansoor didn't quite catch what was said. 'What?' he repeated.

But Rehmat and the others were too busy to reply. Mansoor moved ahead to the anchor post. The clanging continued as the anchor moved down, and the ship slowly moved backwards. The crewmen were busy gauging the depth of the water with oar poles and calling out their finds into pipes placed near their mouths—shallow, one unit deep, two units and so on. The pipes carried the information to the master in the steering cabin overhead, who then mapped out the course and conveyed it to the engineman below through telegraph signals.

•

Mansoor learnt that heavy silting upstream had blocked the course, which had earlier been marked out by hurricane lamps mounted on posts. The master and serang were doubtful about charting a changed course at this dark hour and decided to wait until a viable solution was found.

Mansoor stood at the foremost tip of the vessel and looked far out. To his left lay the riverbank and extensive grasslands. A familiar sight—he knew this area. To the right, all he could see was water, but that was where the silting had happened—a sandbank in mid-monsoon! Ten days or so of sunshine had dried up much of the water, and some earth. Yes, it was possible to encounter a sandbank in such circumstances. He learnt that the ship would remain moored for the rest of the night. At the break of dawn, the lighthouse man would come in a boat, and they would set sail once a new course was charted.

Mansoor walked up to the deck. The passengers were either fast asleep in their tiny beds on the wooden floor or debating possible causes for their sudden midstream halt. Their excited uncertainty triggered various reactions. Those who neared their destination were thankful to have an extra couple of hours' sleep on board the ship instead of having to wait out the rest of the night in a crowded ghat boat where finding space would be almost impossible, thanks to the cargo boat invariably attached to it. Most commodities reached Assam through Kolkata, usually arriving by ship. Dispatch ships towed cargo-laden boats. Once offloaded, they were reloaded with thousands of tea crates before they returned to Kolkata and Diamond Harbour through the Hooghly. Apart from these, 500 to 1,000-tonne boats, solely the domain of Bihari tradesmen, carried foodstuffs into the state.

Mansoor wove his way through rows of passengers in various stages of repose and reached the canvas-walled room where Hindu passengers on board could get a meal cooked by a Bihari Brahmin. Huge pots of rice, dal, fried potatoes and fish curry, cooked on the lower deck, were placed on one side of the room. Diners sat on peeras and were served in large, gleaming brass plates on the floor, the meal costing anything between eight and twelve annas. Mansoor loved the perpetual aroma of this food. The curries in his lower deck dining area had their own unique scents, as did the food the chefs cooked for the few—four to six at the most—first-class passengers on the front deck, usually estate managers—European sahibs and memsahibs. But somehow, to him, the Bihari cook's dishes smelt the best of all.

The canvas flap that served as the diner door was hitched up. Inside, the huge figure of the cook lay asleep on the floor, snoring loudly. Mansoor inhaled deeply and moved on to the stern of the ship, an area reserved for second-class passengers. There wasn't much space here—just two wooden benches along the walls. A small family—perhaps two—could fit in if they made their beds on the floor.

A group that included estate supervisor Borthakur was busy at a card game. They had played into the wee hours and were about to wind up when the ship's sudden stoppage shook them out of their fatigue and inspired them to continue. For a brief moment, Borthakur was distracted from his game—if much time was wasted by this halt, they wouldn't reach Nimati Ghat before dark. By then, the tea-laden tractors and carts on which he could hitch a ride to

Jorhat would stop plying, and he would have to spend another night on a ghat flat. He called out his cards…

•

Back in the cabin, Mansoor found Rehmat stretched out on a bunk. He wasn't asleep; now that the ship was at a standstill, there was nothing for him to do, although, being on shift duty, he needed to monitor the fireman on duty in the fuel chamber.

'Hey, where have you been roaming? Go to sleep,' said Rehmat to Mansoor. He then picked up a bundle from under his bunk, slung a gamcha over his shoulder, and stepped outside. Soon it would be time for the morning namaaz. Mansoor hoisted himself onto Karim Khan's mat-lined bunk and lay down as the commotion outside slowly subsided.

The ship's horn jolted Mansoor awake once again. Through the open porthole, he saw that it was faintly light outside. They seemed to be moving. It wasn't quite daybreak and his duty wasn't until many hours later. He stretched out and fell asleep.

'Hey, wake up. How long do you plan to sleep?' This time, it was Rehmat who made him fumble to a sitting position and rub his eyes. It was bright outside. But wait, the ship was still. Were they at some port? 'Which ghat is this?' he asked.

'What ghat? The ship is exactly where she was last night. She reversed for a bit and stopped again.'

'Why?'

'In these last three hours, there has been silting behind us too. It's going to be tough getting out of here.'

'Wha- ? So what happens now?'

'The lighthouse man is checking the area to see if he can find a way out.'

'And if he can't?'

'A dispatch ship can tow us from a distance. Otherwise they will have to get a dredger from Kolkata and carve out a course. Of course, by then the waters may rise by themselves—if it rains in the hills.'

'Haven't seen anything like this in the last five years.'

'Something like this happened soon after I joined as crew on the *Jamuna*. The signalman made a mistake and we were stuck on a sandbank until a dredger arrived three days later.'

Mansoor left the cabin and surveyed the ship once again. Most of the passengers were trying to gauge the shape of things to come.

The first problem would be food—how long could the one diner and one tea-stall on deck hold out? The ship did not have much extra stock. Many passengers had no money to spare; and the more orthodox ones wouldn't eat out. Besides, maintaining the minimum engine temperature meant using up the stocks of coal.

And these, together, signalled imminent danger.

◆

The *Misimi* lay stranded. The hours ticked by. This could continue for half a day, a whole day or even two, mused Mansoor. However, clouds were gathering over the blue hills on the northern horizon and if it rained there, the water level in the Brahmaputra would rise in a matter of hours; and the ship now lay towards its north bank. But whether they moved or not, the fireman had to be on duty in the boiler and fuel chamber. Mansoor's duty would start in the afternoon.

If only he could get into one of the signal boats and sail around the area for a bit! Perhaps he could even pick up some vegetables on the shore. But wait—why did he need a boat at all? He could easily swim the short distance to the bank. He'd swum longer distances before, spanning the river eight to ten times, non-stop, in his village in Chittagong.

Now that his mind was made up, he could wait no longer. Draping a blue checked gamcha around his waist, he tied his lungi around his head and lowered himself into the water by the anchor chain.

◆

Sloshing through the muddy grassland, Mansoor soon reached the dry riverbank. A tiny lane led through rows of silk-cotton trees and thick shrubbery, straw and thatching grass at their base. Moving along this, he eventually landed near a big river—probably the Kuroi that merged with the Brahmaputra slightly further on. He walked on until he chanced upon a vast open space stretching right down to the river, a thick forest on one side and grasslands on the other. There was a field to one side and beyond that, far away, signs of a village. A row of tall trees etched a dark horizon. Some scattered hutments, a herd of cows or buffaloes...

Mansoor felt a strange, tingling excitement. So much uncultivated land—not an ear of paddy, not a strand of jute! He moved further ahead. Finally, he saw a well-built man coiling ropes beside a rubbish dump outside a long cowshed. He tried to strike up a conversation, but that wasn't easy—Mansoor spoke in his Mymensingh dialect and the man replied in Nepali. Neither understood the other fully but made do by throwing in a few Hindi or Bengali words every now and then. And in spite of his limited comprehension, Mansoor gathered some very important information that steered his life in a totally new direction.

◆

Mansoor learnt that the miles of barren expanse that lay before him had no owner—there was no zamindar and no headman like there was in his village. Whoever wished to raise crops or livestock here could do so. The river he had seen was indeed the Kuroi, and from here until where it met the Brahmaputra, it was flanked by a bank that was legendary in its fertility. Yes, in this place, the Kuroiguri Sapori, every seed that fell to the ground would sprout gold!

Was this a dream? wondered Mansoor. There was land, land, and more land. It could be nothing short of a living dream.

His Nepali friend offered him some thick yellow curd made from buffalo milk, and its creaminess remained on his fingers even after Mansoor wiped them on the grass. He got up to leave. On his way back to the ship, he turned back many a time for yet another glimpse of this vast dreamland. The sight continued to haunt him long after he was aboard the ship.

◆

The *Misimi* lay moored in Kuroiguri for the entire day. Some of the passengers took the signalman's boat—or one that he had arranged—to shore and either walked or made other arrangements to reach their destination. But the others, especially those travelling to the southern bank, had no such option. The south bank was home to the forests of Kaziranga, and it was unrealistic to think of crossing that stretch to reach a road beyond. However, in the early afternoon, the Bihari cook had gone ashore and returned with vegetables from a village further up the northern bank and fish from fishermen's boats. The deck chef, too, managed to get hold of a couple of chickens. Tonight's dinner could be managed all right, although the orthodox passengers would have a problem as their personal stocks of beaten rice were almost empty. Some had brought along no food at all because once aboard, it was taboo to let so much as a drop of water pass through their lips.

As the cooks brought their acquisitions onto the ship, estate supervisor Borthakur bombarded them with questions—what did they get, how and from where, and so on. He ought to eat nothing but the bland ritual food since it was his father's annual ceremony the following day. But he wasn't going to get home in time anyway... He looked at the large silvery fish hanging from the cook's hands and was tantalized by the thought of a good meal later on.

It started raining around midnight and continued to pour almost until dawn. In the morning, the crew were heard saying that since it had also rained through the night in the Dafala hills, the water would flow into the Brahmaputra through the Kuroi and Ranga rivers, as well as some minor streams, and the sand-drifts would soon be submerged. This could take three to four hours, but before long, the ship would find a way out.

On the upper deck, the master's eyes, fixed on the blue hills in the distance, gleamed with hope. Suddenly, he saw two crewmen jump into the water and swim towards the shore, soon becoming almost invisible. One was Mansoor and the other, Kader, the oarsman, who also helped with the anchor. Once Mansoor gathered that they wouldn't be around for long, he wished to see the land of his dreams one more time; and this time, he invited Kader to come along. The latter was hesitant at first, but the promise of creamy milk and yoghurt was too tempting to resist.

Mansoor and Kader couldn't take their eyes off the soft, green, ownerless expanse as they walked towards the buffalo shed. Presently, they saw the Nepali man Mansoor had met earlier, and the two struck up a conversation once again. Mansoor had described his find to Kader the previous evening with unbridled enthusiasm— it was as though he knew more about the lay of the land than anyone else. The Nepali man once again fed them creamy yoghurt to their hearts' content. Then the three of them walked, chatting in their mixed tongues, to a point by the Kuroi about two miles from where it met the Brahmaputra. They noticed that the waters were rising rapidly, frothing as they swirled. Yes, the water from the hills was moving towards the Brahmaputra—its level was sure to rise. The *Misimi* was docked due west of Kuroimukh and they could see wisps of smoke from it. They took leave of their Nepali friend, walked through the undergrowth along the Kuroi and returned to the ship.

◆

Twice every week, for a year after the *Misimi*'s two-day confinement in the sands, Mansoor sailed past the Kuroiguri Sapori. Each time, he felt the virtual softness of the sands below his feet, and they roused in him a tingling lust for the land. He surrendered himself to the dream, like a youth surrendering to the seductive allure of his lady love. One day, accompanied by his young wife Nerisa and four-year-old daughter Hasina, who had left their unknown little village in Chittagong, he boarded the *Dhansiri* and alighted a port short of the Kuroiguri ghat. They spent the night on the shore boat and in the morning, they sailed upstream in a fishing boat to the expansive dreamland.

A month earlier, Mansoor had spent a few days in Kuroiguri with his Nepali friend Kaila and made plans for this trip. He had repaired a part of a cowshed that Kaila had abandoned. Now, depositing their few belongings in this shed, he took his wife and daughter to the banks of the Kuroi and set up a hearth under a huge silk-cotton tree. It was here that Nerisa cooked the first meal in their new home while Hasina amused herself, building sandcastles by the riverside.

Thus began a new chapter in the life of Mansoor Ali and his small family.

Kader Khan had promised that very shortly, he would bring his parents from Chittagong and join Mansoor in the Kuroiguri Sapori. He lived up to his word—and another new family moved in to settle there.

Soon, one more family moved in; then another... And another... Until there were many.

2

The first reasonably populated village, a few miles from Kuroiguri, was Sonaruchuk, home to a young man named Gojen. He lived with his old grandmother, his only family. His mother had died of dysentery when he was little and his father, Holodhor Keunt, had been renowned for his temper...

◆

Khargi mauzadar, the revenue collector, who had risen to the post fairly early in life, was a powerful man in the area, with an ongoing difference of opinion with the villagers regarding the boundaries of their fields. Holodhor and his friends had got their land leases converted from annual to long ones, so the mauzadar kept interfering whenever he got a chance. Holodhor's volatile temper and sharp tongue deterred the mauzadar from accosting them directly. But one day, his hired tea labourers reaped all the grains from several fields and stacked them in his threshing yard, and the same night, several of those stacks were reduced to ashes in a fire. It was nothing short of a miracle that the huge paddy barns nearby were unharmed.

This was Holodhor's handiwork. But although he was accompanied by a couple of other men, he took sole responsibility for the arson, both in his statement to the police and at the trial that followed. His argument was that the task could be achieved by one man; he had taken the lead and there was no reason for his companions to get involved and go to jail. So he entered the witness box alone; the others were absolved.

Holodhor's confession was straight and simple. The only regret he voiced to the police—and later, the magistrate—was that although he had done the right thing by starting the fire, he had made a grave mistake by not targeting Khargi mauzadar instead of the grains. His real job remained undone! He told the policeman: 'Daroga babu, the fire caught as soon as I started it, and I watched the blaze from a distance. That afternoon, the village folk had gathered for the harvest feast. They had stayed up all night watching a bhaona, and after the feast, they were all fast asleep. Khargi mauzadar got his labourers into our fields while they were feasting. You know what, Daroga babu? I felt my chest as I watched the fire—it was the fire in my heart that blazed before my eyes. My eyes—and my whole body—seemed to multiply and dance before me as I craned my neck. I inhaled deeply when the smell of burning paddy reached me. Have you ever smelt paddy burning, Daroga babu? No, of course not. Who on earth would burn paddy, of all things? I was sad. Wasn't some of that paddy from my own fields—the product of the sweat of my brow, of the hot sunshine beating down on Gojen's mother's bare back...? Daroga babu, my mind wilted at the thought. What had I done? I, the demon, had set fire to the goddess of my own fields! What a terrible sin I had committed! How contemptible! My heart trembled, and I could stay there no longer. As I walked home, the smoky scent remained with me. Then I remembered something. You know, when you return from a cremation, a smoky smell remains with you, but that is the smell of burning human flesh, not paddy. Suddenly, Daroga babu, a thought flared up in my mind. Really, Daroga babu, I swear on my son, I felt I should have spared the paddy and burnt Khargi mauzadar alive instead. Then the smell in my nose wouldn't be that of burning paddy, but of burning flesh—Khargi mauzadar's flesh...'

'Shut up, will you? This man simply won't shut his trap!' The policeman pounded the table hard with his fist and the man stopped speaking.

Holodhor was imprisoned for three years. The day after his release, he went to his fields to find that the mauzadar had encroached far into them and raised the boundary fence. Strangely, he had not touched the lands of any of his associates and had no plans of doing so. From the gossip his mother had heard, Holodhor learnt that the other men had fallen at Khargi's feet and declared that although they were instigated by their friend who had spoken of the mauzadar in most uncomplimentary terms, they had nothing to do with him or his deeds. Holodhor forced himself not to react. Since his release, he had sensed a strange aloofness in the villagers' attitude towards him. It was probably because he was now a tainted man, an ex-prisoner.

A more significant event during Holodhor's jail term was the sudden death of his wife. She had had dysentery and had not survived the night. His mother's postcard containing this news had reached him a month and a half later. Once he was back home, his ageing mother and young son did all they could to ease the pain of their long separation, but the house felt empty and he keenly felt his wife's absence. He felt like a misfit in his household as well as among the village folk. A few days later, he left the house on the pretext of going on a pilgrimage, never to return there again.

◆

Gojen's grandmother was sad. Every now and then, she pleaded with the boy, 'Do go and ask around—see if anyone has any news of your father.'

To this, the boy would reply, 'If your son doesn't think of you and return home, why should you worry about him? And if he's passed on to the afterlife, what good will asking around do?' Gojen didn't care to find out about his father. He charted out his own course of life and went ahead accordingly.

Gojen was a late riser. He didn't need to work on his fields—whatever returns he got from his leased-out land was enough to sustain him and his grandmother for the year. He started each day by chopping firewood. When the quota for his home was done, he ambled over to his friends' homes and called out, 'Hey, pass me the axe—let me do some chopping.' This eagerness was triggered not by the need for firewood but by his desire to keep himself fit.

◆

Gojen had chopped a large amount of wood under the jackfruit tree and was sitting with one leg raised onto an old chair on the veranda, kneading a wad of tobacco in his palm. To one side lay the small barn, and under the same roof, his grandmother's loom. Beside these, on three stone hearths, the paddy bubbled in three giant kerahis. Placing the wad of tobacco between his teeth and lower lip, Gojen stepped into the courtyard and looked up at the sky. The sun shone strong, although masked by clouds. No, these weren't rain clouds—these were the flighty clouds that sometimes played hide-and-seek with the sunshine. This was the sort of weather in which the fish swam close to the surface. The Kuroi's banks would be teeming.

Gojen walked to the barn and picked up the long, narrow bamboo he had rested against its wall a couple of days ago. When he saw the boiling paddy, he called out to his grandmother, 'Aai, take this stuff off the fire—the paddy's bursting.' Seeing no sign of the old lady, he mumbled, 'God knows where this one's gone—is she dead or what?' He turned the paddy with a straining ladle, lifted the wok off the fire, holding the edges with the gamosa he was wearing, and placed it on the ground.

The old woman must have gone to pick the fallen paan leaves in the neighbour's areca grove. He had forbidden her to do so many times, but would she listen? No way. Just let her get home today! Gojen shaved the bamboo smooth and heated the joints and crooked parts to straighten them out. He retrieved an old box from inside the house. This contained fishing hooks of various sizes, silk thread and pieces of lead. Tucked away in the veranda roof was a piece of pith for the float. He had his fishing gear assembled in no time. Propping the rod against the veranda roof, he picked up a hoe and a machete and made his way to the backyard.

Beyond the small rear courtyard was a small bamboo grove. The ground here was perpetually covered with dry leaves—a soft carpet that yielded with every step. A dank odour—a sort of darkness—hung around the area. When he was younger, he was afraid to venture here alone, and the only times he had come were with his father. He had also heard that this grove was haunted.

Gojen's paternal aunt, who was married and lived far away, had a daughter named Romola who was about his age. During their childhood, every time they visited, this cousin dragged Gojen to the grove to look for the leafless purple blooms that sprouted from the ground. She also teased him about his fear of coming here alone. Sometimes she picked the flowers by herself, and Gojen was amazed at her courage. This was about fifteen years ago, when they were about nine years old.

Romola was now married and a mother of two. Even so, every time she visited, she took Gojen to the grove, and they laughed at their shared childhood memories. They both felt a strange excitement in its eerie atmosphere. Romola, now a woman in full bloom, still led Gojen by the hand as she had done years ago, and often teased him, pulling his hair or pinching his cheeks to scare him—'Hey Gojen! I'm the spirit of the grove and I'm going to haunt you now.' And they would both burst into laughter.

The grove, therefore, evoked memories of Romola every time Gojen entered it, and the memories tingled his senses.

•

Gojen instinctively knew which bamboos had borer-worms in them. He would listen carefully for the grating noise from within, and when he had cut a few nodes, there they would be. Of course, the bamboo was ruined, and it upset his grandmother. When other boys came asking for the worms, the old lady didn't let them anywhere near the grove and shooed them away, actually giving chase if anyone attempted to steal any. But Gojen chided her, 'All they want is a few worms. Let them take some. Why break your head over it?'

'Doesn't it hurt the bamboo to be hacked like that?'

'Ah! It's not as if anyone's hacking *you*! Hurts the bamboo indeed! Come on boys, I'll get you what you want.' With that, Gojen himself would chop the bamboo and give them the worms. Needless to say, the boys loved him and never failed to inform him when they found a wasp's nest. He would then fish with them at the nearby stream, using the wasp larvae as bait. But that was just to keep them company. For him, real fishing was when he spent an entire day by the Kuroi in uninterrupted solitude. And that was what he would do today.

◆

Gojen filled a length of bamboo with the worms he had gathered and wrapped some fat earthworms in a crocus leaf. He set these beside his fishing rod and, slinging his gamosa over his shoulder, was setting off to take a dip in the pond in his backyard when he heard the bamboo gate being opened. Turning around, he saw Konloura and Rupai hurrying towards him.

'What's the matter, Konloura?' he asked, moving towards them.

'Come with us, Gojen,' said Konloura. 'Khargi mauzadar's men are setting up a fence around the village pond. Many of our people have already assembled there.'

'The mauzadar's men are fencing the pond? But why?' asked Gojen.

'Apparently, according to the last survey, the pond is a part of the mauzadar's estate. Now he wants to make it a part of his backyard.'

Gojen absently looked up at the sky, where wispy clouds floated about in patches. Konloura wondered whether he had heard him at all and tried to draw his attention. 'Look, Gojen, is this right? The pond belongs to the people. That is where we catch the fish for the Magh Bihu feast. In the dry season, the village livestock drink from it. Is it right that a public pond should become private property?'

Gojen shifted his gaze from the sky to Konloura's face, but his expression remained unfathomable. As soon as the other had finished speaking, he said, 'Come along' and strode purposefully ahead, his friends at his heels. At one point, they left the road and cut across a field to save time. Closer to the pond, they heard a loud gunshot from its far side and saw people clambering out of its sloping bank and running helter-skelter across the field, some of them tripping over as they fled the scene.

Gojen recognized his village folk. 'What's the matter? Why are you all running like this?' he asked in surprise as they ran past him.

Most had no time to answer. But one of them turned around from a distance and yelled out a single word—'Mauzadar.' To which another added, 'Gun.'

'Gun?' said Gojen to himself. He looked quizzically towards Konloura and Rupai and then the pond. On its high bank he saw Khargi mauzadar, gun in hand, staring at the field and yelling at the people, 'Don't you know who I am? I'll shoot each one of you if you dare fight my men!'

Gojen moved forward until he was right beneath the mauzadar and scanned the pond's periphery. The labourers had dug deep holes all around and were beginning to plant the bamboo posts, some of which lay stacked near where he stood. His eyes glinted as they moved from the stack to the mauzadar. Khargi suddenly recalled that this was exactly how Gojen's father Holodhor's eyes had glinted as they looked upon him on various occasions.

The mauzadar rested his gun on the ground, nozzle upwards, and leaned against it. 'What, eh?' he asked Gojen. 'How come you are still facing this way?'

Gojen's eyes scanned the fenced portion of the pond once again and then turned to the gun.

'What? Do you have anything to say?' the mauzadar prodded.

'Deuta, why are you getting the pond fenced?' asked Gojen meekly.

'It's mine, so I'm fencing it.'

'But Deuta, all these years, the people here have known that this is a public pond,' said Gojen, his tone unchanged.

'They have known wrong. Now you all know better. This is Khargi mauzadar's pond, and the people have no right over it.' Turning to the Nepali labourers on the other side, he called, 'You all carry on with your work. Nobody will disturb you any more—they've learnt that their bones will be crushed if they venture here.' Lifting the gun onto his shoulder, he started walking back along the bank.

Gojen stared speechlessly at the mauzadar's departing figure. Then he landed a hard kick on the pile of bamboo, scattering the stacked posts. The mauzadar turned around just in time to see him landing a second kick on the pile. Then Gojen stomped away, his two companions in tow.

◆

As Gojen climbed over the bamboo bars and into the walkway leading to his house, he spotted his grandmother stacking paan on the veranda. He moved closer and said, 'Aai, if you go picking paan from the neighbour's garden again, I'm going to finish you right there. Hadn't I forbidden you?'

The old lady continued with her task. Without lifting her head, she replied, 'I only pick the fallen leaves—I enjoy them with my tamul. What's wrong with that?'

'You don't need to know what's wrong. But I say don't do this again. If you want it so badly, I'll plant some in our garden for you.'

'Hear, hear! What have you ever done for me? Your mother died when you were young and your father abandoned us six years ago on the pretext of going on a pilgrimage. I've lived only for you and all I get in return is harsh words.'

Gojen left to bathe even before his grandmother had finished speaking. The old lady wrapped the leaves in a piece of banana leaf, hoisted herself up with some difficulty, and hobbled into the house. A little later, as she served Gojen his lunch, she broached her pet subject once again. 'Please, son. Go make some queries on the west side—perhaps we'll find him somewhere.'

'You think the western side of your land is restricted to the Sonaruchuk village? That my father is whiling away his time at the crossroads and all I need to do is fetch him home? Your son isn't bothered about you—why should you bother about him? If not for his son, he ought to have at least spared a thought for his ageing mother. He was a coward; let him live or die as he pleases. Don't expect me to go asking around for him.'

Pushing a bowl containing some milk and a banana towards her grandson, the old lady said, 'Should you be talking like that about your own father? You are just as arrogant as him!'

Gojen noticed that his grandmother had served him the only banana in the bunch and all the milk left in the brass tumbler. Lately, one of their two cows had gone dry and the other gave very little milk. He knew that the old lady relished her milk-and-banana dessert, without which she considered her meal incomplete. It was from her that he had acquired the habit. Pouring a little of the milk into one of his used bowls and adding a piece of banana he had broken off, he pushed the other bowl back towards his grandmother. 'Aai, this is for you. I'll speak to Kaila in Kuroiguri and ask him to loan us a milch cow. He won't refuse me anything I ask.'

He watched his grandmother prepare the tamul and said, 'Put some away for me too. I'm going fishing now.'

Gojen broke a couple of beedis, poured the tobacco into his palm and added something from a small paper packet. He divided the mixture between four pieces of paper and rolled them into joints. Three went into the beedi bundle, and he lit up the fourth. He put the beedis, a matchbox and his bundle of tamul-paan into the pocket of his khaki pants. These pants, teamed with a short-sleeved kurta, were his angling uniform. He checked the contents of the box which held his spare gear—the hooks, thread, lead, pith—and put it into a sling bag along with the bamboo nodes containing the borer-worms and earthworms. Then, picking up his fishing rods, he set off.

'Aai, I'm off to Kuroiguri. There's no need for you to wait up for me if I'm a little late,' he called from the gate as he replaced the bamboo bar. He knew his grandmother was on the veranda, watching him leave.

As he stepped into the road, Gojen realized that he was finally on his way. The events of the morning—Khargi fencing the pond and the people looking on helplessly—had somewhat dampened his spirits, but they were now beginning to lift. He wondered—was it right that one man should enjoy what rightfully belonged to the people? No, something must be done about it. He was distracted by a familiar sound behind him—that of the steady pedalling of Sarbai Pandit's Hercules bicycle. Before turning to face his teacher, Gojen hastily grabbed the joint from his lips and concealed it in his hand. This was the only man in the area for whom he showed this mark of respect.

'What, eh, Gojen? Off fishing again?'

'Yes, Sir.'

'Lucky young man,' said the teacher as he pedalled away, and soon the sound of the cycle could be heard no more.

◆

Old memories assailed Gojen as he recalled the numerous times that Sarbai Pandit had caned him or pulled his ears in primary school. There was no school in his village, so Gojen had had to troop to one in the neighbouring village in his early years. The sole teacher, Sarbananda Saikia, popularly known as Sarbai Pandit, taught children from about six villages, his being the only primary school in the entire area. He had been teaching in the same school for about twenty-five years now. Except for a few streaks of grey in his hair, the man, like his bicycle, showed no signs of ageing.

Various instances of his childhood association with Sarbai Pandit were fresh in Gojen's mind, especially the events of one particular day.

The boys were divided into five groups, ranging from class three down to the two pre-school years. There was only one blackboard, and the children sat on bamboo or reed mats on the floor. At the board, Pandit was explaining the unitary method to his second standard students and was about to repeat the basics when Gojen stood up and said, 'Sir, I need to go out,' this being the term for needing to relieve oneself.

'Did you understand the problem I was explaining?' asked the teacher.

'I did, Sir. I can solve the rest of the problems in the book by myself.'

'Well, go then.'

Pandit knew that Gojen was not lying. The boy had a keen mind and was quick on the uptake.

As he returned, buttoning his pants, Gojen suddenly noticed that Pandit had left his bicycle, bought only a few days ago, leaning against the school wall. He walked up to it and, holding a pedal, turned the chain backwards a couple of times. Then he loosened it from its cranks and tossed it away. His hands got greasy in the process, so he wiped them on the bicycle seat. Next, he opened one of the tyre valves and scooted to the other side of the schoolroom as the air escaped with a loud hiss. Pandit heard the noise and left the classroom to see what was going on. He noticed the flat tyre and the chain beside it. When he placed a hand on the seat, it became greasy. Meanwhile, Gojen slunk back into the classroom and settled himself on his mat.

◆

As soon as Pandit left the class, the boys began talking. When he returned, he yelled, 'Quiet!' and looked pointedly at Gojen, who was peacefully engrossed in working on a problem on his slate. He wiped his hands on the rag that served as a duster and, turning towards Gojen's class, said, 'You boys take up geography now.'

The students fumbled as they pulled out their geography books. Pandit said, 'Okay, now. Let's begin with a test. Which one of you can say for sure that you can answer all my questions?'

The boys lowered their heads and looked at each other. When Gojen stole a look at his teacher, their eyes met. 'Why, Gojen,' said the teacher. 'You are a bright boy. Why don't you say you can answer my questions? Are you a coward?'

Gojen jumped up. 'I can answer you, Sir.'

'Think about it. Now that you have committed yourself, you must answer as many questions as I choose to ask. And if you have the correct answer for each one, I shall let you all off right away.'

'Yes, Sir!' Gojen was even more enthused by the promise of an early release from school.

The Pandit started, 'Well, then. Tell me, where is the capital of Assam?'

'In Shillong.'

'Who is the inspector of the state's education department?'

'Shri Sharat Chandra Goswami.'

'Who is the present viceroy of India?'

'Lord Lin-lith-gow.'

'Very good. Now answer this. Remember you said you could answer all questions?

Gojen looked keenly at his teacher as he waited. Pandit asked, 'Tell me—how does your school teacher come to school?'

Instantly, Gojen replied, 'On a bicycle, Sir.'

'Now tell me, who let out the air in its tyres?'

Gojen, taken by surprise, stood silent. The teacher prompted him, 'Come on, tell me. You said you could answer all my questions.'

Hanging his head, Gojen muttered, 'I did, Sir.'

'Great. You really do have all the answers.'

'So can I leave now?'

'Sure, you can—you did answer everything. Now, come here for a moment.'

Gojen walked up to his teacher. In a flash, Pandit retrieved a fine cane from behind the blackboard and roared, 'Hold out your hands!' The cane came down several times on the boy's outstretched hands.

Suddenly, as it touched his palm yet again, Gojen caught the cane in a vice-like grip and shouted, 'Sir, I have answered all your questions. I have spoken the truth. Why do you hit me now?'

'What...?' bellowed Pandit as he jumped up from his chair. The other boys were staring at their teacher in pin-drop silence. Glowering at Gojen with bloodshot eyes, he reached out his hand. The boy quietly placed the cane in it and, ready to face another barrage, held out his palm once again.

But Pandit placed the cane on the table, sank into his chair and solemnly told the boy, 'You may go now.'

Gojen returned to his mat. Pandit hung a map of Assam on the blackboard, opened the geography textbook and settled in his chair. Then, noticing that Gojen was still sitting with his head lowered, he said, 'Gojen, I let you off for the day since you answered everything correctly. You may leave.'

Suddenly, the boy broke into tears. A baffled Pandit looked from the geography textbook to the sobbing boy before him and then to the rest of his class. All eyes were fixed on him. The next instant, he shut the textbook, stood up and said, 'School is over for the day. All of you may leave now.'

That day, on the way home from school, Gojen deliberately lagged behind his classmates. After a while, he turned back and sure enough, far in the distance, he saw his teacher pushing the bicycle along. The cycle repair shop was in the next village, and he would need to tow it the entire way.

◆

This was twelve to thirteen years ago. Now the area boasted a number of primary schools. One of the neighbouring villages had an ME—Middle English—school in addition to an MV—Middle Vernacular—school. But Sarbai Pandit continued to teach at the same place, commuting on the same bicycle. Even the pace at which he rode—and the rhythmic sound it created—remained constant.

Gojen stood his fishing rod on the ground and pulled out his bundle of beedis. Now that Pandit and his cycle were out of sight, he felt it was safe to light up once again. The teacher remained in his thoughts as he continued on his way.

In spite of being a prankster, Gojen was one of Pandit's favoured students. This was because apart from being good at studies, he was also brave and outspoken. He had only one failing—his moods. He and the shopkeeper Sharma's son Torun had been selected to appear for the LP—lower primary—scholarship examination, which would be held in an MV school about five miles away. The first two days went fine, but on the third, Sarbai Pandit failed to find Gojen in the exam hall. On making inquiries that evening, he learnt that on his way to the exams, the boy had been distracted by a band heading a procession to a religious fair. Without a second thought, he had joined the procession, attended the fair, eaten the traditional goodies being distributed there and, in the late evening, returned home to study for the following day's exam, the sights and sounds of the band still in his head.

Gojen was just settling down to his studies when Sarbai Pandit pulled him up by the ear. 'Enough, wise man. You don't need to study any more.'

'But I have my literature test tomorrow, Sir,' said Gojen, as though the teacher didn't know already.

'Sure! And of course, the marks for today's test will get filled in automatically, right?'

Pandit, who had heard of Gojen's escapade from Torun, explained to Gojen's father how one day of absence would make the entire exam effort worthless. The highly incensed Holodhor pulled out a cane from the veranda lattice and beat the boy so hard that Pandit had to rush to his rescue. Much later, he discovered that Gojen had scored ninety-eight per cent in each of the first two days' papers.

At Pandit's insistence, Gojen and a few other boys were enrolled in the nearest MV school. They did him proud—all three boys, including Gojen, who qualified for the MV scholarship that year were earlier his students. Gojen continued to excel at studies, though it was his courage and candour that made him more popular.

At the time, the only centre for the scholarship examinations was at the district headquarters about eighty miles away. Memories of that journey remained with Gojen until years later. There were no railway tracks on the northern bank and no bridges across the major rivers except for 'cold weather bridges' in winter. The North Trunk Road was entirely gravelled and only one bus plied on it daily, crossing rivers on large ferries. Besides, with World War II on, the services were rather erratic.

Shopkeeper Sharma happened to know a few barge owners whose fleets brought in his store supplies from the headquarters, via the Brahmaputra. On Pandit's advice, he agreed to send Torun for the exam, and other modes of transport being uncertain, he arranged for him to travel by barge. Once again, at the teacher's request, it was agreed that the other boys would also travel by the same conveyance.

The barge, which was leaving at an auspicious time at daybreak, was docked about six miles from their village. Sharma decided to send Torun in a bullock cart at night itself, and Pandit arranged for Gojen go with him.

After an early dinner, Gojen collected his metal suitcase and mat-wrapped bed-roll and waited, sitting on the bench in front of Sharma's shop, nodding off at intervals. They boarded the cart around midnight. Torun, who had been sleeping at home before the cart arrived, made a makeshift bed by spreading a sheet on some straw, curled up in his blanket and fell asleep almost instantly. His bed-roll—packed in a hold-all—and suitcase lay by his side. Gojen settled by his feet, his belongings beside him, and huddled up in his eri shawl. He tried to sleep, but having helped the cart driver with the preparations for about an hour before starting, he now felt wide awake. Also, there was not enough room to stretch out comfortably, so he remained seated. By the light of the lamp swinging from the cart's canopy, he noticed the sleeping Torun and, picking up a straw, tickled his nose with it. Torun sleepily brushed it off. Gojen smiled and repeated his prank a few times. Then he sat still.

Apart from the sound of wheels on gravel and the occasional 'Hey, hey!' of the cart driver urging his animals on, there was silence all around. Through the canopy, Gojen suddenly spied the night sky, studded with stars. While he was still in primary school, Sarbai Pandit had once visited his home in the evening and acquainted him with many of the major constellations. He could identify these fairly easily, but never before did he have the opportunity to gaze at the midnight sky like he did now. True, many a time, he had walked home late from a bhaona in another village, but then he was either too preoccupied with the dramatic characters or too drowsy to notice this spectacle.

Jumping out of the cart, Gojen took in an unhindered view of the velvety darkness. The path was flanked by vast paddy fields on either side, and above them, wherever he looked, was the great expanse of the night sky with stars blinking bright. How beautiful! He followed the cart on foot—this was far better than being cramped inside!

3

After three days and two nights of sailing on the Brahmaputra, Gojen and his co-examinees arrived at the district headquarters. It was exciting to be in a real town for the first time; but for Gojen, his voyage on the Brahmaputra was even more so. Every moment of that trip was memorable—the red sun rising from the misty horizon, the soft afternoon sunshine growing brighter before fading into a vividly coloured sunset; and the deepening blue of the sky as the stars started adorning it. These sights remained imprinted on his young mind and continued to excite him in later years, just as they had done then.

After qualifying for the scholarship, Gojen was persuaded by Sarbai Pandit to enrol in the fifth standard in the newly started ME school. Since he had cleared his MV, all he needed to study was English, attending the classes in the third, fourth and fifth standards, after which he could go home. The early break from school left him with plenty of time to while away; as a result of which he discovered some new interests, especially at the weekly market at Roton Pukhuri.

The market was a fairly big affair, and every Saturday, Gojen rushed there immediately after school. People from about twenty-five villages walked eight to ten miles to assemble there with their wares, and labourers and clerks from the large tea estates not too far away visited routinely. In addition to trading, it provided various forms of amusement—magic shows, bioscopes, bear and monkey acts, canvassers building up a clientele for their products—the list was endless. Then there were the rows of food stalls, where one could find a wide range of delicacies. It was more a fair than a market.

Except in a few orthodox Assamese villages, there was no taboo on women moving around freely. So women of all ages from the neighbouring Nepali villages and tea estates came to the market as did their men, and many romances bloomed.

◆

The Roton Pukhuri market was about three miles from Gojen's route home. Every Saturday, as soon as he arrived, he walked the entire length and breadth of the market several times, trying to extract the maximum possible excitement from its various people, goings-on and colourful mystery. Then, finally, he settled down in a special place—one to which he drifted very naturally after the first few visits.

This 'special' place happened to be a spot at which people gambled over a game of dice. For quite a few days, he observed the way the game was conducted and one day, very hesitantly, he placed a one-anna piece on an empty square. Making strange sounds in his throat, the gamester shook the dice in a leather box, inverted it and lifted it slowly to add to the suspense. Then he removed the money from all but Gojen's square and another, and placed a four-anna piece beside each of the one-anna pieces in these two. A man cleaned out the money from one, and those huddled over the game looked around to see who had won the other. Gojen stood undecided.

'Whose loot is this—and why haven't you taken it? If you don't, I'll clear it off, I swear...' Just as the gamester reached out for the money, Gojen made a grab for it. His heart thumped, an unknown thrill coursed through his being and his throat went dry. All eyes were upon him—some advising, some critical, some taunting... Presently, the betting started again.

Gojen broke into a sweat. The gamester turned to him, looked him in the eye and said, 'What are you waiting for? Bet.' Suddenly enthused and fearless, he tossed the four-anna piece in his fist onto his earlier block. That evening, when he returned home, he had four rupees and twelve annas in his pocket.

In a few years, Gojen became a hero among the Saturday market gamblers.

Another spot that attracted Gojen was the country liquor den on the fringes of the market. Initially, he was amused at the intoxicated antics of its customers, which he watched from a distance because he couldn't bear the smells of spirits. But soon, he got used to them. Many a time, he lent a hand to a teetering sot, helped break up brawls and assisted the hassled wives of drunken labourers. And before he knew it, he had changed from a mere spectator to a member of the liquor-den community.

But things did not end there.

•

One day, elated by a big win at dice, Gojen was persuaded by some of his much older cronies to treat them to a round of drinks. He had done this on two earlier occasions, but the thought of sipping the spirits had never crossed his mind—it wasn't worth it! But that day, for some unknown reason, he gulped down half a bottle in his happy state. Suddenly, the joy of winning multiplied manifold inside his head and spurred him to polish off the remainder quicker than his mates.

Then he rose to get himself another bottle.

Gojen had stopped attending school quite some time ago, least concerned about what anybody had to say. Only Sarbai Pandit chided him occasionally. But one day, the teacher, too, realized that he no longer held any power over the boy—and he had good reason to believe so.

•

Musing over Sarbai Pandit's affection towards him, Gojen continued on his way and soon found himself approaching the temple of the goddess. He bowed his head in obeisance. Then he recalled that Bapudeu, the temple priest, had not been keeping too well—he had occasional bouts of vertigo. Gojen had met him on his way to the kabiraj—the Ayurvedic doctor. Bapudeu was returning with his medicines and the boy had helped him carry his bags, chatting with him on the way.

Gojen was fascinated by the priest. Every time the man donned his red dhoti and sador, applied the red vermilion mark on his forehead and sat rapt in front of the goddess, Gojen stared at his bony face, trying to gauge what was going on in his mind. Before him was the image of the dark goddess, red tongue thrust out, holding a severed human head by the hair in one of her four hands. But somehow, Gojen was always more captivated by the older man's drawn countenance and his small eyes, bright and keen though set deep in their sockets. He had first noticed that piercing look one day about eight years ago...

4

In the small thatched house by the temple, Bapudeu lived with his only daughter, Joba. Her mother was the daughter of the earlier priest. Bapudeu had studied the scriptures in a Vedic school and soon after coming to the temple, had become an able assistant to the senior priest who taught him all about conducting rites and rituals. Then, entrusting their daughter's hand in his, the old man and his wife moved to the Kamakhya temple in Guwahati, and eventually settled in Kashi.

In the early days, Bapudeu received about two letters a year from his father-in-law. Then, one day, a letter informed him that his mother-in-law had died. After that, the mail got more and more infrequent, until he had no news of the old man at all. Meanwhile, one day, when Joba was about nine, her mother suddenly began vomiting blood and passed away too.

Bapudeu was highly perturbed—how would he look after his work, home and the motherless girl at the same time? Apart from his temple duties, he was summoned to perform some ritual almost every day, keeping him away from home for long hours. Sometimes he took Joba along, but this wasn't always possible. He also worried that the girl was fast approaching puberty—the physical changes were obvious—and he needed to get her married before that happened. In those days, a Brahmin family with an unmarried mature girl was shunned by the rest of the community. Being the temple priest, if he were to find himself in such a situation, Bapudeu would need to leave his calling and move elsewhere. But where could he go?

As if in answer to his prayers, Gojen arrived to ease his tensions.

◆

Right by the temple, there flowed a small river whose curve formed a lagoon-like inlet. On the bank was a huge fig tree. Gojen often sat in its shade when he came fishing at this spot. He had been a keen—and regular—angler ever since his school days; and in the course of time, his fishing excursions extended to include visits to the temple and the priest's home. Bapudeu fed him prasad from the temple, Joba made him tea and he gave them some fish from his day's catch. When Joba went down to the river to bathe or to fetch water, Gojen teased her and engaged her in light banter. Sometimes she tossed a piece of earth to the spot where he had laid his lines and he retaliated with mock anger.

Joba happened to be one of the few girls whom Sarbai Pandit had convinced to attend school, although they all gave up after a year or two. It was in primary school that Gojen had first met her and a deep bond was forged between the two—an innocent bond of two young minds. Joba was about ten then, and Gojen, still in school, was thirteen or so.

One day, Bapudeu had asked, 'Gojen, are you attending school regularly?'

'Yes, I am, Deu.'

'If you happen to have a holiday, do come over and spend some time here. It will be of great help to me.'

'Of course, Deu. If there is anything you need me to do, I'll take the day off.'

'Not at all. No playing truant from school. I am only asking you to come on holidays. The problem is, ever since this girl lost her mother, I have been towing her around every time I am called out on work. But she's growing up and I can't do that all the time. If you are here, she'll be safe at home.'

Without a second thought, Gojen agreed to come.

But Bapudeu's prime problem was yet unsolved—that of finding a groom for his daughter before she became a woman. Every morning, he fell at the feet of the goddess and begged her to deliver him from his dilemma. And one day, his prayers were answered.

•

Late one night, Bapudeu was woken by a suppressed voice calling, 'Khura? Khura, can you hear me?'

Try as he might, he could not recognize the voice. Nor could he recall anyone who addressed him as Khura—Uncle. He remained still, but the voice called once again, 'Khura, please open the door.'

'Who is it?' asked the priest, stepping out of bed—someone must have died and he was wanted for the cremation! But he had stopped conducting those rites some time ago because that meant he had to abstain from conducting the daily worship at the temple as well as other rites for the entire period of ritual mourning. When his father-in-law was around, they split the duties between the two of them. Now, although everyone knew he would refuse, they bothered him all the same! But why was he being addressed as Khura?

Lighting the lamp, he went up to the door. 'Who is it, eh? I don't do cremations any more.'

'It's me, Khura. Hurry up and open the door. It's not about a cremation.'

Bapudeu opened the door and, by the light of the hurricane lamp he raised, looked into the lightly bearded face of a man about twenty years old.

'Who are you, son? And at this hour?'

'I'll tell you everything. But can I come in first?'

'In...? Well, I suppose it is all right.' He scanned the youth from head to toe and reluctantly let him into the house.

The youth shut the door after him as soon as he entered and latched it with its bamboo crossbar. Then, setting his bag on a bench, he sat down and said, 'I'll tell you all, but could I have a glass of water first? I'm parched.' Bapudeu brought him water in a ghoti and he glugged down the entire contents.

Joba, now awake, got out of bed and stood quietly at the door to the sitting room. Over her red frock, she had tied one of her mother's old mekhelas at her waist and draped a gamosa like a stole on her chest. The young man saw her as soon as he had finished drinking the water.

'And this is…?'

'My daughter.'

'Anyone else at home?'

'No one else. Just me and Joba—just the two of us since her mother left for her heavenly abode last year. Now tell me, who are you? And where have you come from in the middle of the night? Will you stay or leave? And why are you here?' After this barrage of questions to the young man, Bapudeu turned to his daughter— 'Joba, go back to sleep now.'

Joba had been staring intently at the man, curious about his identity. It was strange that someone should visit them at this late hour. She was loath to return to bed, but another meaningful glance from her father made her obey his order. Lying on a bed in the next room, she strained her ears to catch every word that was spoken between the two men.

The young man's name was Modon Bhattacharyya and he was the son of Tolen Bhattacharyya, one of Bapudeu's classmates from the Vedic school. The father now taught Sanskrit at a high school and it was from him that Modon had acquired Bapudeu's address.

It was 1942 and India's freedom movement was at its peak. A secret leadership directed the revolution. The Second World War was on too, and cantonments of the friendly forces were scattered all over.

Modon should have appeared for the IA examinations that year from Cotton College, Guwahati. But, like many of his fellow students, he boycotted the exams and, returning to his village, plunged into the movement. Thanks to his acumen, he was deputed to the secret service, where he needed to carry messages and instructions from one place to another. He was in constant touch with the three leaders of the movement and served as the sole means of communication between them. Now one of them had sent an important message for three people from three neighbouring villages. He had no idea about the lay of the land and had set off secretly, away from the prying eyes of the police and the army, with the only knowledge that one of his father's classmates was a priest at a temple to goddess Chandi somewhere in the area.

Without making his mission public, Modon managed to inform Bapudeu about the gravity and secrecy involved, and requested his cooperation in arranging the meetings. Although hesitant at first, something in the youth's demeanour soon put the older man at ease.

Modon had left his village at dusk and crossed the Kuroi by boat. At Kuroiguri Sapori, he had wended his way through some new Muslim hutments and come to a few Nepali homes, at one of which he had eaten his fill of beaten rice and curd. Taking directions to the temple from them, he had waited until the villagers were asleep and walked there under the cover of darkness.

So the man had eaten. There was no need to cook him a meal, mused Bapudeu.

The priest's thatched house had three rooms—the far one, a kitchen; the centre one, the bedroom and the one in front, the sitting room, furnished sparingly with a mat-lined cot. A mattress was spread on this to serve as a bed for Modon. Bapudeu could not remember when he last had a live-in guest. True, there were plenty of visitors to the temple around Kali Puja, which was celebrated in a big way, but the priests' assistants who needed to stay over slept in the temple. Anyway, though he floundered at first, he was soon ready to accommodate his visitor.

The night wore on. Bidding Modon good night, Bapudeu returned to bed. As he reached out to turn off the lamp, he noticed that Joba's eyes were open wide, staring at him.

'Hey, why aren't you asleep yet?' he asked as he blew the lamp out. As he tried to sleep, Modon's words kept ringing in his ears. One thought dominated all others—this young man, the son of his old classmate, was a Brahmin—healthy and handsome too. He peered through a gap in the reed walls and saw that the guest was sitting on his cot and, in the faint light of the little lamp, scribbling something into a small book. That must be his diary! He peered again and took note of Modon's features—gleaming eyes, a bright face and a physical structure that indicated robust health. He should be about twenty or so—and Joba was about ten. If he could have the wedding solemnized now, Modon could take her home anytime after she attained puberty. He fell asleep visualizing the wedding.

The following day, it was arranged that Modon should meet his three contacts at the temple. There was no point going to their homes—they were hardly ever in, preferring to carry out their secret errands on the move now that the police had their eyes on them. There was no police outpost in the vicinity, but who knew who could have been bought to spy on them? Also, being a newcomer to the village, Modon would draw undue attention; so it was better they were called here instead.

But who would summon them? Bapudeu offered to go after finishing his duties at the temple, but Modon refused to inconvenience the older man by making him walk the four or five miles. They could ask a visitor to the temple, but then, who could vouch for that person's integrity? Finally, Modon decided that if need be, he himself would venture out.

Right then, Joba called from the next room, 'Pitadeu, Gojen will come fishing today.' She was chopping vegetables in the bedroom, having moved there from the kitchen to listen in on the men's conversation.

'How do you know he'll come today?' asked Bapudeu from the sitting room.

'He told me so when he brought us the custard apples from his garden yesterday evening,' replied Joba from across the wall.

'The problem is solved, my boy. Now all we need to do is wait for Gojen to arrive.' Bapudeu sounded relieved as he addressed Modon.

'Who is he?'

'A young boy we know. Was a bright student—got a scholarship in MV, enrolled for ME, completed the English courses, but didn't appear for the exams. Heard he has picked up some vices lately. But he's a true worshipper of the goddess and comes here regularly. And to this day, we haven't seen any bad trait in him. He's very fond of Joba and me.' Bapudeu filled in some more details about Gojen and assured Modon that they couldn't find a more reliable errand boy.

The three men met Modon in Bapudeu's house. The meeting started at dusk and continued well into the night. They discussed and analysed the plan of action suggested by the secret head office, carefully assessing their chances of success and failure. Modon also acquainted himself with the prevailing political environment of the area and the trio's views on the course their movement should follow. The discussions also included the availability of reliable manpower in the event that the ongoing non-violence needed to be replaced by armed revolt.

Bapudeu did not take any part in the deliberations; nor did he voice his opinions. He merely dropped in for short periods between his temple duties.

But Gojen, whom Modon had asked to remain on the veranda to keep an eye out for policemen or spies and signal them at the appearance of either, strained to hear every word that was spoken inside. Modon spoke softly, so much of what he said remained unclear. But from what he heard, Gojen realized that they were planning an event of great significance. There was talk of involving each family from about a hundred and fifty villages to the east of the Kuroi in age-specific tasks. They would recruit youngsters into troops, each with a chief of their own. One of the three men present would be the chief for the entire region.

Gojen heard his name being mentioned a couple of times. People from thirty to forty villages in the direction of his home would walk to the police lock-up. They would be joined by residents of another forty to fifty villages and together, in thousands, they would march to the police station. Policemen would, in all probability, try to stop them with lathis, guns and bayonets. But the people, especially the younger troops, would brave all—even bullets—and march into the compound to raise the tricolour flag on the station roof. People could be injured or even killed in the process. The provision for medical treatment in such cases was also discussed.

Gojen was aware of the Quit India movement of the Indian National Congress and the fact that Gandhi, Nehru and many others were in prison. He also knew of India's neutral stand on the World War. He had gathered his information from the Bengali newspapers he sometimes saw at the kabiraj's clinic—papers that Jadob Bora routinely read out loud in the evenings—and from public speeches made by local politicians. But these things happened far away; they involved other people. Now, on hearing Modon and the others, he realized that these events were coming right up to his door. He could be among those marching in to hoist the flag, one of the injured or even dead! His entire body—right from his toes to the ends of his hair—tingled in anticipation.

◆

From the bedroom, Joba was listening too, except when she was in the kitchen making tea, or at the veranda, trying to converse with Gojen. Rapt as he was in trying to overhear the discussions, he showed little encouragement and she had to return inside. Every now and then, she peeped through a crack in the wall to watch Modon. His mannerisms, his rosy countenance, his shining beard and his voice held her spellbound and she often lost the thread of the topics they discussed—much of it was beyond her grasp anyway. Now on the threshold of womanhood, a face etched itself on the misty mirror of her mind and refused to be erased.

◆

Bapudeu's kitchen was tiny; so guests were sometimes served their meals in the small space by the temple. Joba swabbed that floor, set out the peeras and two ghotis of water, served the meals in two plates and bowls and called her father and Modon to dine. As they ate, she stood at the door watching them, and blushed when the guest complimented her cooking.

'She can somehow manage the basic rice-and-curry meals and sometimes helps me when I cook the bhog for the goddess. But unfortunately, she couldn't learn any weaving or sewing. She dropped out of school when her mother died, though she did study until the second standard,' said Bapudeu.

'That's not right. Joba shouldn't have given up her studies.'

At once, Joba retorted, 'Not that I wanted to quit. It was my father—he said "You're a girl, this is enough" and made me give up.'

'There's nothing different about being a girl these days. Everyone's the same. Haven't you heard of Sarojini Naidu, Vijaylakshmi Pandit or Aruna Asaf Ali?'

'Why, even in ancient times, Gargi, Leelavati and Maitreyee were as academically accomplished as any man,' replied Joba.

'There—so you know already. So why can't you be a Leelavati or Gargi of our times? I would say resume your studies, Joba.'

'That may not be possible now. She's already had a break of two-three years. Now it's time to think of other things. Here, Joba, pass this bowl of curd to him. I won't have any now, so let him finish it.' And Bapudeu deftly diverted the conversation.

Joba finished her own meal, did the dishes, cleaned the kitchen, washed her feet and got into bed. While wiping her feet on an old gamosa, she heard her father ask Modon, 'Son, your gotra is Bharadwaj, right?'

'No, it's Maudgalya,' replied Modon as he sat on the bed and folded his kurta.

'Oh, oh. I thought your father had mentioned otherwise.'

Modon immediately caught on to the fact that this was a ruse. It was unlikely that his father had discussed their descent over twenty years ago; and even if he had, it wasn't possible that Bapudeu would remember, unless the topic had come up in a special context.

After a while, the priest asked, 'Modon, would you by any chance remember your astrological chart? If not, at least your star, your sun sign…?'

Modon took some time to answer. He slowly folded away his kurta and placed it in his bag. Bapudeu was disconcerted by the young man's attitude. Finally, Modon looked him in the eye and said, 'My birth sign is Scorpio and my star is Vishakha. I have guessed the reason for your wanting to know these details, so if you don't mind, instead of beating around the bush, I'd like to tell you something.' As the older man looked at him in stunned silence, he sat comfortably on the bed, nestled a pillow in his lap, and resting both elbows on it, started…

'Right now, the duties we have taken up for our nation call for instant decision-making, which has become our second nature. If you had been here during our discussions this evening, you would have noticed that we made many resolutions—hasty, but not rash. Each was well thought out. But wait, I promised not to beat around the bush. Well, a little while ago, while we were having dinner, you happened to make a statement concerning Joba—that it was time to make other plans for her. I picked up the hint and have been thinking over it for the past half hour and yes—I will marry your daughter.'

Bapudeu almost jumped out of his old chair. Then, gripping both its arms, he slowly sank back. After a moment, he said, 'Wait a minute, let me do a cursory matching of your horoscopes first,' and he made to go to the other room to fetch a paper and pencil.

'Wait, Khura. You can match the horoscopes later. I haven't finished speaking.'

Bapudeu sat down once again. Modon said, 'I will certainly marry Joba, but not right now.'

'Not now?' asked Bapudeu, the question reaching his eyes.

'Yes, in a few years' time.'

'A few years! But this is the most difficult year—the crisis is at hand and I'm dying with worry.'

'You don't need to worry any more, Khura. I have given you my word—I will marry Joba. Just wait a few years until we earn our country her freedom. We will start our married life in an independent India.'

'But you don't understand, Modon!'

'Of course I do. You are worried about Joba's approaching puberty, right? That's exactly what I'm trying to say—I will marry her on one condition. Let her attain her womanhood in full. Only then will I make her my bride and take her home.'

'How can you flout all tradition like this? All right, you don't have to set up home with her right away. That can wait a couple of years. But how can I not get her married while she is yet a minor? What are you saying? How can I keep a grown-up unmarried girl at home? I have responsibilities—the temple, rituals, social ceremonies...'

'Listen, Khura. The root of the problem is that in our society, no man comes forward to marry a girl who has already grown up. But I promise you I will make your grown-up daughter my wife. I don't care about baseless social norms. And in the last half hour, I have decided that the girl I marry should necessarily reach her womanhood, no matter when the wedding happens—which is why I am proposing this for Joba.'

'This is a very difficult proposal, Modon. The Brahmin society will taunt me as non-orthodox. Besides, I haven't matched your horoscopes yet, though going by your birth sign, it doesn't seem to be a problem...'

'Let me also tell you this, Khura. Whether the horoscopes match or not, if you don't mind entrusting your daughter's hand to me, not only will I wed her, we will also have a long and happy married life. Now everything depends on you.'

As Bapudeu left his chair and moved towards his bedroom, he said, 'All right, Modon. Go to sleep now. It's rather late—and you said you have to leave at dawn, right?'

'Yes. If I can make it to Kuroiguri before daybreak, there will be nothing to fear. But if you feel you need some more time to decide about Joba, I will stay here for the day, leave at dusk and make my journey in the night.'

'We'll see, son. Go to sleep now.'

By the light of the dim lamp, Bapudeu noticed that Joba was lying still, apparently in deep slumber. Reluctant to check, he blew out the lamp and got into bed.

In the sitting room, Modon was making entries in his diary. In the faint reflected light, Bapudeu gazed at the rafters as he lay wide awake and wondered what those entries were about. But soon, the writing was done and the light was turned out.

'Vande Mataram'—Bapudeu heard Modon utter the words in a low, clear voice. He had heard something similar last night too, but could only make out the words now. So the last thing Modon said every night was 'Vande Mataram', just as he himself said 'Ma Chandi'! Everything about the man was different—and difficult to accept. His hopes of the early evening were shattered by what he had just heard. Modon had asked him to think about his proposal; but what was there to think about with such unorthodox suggestions? It was impossible! It would have been ideal if things had worked out, but not this way. This was simply not possible!

'Are you asleep, Modon?' he called softly.

'No, Khura. I've just lain down. Not that I take long to fall asleep.'

'I need to tell you something, son.'

'Go ahead, Khura.'

'You may leave in the morning—you don't need to wait until dusk. I withdraw my proposal for the time being.'

'Of course, no problem. You too should sleep now.'

The darkness in the two rooms suddenly grew grave and obliterated the sound of Bapudeu's sigh.

♦

When Gojen came by in the morning, he got to learn from Joba that Modon had left at the crack of dawn. The news disappointed him, because he wanted to meet the man, tell him that he had heard most of what was said the previous day and ask if there was any way in which he could be associated with their cause. He asked Joba about all that had transpired after he left. In her naïve way, she told him whatever she had heard from her bed—about how her father had offered her to Modon in marriage, how he had agreed, but asked to wait a few years, how her father wanted her married immediately...

Gojen heard her out and said, 'Modon Kokaiti is right. Is this any age for you to get married? If someone like him has agreed to marry you, that's great. Why is Bapudeu trying to rush things?'

'You won't understand these things. They can't postpone my wedding for too long.'

'What is there to understand? In my village, there are several girls my age—and they are not married!'

'Don't you know things are different for us Brahmin girls?'

'God knows what's different! Wait—I'll talk to Bapudeu. I'll tell him that he should get you married to Modon Kokaiti—never mind when that happens.'

'You know, Gojen, I'd love to be married to him. But will Pitadeu compromise on his beliefs?'

'You don't worry about it. I'll talk to Bapudeu right now, even as he's out picking flowers for the goddess.' Saying this, Gojen swooped towards the garden.

A little later, Joba saw a seemingly worked up Bapudeu rushing towards her, shouting from the distance, 'So, Joba, what have you been saying? What have you told Gojen? You sinner—what words have you spoken?'

From her father's demeanour, Joba gathered that Gojen had made a deadly mistake. She quickly disappeared into the house.

'Joba! Come out, will you? What have you said?' screamed her father. Then he suddenly turned towards Gojen, who was waiting not too far away. His eyes blazed as he spewed, 'You petty fellow! You come here pleading her case! You're yet a baby and you speak such vile stuff! Get out of here. And beware—if I see you in the temple compound again, I'll hack you in two. Get lost, you devil, you...!'

Gojen looked straight into Bapudeu's eyes before lowering his head. Then, slowly, he turned around and walked out towards the road.

5

Gojen often remembered the embers in Bapudeu's eyes that day. Now, of course, there was no trace of that fire—it was always a placid, serene look, like that of an innocent child.

Resting the fishing rods by a tree, Gojen put his shoulder bag on the ground and proceeded towards the temple. After bowing at the threshold, he noticed that Bapudeu, clad in his red priestly garb, was readying himself for the daily worship. At that very moment, he was putting two red vermilion dots on the two ends of the machete he used for sacrifices. Gojen stared with wonder at the shiny broad steel blade—he was always fascinated by its power.

'Bapudeu,' he called softly.

'Oh, Gojen.' The priest continued with his preparations.

'How come you're late today?' asked Gojen humbly.

'I've been feeling a little tired lately. Besides the devotees are all busy with their harvesting.' Bapudeu's voice was feeble.

'Aren't the kabiraj's medicines working?'

'I suppose they are. The acidity seems less, but I'm still averse to food—I don't feel like eating anything at all. The tablets are also over.' The priest sorted out the holy grass.

'You should have got some more and continued with the medicine.'

'No, forget it. I don't need the kabiraj's treatment any more. The mother goddess will deliver me from all this through her infinite powers. And if she feels that it is time for me to leave this world, then so be it.'

'But Deu! The goddess can only give her blessings. How can you cure an illness without any medicine?'

Even before Gojen could finish, Bapudeu roared, 'Gojen! Don't sit there in front of the goddess and speak so boastfully! When you say she can only give blessings, you undermine her powers. Kneel down right now and apologize to her! It was only a slip of your tongue. May she forgive you. Now, kneel!'

Gojen wondered what he had said to offend the goddess; and when he did kneel, his only thought was, 'O goddess, I know not what I have said. But I had not the slightest intention of offending you—I wouldn't dare. Please forgive me.'

As he rose, he saw that Bapudeu was deep in prayer, palms folded and eyes closed. After a while, the priest opened his eyes and said, 'I too have prayed to the goddess—"O mother, he is an idiot; please don't take offence at his words." Now go out and wait. Once I'm done, you can have some bhog.'

'No, Bapudeu. I'm on my way to Kuroiguri for some fishing. I'll leave now.'

'It's not a good thing for you to go to fishing in Kuroiguri all the time—that too through all those new Muslim settlements. Anyway, get going if you have to. I'll save some bhog for you.'

◆

As Gojen left the temple, he suddenly felt cheerless and anxious. Why did Bapudeu call him an idiot in front of the goddess? How could that be? It wasn't fair! Should he go back right now and confront him? No, let it wait. It wouldn't be proper to do that in the presence of the goddess. On his way back from Kuroiguri, he would definitely bring up the subject and ask Bapudeu how he could consider him an idiot.

Then again, he realized that he ought not to do anything to hurt the man. In the last few years, the tragic events in Joba's life had cast such a pall of gloom over him that he couldn't cause him any more pain, whatever the reason.

Picking up his things, he set off towards Kuroiguri, taking a shortcut at the big banyan tree through a small lane skirting a stream. There was a forest on the way and the track got muddy in the monsoons, but that never bothered him. He was familiar with every aspect of these lanes, which had roamed since his childhood. He wondered if he should light another of his bhang-filled beedis, then decided against it. The sun was too hot. He lit a regular beedi and went on, the spring returning to his step.

A little further on, after he had crossed a couple of fields, he saw Pitkon, Ramchandra—son of Durgi mahajan and nephew of Khargi mauzadar—and the mahajan's ploughman(there are three men here, not two). Pitkon and Ramchandra seemed to be engaged in a war of words. Setting his things down by a tree on an anthill, Gojen plodded through the muddy field until he reached them. 'What's up, Pitkon? What's all this about?'

'Just look at them, Gojen!'

'What's there for anybody else to see? Make sure the fencing stakes are set properly,' Ramchandra said to Pitkon through clenched teeth. 'As for you…' This, to him, was an inopportune time for Gojen to land up.

'What, Ram? What fencing are you talking about?' asked Gojen.

'None of your business,' replied Ramchandra without looking at him.

'Really? Of course, it's none of my business.' He smiled, and with a meaningful glance at Ramchandra, turned to Pitkon. 'What, eh, Pitkon? What's the matter?'

'Just look, Gojen. For a week now, not a drop of water has entered my fields! They don't need all the water they have; so they've cut a canal to drain it to the roadside, but they won't give me any. What sort of justice is this?'

'Hey, shut up! Don't talk about justice!' roared Ramchandra. In the same tone, he chided his ploughman, 'You idiot! What are you gaping at? Why don't you hurry up and plant the stakes?'

Gojen chipped in, 'Hey Pitkon, why do you comment on the mahajan's son's wisdom? They have such high thinking! So Ram, will you remove this block now?' From his tone, Ramchandra gathered that the situation was getting serious. He looked at the ploughman busy fencing the muddy blockade. Pitkon looked at Gojen.

'You know what, Pitkon? Forget this blockade. After all, it is the mahajan's son's idea. You just cut a canal through this lane. Go get your spade—I'm right here.'

Pitkon looked from Gojen to Ramchandra and back again.

'Come on—cut away,' Gojen commanded.

'I wonder what the mahajan will do once he hears of it,' Pitkon hesitated, a helpless look in his eyes.

'Hmph! These curs will carry on with their tails between their legs for fear of the mahajan and the mauzadar! Come on, pass me the spade.' Gojen grabbed the spade from Pitkon and proceeded towards the ploughman.

'Now that you guys are so adamant, let me get rid of this blockade itself. Hey, move!' He pushed the ploughman away. The man lost his balance and just managed to avoid falling into the mud. Gojen pulled out the stakes and cut through the blockade and the lane to create a large canal.

'Wait, I'll tell my father.' Ramchandra, followed by his ploughman, crossed the fields and moved towards the main road.

'Go tell your father. Tattle to your uncle too. Let them impale me on a stake. But,' Gojen raised his head from his hoeing 'if you try to block this canal, I'll chop off your head and bury it right here under the blockade.' He stood leaning against the spade as the water gushed over his feet and into Pitkon's field.

◆

Gojen picked up his bag, raised his fishing rods onto his shoulders and started walking again. He soon came to the rows of silk-cotton trees. In spring, it was a spectacular sight when the trees were in bloom—as though the sky was on fire with the blossoms for what seemed like miles. Until recently, this area had been a dreaded forest. Beyond it, along the Kuroi and right up to the Brahmaputra, tall grasses grew thick and wild. When Gojen had first come fishing in Kuroiguri with his uncle, they couldn't take this route because tigers, bears and other wild animals roamed freely in the area.

He had heard that Khargi mauzadar came to the forest on elephant-back to hunt deer. Khargi's brother Durgi—Ramchandra's father—was supposed to be the better hunter. Gojen remembered how, many a time, he had accompanied the villagers to the mauzadar's courtyard to view a large tiger the latter had shot. He also recalled a white sahib and his wife from a nearby tea estate coming there once. The tiger was huge, but the villagers were more interested in the couple. That was also the first time Gojen had seen white folk. The cigarette-puffing memsahib's long bare legs and rosy face left a deep imprint on his mind.

Years later, on his way back from the Saturday market, he often saw white couples riding to their club in their cars, and some of the faces became quite familiar. But later, especially after meeting Modon in Bapudeu's home and hearing of the chain of events in the quest for independence, he gathered that these people were exploiters. And one class of people—the likes of Khargi mauzadar—were doing their society a grave injustice by being hand-in-glove with them. They ensured that the rich got richer while the poor remained poor. No wonder he felt such disgust when it came to Khargi and his associates!

Looking around him, Gojen saw that a number of silk-cotton trees had been felled lately. He had heard that some matchstick company in Dhubri had bought the wood from the government at a throwaway price and were shipping it to their factories in huge boats via the Brahmaputra. If this systematic felling continued, the vista of flaming skies would be gone for ever. He felt depressed at the thought. The wild animals had already abandoned this area and moved across the river to the forests of Kaziranga. That wasn't right either. The only advantage of the tree felling was that it now provided him with a shortcut to Kuroiguri.

As the forest grew sparser, the grasslands beyond them seemed thinner too. There was a reason for this. Through the sandbanks of the Brahmaputra, ten to fifteen rural Muslim families had moved in to settle in the area and had cleared the grasslands to grow mustard, pulses, vegetables, and some jute and sugarcane in between. The land was extremely fertile—seeds sprouted almost instantly into robust crops.

The silk-cotton grove spread over a small hillock and the path ran through it. Now, from the cleared patch, one could see the Brahmaputra on one side, its far bank invisible to the eye, and the Kuroi on the other, flowing to merge with the larger river. The new settlers had toiled hard to clear the space between the two rivers— and now it teemed with different crops in various hues. The sight fascinated Gojen and he paused to look every time he passed this way. Far away, closer to the Kuroi, was a huddle of hutments— the village of the new settlers. A little further off were the cow and buffalo shelters run by the Nepali families.

On his frequent trips to Kuroiguri, Gojen had forged a deep friendship with most of the settlers; but he was closest to Mansoor Ali. Initially, they just shared a casual acquaintance, exchanging a few words every time Gojen passed him and his companions as they worked in their fields. But a certain event brought them closer.

♦

One day, as Gojen sat fishing by the Kuroi, the clear sky had suddenly clouded over, and in a matter of seconds, he found himself in the middle of a huge thunderstorm. He was rushing towards the hutments not far away when he heard a little girl crying somewhere behind him. Turning back, he saw a girl of about six or seven running his way through the chilli fields. The rain fell in sheets, the wind blew strong and the hail beat down ruthlessly. The girl was obviously terrified. Gojen stuck his fishing rods vertically in the soft earth and gathered the child into his arms. Covering her head with one of his hands to protect her from the hail, he continued to run.

'Which is your house?' he asked her.

'That one.' Still clinging to Gojen, she pointed to a hut in the cluster not far away.

As he charged through the rain, he managed to ask her, 'What's your father's name?'

'Mansoor', she replied.

Gojen remained in Mansoor's hut until long after the storm had abated. He changed into a lungi his host lent him and dried his own wet clothes over a fire that his hostess lit for him in a wok on the veranda. Chillies and pulses which had been spread to dry on the courtyard were still a little wet in spite of being gathered in as soon as the rains started—the chillies would be fine, but some of the pulses would go waste. Who would imagine that the bright clear sky would break so suddenly?

Mansoor told Gojen about his life. His full name was Mohammad Mansoor Ali; he was a petty worker on the *Misimi* before he settled here and took up farming. Life in their native village was full of hardships—they had to fight floods for the greater part of the year, an exercise that toughened them. So several other families had followed him here and were able to replace the wilderness with crops.

Living next to the Assamese villages and interacting with their people at the marketplace had made Mansoor familiar with their language, though he spoke it hesitantly. When the monsoon was at its peak and Kuroiguri's sandbanks were flooded, he and his companions worked as day labourers in the Assamese villagers' fields. The Saturday market was also a great unifier of the two communities.

Gojen learnt that apart from Mansoor, there were only two other people in his family—his wife Nerisa and his daughter Hasina. It was a small, happy family, except that Nerisa suffered from a pain in her abdomen, which was why she couldn't have any more children. The woman blushed at her husband's candour in front of a stranger. She jumped up from where she was scooping the damp pulses into a basket and, casting a meaningful glance at Mansoor from under her veil, went inside.

Hasina was the apple of her parents' eyes. She was so perky, she spent most of her time roaming the neighbourhood, visiting somebody or the other. When the storm broke, her parents assumed that she was in somebody's home, which was why they weren't worried. How would they know that she would venture out to the riverbank by herself? Served her right! If it weren't for Gojen, she could have been badly injured in the hailstorm.

However, she was a bright child. In their little village, there was a slightly literate person named Rezak Ali who could read Arabic, Parsi and Bengali, and had recently taught himself Assamese, its similarity with Bengali being of great help. Ali had rounded up a few boys for tutoring and lately, Hasina had also started taking lessons from him—not at the same time as the boys, of course. As if on cue, the little girl wrote her name on her slate and showed it to Gojen. He said, 'Wow, that's great.' Then, writing his own name below hers, he said, 'Come on now—read this.'

Hasina turned the slate towards herself and, carefully pronouncing the letters, read, 'Gojen Keunt.'

'Wow! You're going to be quite a scholar some day. Tell you what—I'll get you some of my books which must be lying around somewhere, and you can read those—you will read them, won't you?'

'Hm,' said Hasina absently as she copied Gojen's name on the slate.

Mansoor asked Gojen if it was alright for him to have a cup of tea at their home. Gojen replied, 'Why just tea?' He would have anything they cared to offer him. But they hesitated to do anything of the sort. Pouring tea into a brand new glass tumbler, Nerisa brought it to him.

His clothes were not quite dry but wearable, so Gojen changed back into them, standing behind a wall. Then, with a request to Mansoor to fetch his fishing rods from the fields at a later time, he prepared to leave. He fondly stroked Hasina's head—her hair was still damp—and her soft cheeks which felt like petals under his fingers.

It was clear once again, but almost sunset. He would have to cross the forest and the wooded hillock before the light faded. Then he would have nothing else to fear. The forests still saw the occasional lion, or so he had heard. Saying his goodbyes, Gojen returned homewards.

This was about eight years ago.

6

Gojen transferred the fishing rods from his right hand to his left. He gently stroked his right palm. Ever since the day he had caressed little Hasina's cheeks, he always felt their petal-like softness on them. He recalled one other incident involving her, which occurred a year or two after he rescued her from the hailstorm.

He was on his way to the Saturday market as usual, that being his sole mission since he had given up attending school. His chief attraction remained the dice game. He wasn't the lead gamester yet; he simply laid his bets along with other players—and won most of the time. The winning really excited him—the money didn't matter. Many of his co-players were financially broke—they couldn't afford medicines for an ailing family member, clothes for their children or essentials for a ritual or wedding in the family. Gojen distributed his winnings among them before he returned home.

The pleasure of winning at dice was akin to that of catching a large fish. Once he had checked out how big, and of what species and weight the fish was, he lost all interest in his catch. He often gave it to people he met on his way back, happy to eat the frugal meal his grandmother fed him, happy that he had his bowl of milk and banana to wind up.

That day, before he sat down to his game, he took a tour of the vegetable market. His grandmother had asked him to pick up some sticky rice and sesame seeds. He replied that he couldn't possibly lug the items all the way, so she should ask their field workers to get the rice and he would ask Mansoor to deliver the sesame at their door. Gojen always spoke harshly to his grandmother, but if she ever asked anything of him, he never let her down, which was why he decided he had better see Mansoor before he started gaming. Else, this errand would never get done.

From a distance, he saw Mansoor sitting behind piles of red chillies and onions. And next to him—wasn't that Hasina?

Hasina had always pestered her father to let her come to the market, and today she had got her way. It was six to seven miles from Kuroiguri and she, like her father and his companions, had to walk the distance. The men, of course, came every week. There were plenty of buyers, so there was no dearth of sellers at this large marketplace—they came from far and near.

Gojen came up to Mansoor and, looking at Hasina, said, 'Bhai, how come this one's here today? What, eh, Hasina? How come you've landed up at the market?'

Hasina sulked silently. 'What's the matter with her? Why isn't she saying anything?'

Between attending to his buyers, Mansoor explained that, delayed by his little girl's pace, he had arrived late. The place was already crowded and he couldn't leave his wares—or his buyers—to show her around.

'Hey, come with me,' said Gojen.

Hasina looked pleadingly at her father for his go-ahead.

'Go with Gojen bhai. And no more of that long face!'

The girl rose. Gojen took one of her hands in his and showed her the entire market—right from the livestock section to the fish and swine sectors—twice or thrice over. Hasina lingered longest at the trinket stalls. To another side were the cockfights, dance programmes performed by men dressed as women, canvassing magicians, bioscopes—she took her time over these too. This was her first experience of anything so colourful and fascinating, and she was spoilt for choice. Sitting on a bench at an open tea stall, she jumped in joy when she saw loopy jalebis frying. She ate quite a few of them with relish—all paid for by Gojen.

Wearing the red ribbons and glass bangles that he had bought her, she returned to her father. Gojen mentioned the sesame and went to his gaming den where people were already gathering.

When the market was about to wind up, Mansoor and Hasina went over to take leave of him. Too busy with his game to look up at them, he pushed a couple of coins into the girl's hands and, still without turning back, said, 'Bhai, you carry on. I'll leave shortly.'

Mansoor stacked his two empty baskets together and hung them on one end of his bamboo shoulder beam. He put his day's purchases into the baskets—a sari for Nerisa, a new dress for Hasina, a new machete, a pot of jaggery, a ball of washing soap and a few other miscellaneous items. He had also picked up some medicine for Nerisa's pain from a fakir he sometimes saw in the market. He would need to buy the week's provisions of mustard oil, kerosene, salt and so on from the only store on the way. This being quite a distance from his little village, it had become customary for him and his companions to pick up their weekly needs as they trudged home every Saturday. Hasina followed her father out of the almost quiet marketplace. She turned to look back and felt suddenly depressed.

A little away from the eastern side of the market was the pebbled lane of the local board. Traders on foot, on cycles and in bullock carts were returning home after winding up their day's business. Hasina walked close to her father, a half-eaten biscuit in her hand. At times, she ran far ahead and waited for him; at others, she lagged behind. After a while, she saw a wooden bridge and ran to get on it. The very next moment, her foot got caught between two slats, causing her to trip and fall to the ground. She let out a scream that brought Mansoor rushing to her. He thumped her back, lifted her up and said, 'Didn't I tell you not to run? Now look what's happened!'

Hasina sat down and rubbed her foot as she cried. It really hurt. Mansoor stroked the sore spot and then lifted her up. She continued to sob, but hobbled along, holding on to one of his arms. A little later, she sat down again and screamed, 'I can't go any further!' Her ankle was beginning to swell. As Mansoor stroked it once again, he wondered how they could proceed. Carrying her in his arms, or even piggyback, was out of question—he already had a quite a load to haul. He looked around helplessly.

A cycle was approaching from the direction of the market. But as it drew close, Mansoor noticed that the rider was a cloth merchant and he had large bales of his merchandise strapped both in the front and back—there was barely enough space for him. He also needed to ride carefully, without looking left or right, if he had to maintain his balance. So all he got from him was a sidelong glance. Then he noticed a bullock cart coming their way.

After a little negotiation, Hasina was lifted into the cart. But a couple of miles down the road, at a Y-junction, it needed to go in a different direction; so she was duly offloaded. Leaving her moaning under a banyan tree, Mansoor tried to figure out what he could do. He thought he saw Gojen approaching from the distance—yes, it was him. As he drew closer, he was surprised to see them and asked, 'What, Bhai, have you only come this far?'

He heard Mansoor's story and checked Hasina's ankle—it was quite swollen. Looking up at the setting sun, he said, 'It's almost sunset and at least four miles to Kuroiguri.'

'What can I do now? And I also have this load on my shoulders!' cried Mansoor.

'Our home isn't too far from here. Let's take her there.' Gojen slowly lifted Hasina to her feet, and the girl looked beseechingly at him. 'Here, Hasina—hop on to my back.' She was a little hesitant, but he crouched low, held her hand and said, 'Come, now. Hop on.'

Once she straddled his back, he carefully moved her injured foot to a comfortable position and moved forward. Mansoor followed a few steps behind them.

'I wonder how much longer I'll have to carry you around! The last time, you were caught in a hailstorm, now you've broken your ankle—what's next?'

The flame of the earthen lamp lit by the tulsi plant in the evening cast its glow over Gojen's courtyard. Standing in the light, with Hasina still on his back, he called, 'Aai, please get the lamp and come over.'

The old lady, holding a feebly lit lamp in her hand, stepped out on the veranda. 'So you're home, my boy?'

Gojen gently set Hasina down, and she hobbled over to stand clinging to Mansoor, putting as little weight as she could on her injured foot.

'Wait, I'm coming,' said Gojen's grandmother as she stepped down into the courtyard.

'Aai, this is Mansoor bhai, and this is his daughter Hasina. They had come to the Saturday market and she sprained her ankle on the way back.' Gojen unrolled a mat on the veranda and said, 'Bhai, get her here.'

'Wait, where do you think you are calling them?' said his grandmother through clenched teeth. 'You want to taint the mat on which I dry the boiled paddy?' Instantly, she picked up a sack from a corner of the veranda and, taking it to the courtyard, spoke to Mansoor, 'Wait right here. You don't have to make her limp all the way there.' Then, spreading the sack near the girl, she said, 'Now make the girl sit down.' She looked at the girl's foot from a distance and cried, 'The poor dear! Her foot is badly swollen!'

The three people around her discussed Hasina's condition. 'You know what, Bhai? Stay here tonight,' advised Gojen. 'How do you expect to take her that far?'

'My woman will be alone at home and she'll be worried. I could have sent a message through my companions, but they have all left.'

The old lady intervened, 'I know. Look at the poor girl and her broken foot! But wait, where will they sleep?'

'We'll manage somehow. Won't we find any room in this huge house? If we don't, we can make arrangements on the veranda,' said Gojen.

'Well, I don't know...' The old lady gripped one side of her waist and walked inside.

'Otherwise, Bhai, you can go and leave Hasina here. Hey, will you stay with us—alone?' he teased the girl.

Hasina clung more tightly to her father and said, 'No, I want to go home.'

'Go then—if you can, with your broken leg,' teased Gojen.

Hasina looked at Gojen and then lowered her head. Mansoor tried to reason with her. 'Stay, Hasina. Nothing will happen. Gojen is here; so is Aita. I'll come tomorrow morning and fetch you.'

The girl looked once again at Gojen—he smiled and indicated with his eyes that she should agree to stay. She smiled back at him and slowly loosened her grip on her father's arm. Mansoor gently stroked her hair and took leave of his hosts.

After a while, Gojen's grandmother brought a mixture of freshly pounded turmeric and mustard oil in a bowl and called to Gojen from the veranda, 'Bring her here, my boy.'

Gojen gave his grandmother a perplexed look. Had he heard right?

'Never mind—she'll sit only at the veranda,' the old lady confirmed.

Hasina stood up and, holding on to Gojen, who carried the lamp and the sack in one hand, limped to the veranda. He then left her there and went to wash up. She took some of the turmeric paste from the banana leaf on which it was given to her and massaged it over her swollen ankle. The old lady watched from a distance and tossed a pouch, filled with fallen hair and dipped in oil, towards her. 'Here now. Rub this all around the spot.'

Hasina tried to tie the cord on the pouch and burst out crying when she was unable to do so.

'Gosh! This girl's really useless. Come now, stretch that leg a little.' Seeing that her verbal instructions were not working, the old lady put aside her reservations and lifted Hasina's injured foot onto her left palm. With her free hand, she picked up some more of the salve and applied it to the swollen ankle. Gojen, just back from his washing and about to call out to his grandmother, stood speechless as he witnessed the sight on the veranda. It was unbelievable! At a loss for words, he simply said, 'Aai, I'm off to see the kabiraj. Let me see if he has anything for her pain.' Then, turning to Hasina, he said, 'Hey little girl. Now that Aai has given you her medicine, you'll be perfectly alright. So no more crying. I'll be right back— you stay here with Aai.'

◆

From the lane itself, Gojen saw the daily assembly in front of Dharmananda kabiraj's shop. It began with a reading of the Bengali newspaper *Dainik Basumati*. The kabiraj's uncle was, at one time, the personal physician to the king of Coochbehar, and it was from him that a young Dharmananda had learnt his Sanskrit and Ayurveda. Around the same time, he had started reading the daily paper, a habit that he had not forsaken for a single day in all these years. It took seven days for the paper to reach him by post from Kolkata. But being a daily, every day's news felt fresh—it was just that each day in the reporting world began a week later for him.

The post office was about three miles away, and the postman visited the village once a week, and that too, only if necessary, for the villagers had almost no contact with the outside world. The only letters that came in were for Sarbai Pandit's school, the kabiraj's clinic and Khargi mauzadar's home. Khargi had his daily mail picked up by a peon; and it was through a secret arrangement with this peon that the kabiraj received his paper every day. The mail, despatched by ship the previous day, reached the post office from the mail port only by evening, and it was the next morning before it was sorted and delivered. Most of it was for the tea estates and Marwari traders, and they had theirs collected too.

The kabiraj received—and read—his paper in the morning. In the evening, it was read again by the group of people that routinely assembled at his clinic veranda, with a person named Jadob Bora taking the lead. Apart from some elderly and middle-aged men, there were a couple of youths who formed the party. These youngsters were great fans of Jadob Bora and aided him in all his 'social' pursuits—good and bad. They had no interest in the reading and got involved only later, once the older members had left and Bora's discussion of his action plans started.

Jadob Bora held certain powers. He belonged to the elite group of two or three people before Gojen's time who were familiar with the English language. His sister's husband was a clerk at the court in the district headquarters. He had stayed with them while studying in high school, but failed to clear the matriculation exams. So he had returned to the village, stayed home and plunged into social work. He had inherited some land when his father died, and while his two brothers leased some of it and cultivated crops in the rest, Bora roamed the area on his bicycle and cultivated the powerful local officials.

His closeness with the local who's who helped him play a pivotal role in society. He was routinely called upon to organize public functions, or at least assume some position of responsibility. A few years ago, he had also involved himself in the Quit India movement. But drawn into the cesspit of local politics and weighing the risks involved, he made sure that he came to no personal harm. It was his calculating mind, more than his wisdom—and, of course, the musclemen who hung around him—that enabled him to wield some power among his people.

After completing his public and private duties for the day, Jadob Bora made it a point to stop by at the clinic on his way home. Sitting in a chair hastily vacated by the kabiraj, he would pick up the day's copy of *Dainik Basumati*. The wooden benches seated customers and patients during the earlier part of the day; but since there were no such people coming at this hour, they served as seats for the people who gathered for the news bulletin and gossip.

Bora would scan his audience, make a few introductory statements and then start reading. The kabiraj was the only person present who realized that there were many errors in the way the Bengali words were pronounced. Sometimes he explained the meaning of an unfamiliar word and when Bora had difficulty reading a certain word, he chipped in with it. Sitting on a stool, he listened to the entire session although he had read the paper already. He felt privileged that the *Dainik Basumati*, which benefited him by keeping him abreast of what was going on in the outside world, was something he could share with luminaries like Jadob Bora and his companions.

♦

Bora was reading *Dainik Basumati* in the dim lamplight as his audience listened in rapt attention. Gojen heard words like 'Sir Stafford Cripps, Cripps Mission, Gandhi-Jinnah dialogue, Viceroys' Summit' and so on. He quietly stole up to the kabiraj and sat next to him on the bench. The man gave him a sidelong glance and returned his focus to the news.

'Dharmadeu,' murmured Gojen. The man pretended not to hear him. The reading continued. After a while, Gojen repeated, 'O, Deu.' No response. Then, suddenly, in a loud voice, he called, 'Dharmadeu!'

Bora stopped reading, raised his head and saw Gojen. All eyes were fixed on him. He stood up and looked at the kabiraj, who said, 'What are you shouting about?'

'Get up—I need medicines,' said Gojen gravely.

Gesturing with a finger, the kabiraj bade Gojen to sit. 'Sit for a while. I'll give you the medicine later. I'm listening to the news. Read on, Bora.'

'I say, get up!' Gojen glared at the kabiraj. Though slightly shaken, the man tried to cover that up and rose slowly. 'These pests!' he muttered as he shoved his way past Gojen. 'You carry on, Bora.' Bora raised his head slightly and cast a sidelong glance at Gojen.

The kabiraj entered the side chamber, which was lined with neatly labelled glass and china medicine jars in various shapes and sizes. An old desk, darkened with age, held wood and stone gadgets for mixing and pounding. Turning to Gojen, who had followed him in, the kabiraj handed him some balm and a few tablets and said, 'I'm giving you these on the basis of what you have told me. Actually, there is no medicine for broken bones—they have to heal themselves. These are just to relieve the pain. The tablets have to be taken three times a day, two at a time, and the balm needs to be applied lightly—no massaging. And take care that it doesn't enter the eyes or mouth—it's poisonous.'

Gojen took the medicines and said, 'And my stuff?'

'I won't give you any.'

'Why? Why do you refuse me? What's different about today?'

'It's not just today. You know I don't ever like giving it to you.'

'But I get it anyway; so give me some now.'

'You stubborn creature, why don't you try and understand? If you have it regularly, you won't be able to give it up later—you'll get addicted.'

'What happens to me is my business. You don't need to worry about it. Now give me one anna's worth.'

'I'm telling you there's no need for it. Now run along.' Gojen reached out and removed a bottle from a shelf. In a swift move, the kabiraj retrieved it from him and said, 'Wait, wait—I'll give you some.' He took out some powder from the bottle with a stone spoon, wrapped it in some paper and handed it to Gojen.

As Gojen passed the group outside, Jadob Bora raised his eyes from the paper and called out, 'Is that you, Gojai?'

Gojen retraced his steps and addressed Bora very seriously. 'Kokaideu, I have told you this many times before—my name is Gojen, not Gojai. If you have a problem addressing me by my proper name, I'd rather you didn't address me at all. I'll survive that.'

'Really? But why all this hurry?'

'I have some important work.'

'Where? At Moti mistry's?'

'Moti mistry's wife is waiting with her fish fry, peanuts and glasses of country liquor. It's you who ought to be rushing there,' said Gojen as he walked away.

Bora jumped out of his chair and barked at Gojen's retreating back, 'Hey! Mind your tongue. Don't you know who Jadob Bora is? You're trying to act the goon, eh?' Gojen felt strangely gratified at the degree of the man's displeasure and smiled to himself. Then, suddenly, he got angry—how dare Bora, of all people, taunt him about his visits to Moti mistry's home?

◆

From a distance, Gojen heard the strains of a flute. He knew that Konloura, Rupai and Dino were at their regular rendezvous at the wooden bridge over the little rivulet that flowed through their village. Rupai played the flute beautifully, picking up tunes with ease. These three were Gojen's only friends in the village. Konloura was about his age and the other two, a couple of years younger. Thanks to his fearless nature, they hero-worshipped him. He didn't spend too much time with them, mostly preferring to remain by himself. But whenever he needed a friend or confidante, these were the three people he turned to.

In the faint moonlight, they recognized Gojen while he was yet some distance away. Rupai stopped playing, and Konloura called, 'Come, Gojen.' And, as he approached, 'We have been waiting for you.'

'Why?'

'We need to go dig potatoes for the Magh Bihu feast.'

Rupai piped in, 'We thought we should hit Durgi mahajan's garden tonight.'

'I'm not into all this potato-and-vegetable-stealing business. As it is, I've just had a spat with Jadob Bora,' said Gojen gravely.

'Why? What happened?' asked Konloura.

'These days I go to Moti mistry's for country liquor. Yes, I do go there—what's his problem? He goes there too—have I made any comment on that? He is a gentleman, a leader. And you all remember this—don't hang around with me. I'm a disreputable guy—a goon!' Gojen was angry and restless. He walked away.

From the gateway, Gojen saw Hasina having her meal at the veranda. When he came closer, he noticed that she was almost done—her banana leaf was almost empty. By her side was a wok with some dying embers, a bottle of old ghee and a few medicinal leaves. Aita sat by her side, goading her on, 'Eat up, my girl. Don't waste the food.'

Gojen went up to the veranda and asked, 'So, Aai, you've served her dinner already?'

'Actually, there were enough leftovers from lunch. And the poor child hasn't had a meal the whole day. The pain is also getting bad. So I thought, let her eat and try to get some sleep if she can.'

Gojen set the medicines on a plank and repeated the kabiraj's instructions to his grandmother. Hasina rolled up her used banana leaf with one hand, wiped the floor with a handful of water from the other and, holding on to the old lady, went to toss the leaf in the garbage pit. Then Aita poured a bit of water for her to wash up and wiped her dry with the end of her sador.

Gojen sat in an old chair and watched the goings-on. When Hasina returned to the veranda, he asked, 'Aai, where will she sleep tonight?'

'Inside. Where else? I've made a bed for her in the sitting room.'

'Really?' He entered the sitting room—two long benches on two sides, an old chair, a few low stools and two raised peeras. And, in the middle, a bamboo mat covered with a mattress, an old sheet and a pillow.

'Aai, you've made a bed on this mat?' asked Gojen. He felt strangely elated at his observation.

'Never mind. She's yet a child. Later, I will wash everything—including the mat. Get me some holy water from Bapudeu and I shall sprinkle some all over.' Saying this, the old lady applied the balm on Hasina's ankle, made her drink some water and swallow the tablets and then helped her lie down. Gojen sat on the bench and watched his grandmother in awe.

'Now that I've been dirtied, I have to bathe before I enter the kitchen again. You stay with her,' said Aai, and proceeded towards the well.

The next afternoon, Mansoor arranged for a bullock cart and took Hasina back to Kuroiguri. Gojen's grandmother sent her off with some coconut sweets, ground rice cereal and a hand of bananas. Gojen stared in disbelief.

◆

After this incident, a strong bond developed between Gojen's family and Mansoor's. The latter brought them produce from his fields, and Aita always had something to send for Hasina. On Magh Bihu, Mansoor and his family visited Gojen's home and brought them sesame, pulses, sweet potatoes and other vegetables. Every time he came over, the old lady served him his fill of a variety of home-made snacks and cereals. For Bohag Bihu, she wove a small embroidered mekhela for Hasina, a gift that pleased the child no end.

Gojen wondered at his grandmother's special fondness for the girl. He also noticed the changes in her in the eight years since he had first carried her on his back—were they only physical, or had some unseen power changed her as a person too? For, these days, she seemed much more reserved when dealing with him, although she remained the same with her father. Girls in Muslim homes were brought up rather strictly, but in Mansoor's family, the rules had been relaxed for Gojen. Hasina now wore a burqa, but when he was around, neither she nor her mother donned one. He smiled as he recalled the first time he had seen her in one. The moment she took it off, he sighed in relief and said, 'Thank god! I thought you'd die of suffocation in that thing.'

Yes, Hasina had changed. If, for some reason, he had to carry her piggyback again, would he be able to do it? Gojen smiled at the thought.

7

Lost in thoughts of Hasina, Gojen hardly noticed that he had crossed the fields and reached the Nepali village in Kuroiguri. He was close to the first of the settlers in the region—the Thapa brothers Durgaram, Bishnuram and Tikaram, popularly known as Jetha, Chaila and Kaila. One day, Jetha told Gojen how they came to this place and, in time, became one with it.

A Chinese carpenter had come to make crates for the Rangajan tea estate with two Nepali youths from Doomdooma to assist him. For some reason, he got into the bad books of the new estate manager and, when he was sacked, left for another place, leaving his assistants behind. Back home, their occupation had been to hew large trees with a huge saw which they both wielded from either end. It was strenuous work and the carpentry job had seemed attractive. But now, left with no other means of earning a living, they decided to go back to their old occupation. They had befriended some local people during their visits to the Saturday market, and it was here that they bought themselves a second-hand saw to start their trade.

It was in their quest for work that Jetha and Chaila landed up in Khargi mauzadar's courtyard one day. Behind the mauzadar's huge compound flowed a small river, beyond which there were thick woods—perhaps he would care to have a few of those trees felled? After two hours, the man gave them an audience and turned them away, saying he had no such plans. Then, on second thought, he summoned them back.

The mauzadar owned a herd of about twenty buffaloes—male and female, young and old. He had housed them on the sandbank of the Brahmaputra. The young man to whose care he had entrusted them had left, reliable help was not available and the herd had been much neglected in spite of moving it to his backyard. Also, tigers roamed the forest, especially during the monsoons. The herd tended to stray as soon as it was set free, and a couple of calves inevitably fell prey to the beasts.

The mauzadar had been planning to relocate the herd to the Kuroiguri area. He had heard that Nepali people were experts with livestock. And now that two of them had appeared at his doorstep, he decided to enlist their services. Jetha and Chaila acquainted themselves with the tasks involved in looking after the animals and, a few days later, set up a thatched house and some long sheds in the best part of the Kuroiguri sandbank. Then, leaving a brace of buffaloes for tilling the land, they moved the rest to their new settlement and took on the entire responsibility of looking after them. One day, they were joined by their younger brother Kaila.

That was many years ago. Eventually, the three of them got married and had families of their own.

Meanwhile, when the match factory decided to use the silk-cotton wood from the area, it brought in some more Nepali labourers to do the felling, and some of them stayed on after the company camps broke up. It was as though the scent of the Kuroiguri land had cast a spell on them and bound them to it. A few more huts came up beside the ones erected by Jetha, Chaila and Kaila. The new settlers also started breeding livestock and supplying milk and dairy products to the tea estates' sahibs and babus, and to the trading communities nearby. And a small society of hardworking Nepalis came into being.

Jetha and his brothers added a few buffaloes of their own to Khargi mauzadar's herd. They also became owners of a stretch of cultivable land. Inspired by their success at growing paddy, the other families toiled hard and cleared the grassy wastelands bordering those fields. It was low-lying land, which remained submerged for long periods during the monsoons. They cut canals, built dykes and in about two years' time, turned the stretch into lush rice fields. The sweat of their brows and caked blood from endless mosquito bites blended with the earth and transformed it to its green-and-gold majesty.

Although they had their own settlements and livestock sheds in Kuroiguri, the Nepalis who farmed paddy built some temporary shelters closer to their fields. Over a period of time, more of these came up and the erstwhile temporary dwellers began staying there permanently. This became the second Nepali village in the area and came to be known as the Doloni—the grassland—village.

But this village had a secret history.

It all started with Jetha's livestock farming, first for Khargi mauzadar and later for himself. His venturing into rice cultivation became possible because Khargi made over a stretch of land to him. This largesse was triggered by an infamy—a scandal that the mauzadar's family would go to any length to keep under wraps.

◆

It was some time ago, when Khargi mauzadar's adopted son, Swargaram, was still alive. The young man was the perpetrator of many a scandal; and there were many family secrets associated with him being an 'adopted' son.

Khargi's real name was Khargaram Singh, and his surname left room for speculation. He was a third-generation resident of Assam—his grandfather had moved here from their native Bihar and, through the good offices of a white officer, had acquired the mauzadar's post in Bishnujan. The post was then inherited by Khargi's father, Gargaram, before it was passed it on to him. Now close to seventy, Khargi was a man strong and healthy for his age.

Despite his alien roots, Khargaram was Assamese to the core, both in thought and deed. In fact, his wife, Chandraprabha, was the girl he had eloped with when she had come to the banyan tree to dance the Bihu. Not that his father should have allowed such an alliance—it was unthinkable that a member of the mauzadar's family should marry a penniless village girl, that too after eloping with her. But a chain of events made him concede to circumstances.

Except for a few villages of lower Assam, the zamindari system was unheard of in the state. But the mauzadars of the British era were no less than zamindars—their assets and lifestyles, though not quite comparable, were far above the reach of the common masses, whom they exploited as a matter of right.

Khargaram and his wife were distressed that they were childless even after many years of marriage. When all hope was lost, they decided to adopt Chandraprabha's distant nephew. They named the boy Swargaram.

Khargaram and his father had little formal education. In those days, it was Bengali that was taught in the schools. A priest from the Jagannath temple in Puri, who knew some English, visited the mauzadar's estate every year to distribute the lord's prasad in the neighbourhood and to collect donations. It was from him that Khargi learned some English. After a while, the priest's visits stopped, and with them, Khargi's English tuitions.

But when it came to Swargaram, all arrangements were made to give him a sound education. He was initially tutored at home; and at about twelve years of age, was sent off to boarding school in Kolkata. Khargaram had a distant cousin in the city who owned a fleet of about twenty large steamers which brought in goods to Assam through the Padma, Hooghly and Brahmaputra, and took back tea crates, jute and wooden planks. This cousin became the boy's local guardian.

Swargaram came home for two to three weeks during each summer vacation. These visits caused a stir of excitement not only in the estate and its surroundings, but in the nearby villages too. Many events took place in the area during these periods, and at the core of each was Swargaram Singh.

♦

One summer, when Swargaram Singh was seventeen or eighteen, he started taking driving lessons in the Ford that his father had bought from a white tea estate manager. The very first day, he ran over a cow and a calf before landing the car in a ditch. So the villagers had to keep their livestock within their compounds for the entire period of that vacation, and they chanted their prayers and made way for Swargaram every time they saw the car in the distance.

Another time, it was horse riding. Like his angling and shooting expeditions, his trotting through the village roads on horseback created a stir among the local people. He frightened them. With every passing year, he consolidated his image as the village hero—or rather, the villain. His visits threw life in the entire mauza off gear, and everyone—right from the labourer to the highest official—needed to exercise utmost caution at all times.

Swargaram also forged a relationship with Jetha, but it wasn't a pleasant one. The latter had heard about the young man's tyrannical exploits—shooting without provocation at the crowd that gathered to see a slain tiger, bashing a driver to death over a trivial matter and attempting to rape his wife, terrorizing locals until they relocated—the list was endless. And one day, Jetha's family became victim to Swargaram's venom.

One permanent item on Swargaram's agenda was to go angling and picnicking, and his preferred spot, almost always, was the Kuroiguri sandbank. Each time, he stopped by at Jetha's place, bossed around for a while and left with whatever provisions he needed for his outing—a boat, vegetables, curd, cream...

On one of these visits, he happened to set his eyes upon Suramaya, the stunningly beautiful young girl who happened to be the wife of Jetha's challenged younger brother. Swargaram was familiar with most of the brothels, hotels and clubs of Kolkata and had roamed all the villages within miles of Bishnujan. But he had never before seen a woman so beautiful. She could make the blood rush in any man's veins!

As he sat fishing, the image of Suramaya kept haunting him like a large silvery fish, and he thought of ways in which to land this one. He knew not if fish bit on his bait or skirted it—all he could think of were Suramaya's curves and the promise in her full breasts. After some time, he decided that she had surely arrived in

Kuroiguri because she was destined to become his. It wasn't fair that this golden girl be wasted on a half-wit! He resolved to rescue her from her fate and set about planning his moves.

Meanwhile, the premonition of impending danger loomed large over Jetha and his household. He hit out at Chaila for no particular reason and chided Suramaya at the slightest pretext. It was a heavy, clouded sort of atmosphere that surrounded Suramaya—the sort that precedes an earthquake. Swargaram became a daily visitor to Kuroiguri. As keeper of the mauzadar's livestock, Jetha naturally played host to anyone visiting from his home, and Swargaram took full advantage of that tradition. Earlier, he would drop in on his way to the river; now he remembered to also stop by on his return. Using his cunning, he befriended Chaila, for whom he frequently brought expensive gifts. Initially, the rest of the family looked on it as sympathy for the simple man. But slowly, that changed to mistrust. They tried to warn Chaila, as they strove to put a finger on the imminent crisis.

But when it did come, it took everyone by surprise.

◆

Three days before the end of his son's vacations, Khargaram got ready to drive him to the district headquarters, like he always did, so that he could catch a train from there. As they were about to leave, a pensive Swargaram declared that it would be a waste to drive all the way for just one person's convenience—he could take the bus that plied every alternate day. The owner, Kanubabu, who drove the bus himself, would make room for him; besides, he wouldn't even charge him the fare.

Khargaram was impressed. So his son was getting responsible at last!

Swargaram set off in the bus; but two hours down the road, he got off, telling Kanubabu that since there were yet a few days before his college started, he would spend some time with a relative. Kanubabu found no reason to doubt him.

On the fourth day after Swargaram left home for Kolkata, Jetha brought a piece of news to the mauzadar—his sister-in-law,

Suramaya, wife of his younger brother Chaila, had been missing since the previous day. They had searched the whole of the Kuroiguri area, but there was no trace of her.

The mauzadar smiled and said sarcastically—'There! You got such a beautiful girl to marry that idiot brother of yours. How could you expect him to douse her fires? She must have run away with some young man who could satisfy her.' But little did he expect what came later.

Jetha said that the 'young man' in question was possibly none other than the mauzadar's adopted son Swargaram.

In an instant, Khargaram's smile disappeared, making way for intense anger. He glowered in rage. How dare Jetha cast aspersions on his family like this? How could he voice such baseless allegations? He threw the man out of his compound. But moments later, he felt a strange uneasiness and mapped out a plan of investigation.

He got to learn from Kanubabu how Swargaram had gotten off the bus after a two-hour ride. Following this clue, it emerged that he had boarded a ship. Finally, the probe led to Rangapara, where the police had picked up a young couple on suspicion, and it turned out that the two were none other than Swargaram and Suramaya.

The mauzadar immediately put his son on a train to Kolkata, locked Suramaya in the woodshed behind his house and sent word to Jetha. While the latter decided that his family would have nothing to do with the characterless woman, Chaila arrived at the mauzadar's home and cried out that he wanted Suramaya back—he would take her home!

Finally, the mauzadar made an offer—he would make over a stretch of the grassland by the forest to Jetha. He could re-settle his brother and sister-in-law and also start cultivation there. The lure of immediate assets was too strong for Jetha to resist; so he readily agreed to the proposal. The mauzadar heaved a sigh of relief that the scandal would die a natural death at this very point.

◆

One day, a small hut came up beside one of the vast grasslands by the forest. Chaila and Suramaya set up home once again. But the man's physical and mental abilities were not adequate to clear the wasteland and convert it to farmland. So his brothers took it upon themselves to develop the land they now owned, Jetha making the daily trip from Kuroiguri.

In the next five years, Suramaya gave birth to three children. The pregnancies and other health problems took their toll and left her a thin and ghostly shadow of her former self. One morning, Chaila failed to rouse her from her sleep. He sat by her inert body and wailed.

It was impossible for Chaila to bring up his three children by himself. So the house was extended and made more habitable, and Jetha's family moved in. some time later, Kaila and his family joined them. Only Maila remained to look after the livestock in Kuroiguri.

That was the history of Doloni village. Though built upon a scandal, it became a blessing for the simple folk who made it their home. And although some of the Nepali folk stayed back in Kuroiguri with their cows and buffaloes, most of them relocated to the adjoining area, creating a village of their own.

8

Gojen was startled back to the present by a flock of teals suddenly flying out of a marsh. All this while, his mind was occupied by the history of the Nepali villages. He had heard the stories many times, on different occasions, from Jetha who, along with the rest of his family, had come to be considered a pioneer of sorts in the last twenty years or so.

Gojen shifted his fishing rods to his other shoulder and looked up at the sky, trying to gauge the time. There was yet some time until noon. It was around half past nine when he crossed Sarbai Pandit on his way. So it couldn't be more than half past ten now. He had already come past the woody hillock. There in the distance was Mansoor bhai's hut, the Kuroi flowing behind it. Before Gojen lay the vista of green crops, behind which were grasslands, then a stretch of silver sand followed by grey water and farther away, a black outline—the Kaziranga forest—with the blue sky above. His eyes feasted on the colours. They stoked his mind and he walked ahead, faster than before.

It was his habit to first drop in at Mansoor's home to check on Hasina—and on Nerisa's health—and to take along some cucumber, carrot or whatever was available, wrapped in a plantain leaf with salt and chilli, to eat while he was fishing. He enjoyed watching how all three members of Mansoor's family busied themselves with arranging these. If it took longer than expected, Hasina delivered the bundle to him by the riverside. Even otherwise, she occasionally dropped by to check how many fish he had caught. Gojen, loath to have his concentration broken, was visibly irritated by these visits—and this amused the girl no end.

He was smiling at his thoughts as he entered Mansoor's courtyard. But how come it was empty? There was always someone, if not all three of them, around at this time! Sensing something amiss, he stood his fishing rods against the wall, set his shoulder bag on the ground, went up to the door and called from the veranda, 'Bhai!'

Hasina rushed out. It was as though she was impatiently awaiting his arrival. 'Come in quickly,' she said excitedly, 'and see what's happened to Ma-jaan.'

Gojen realized that he had walked into a serious situation. 'What's the matter with her?' he asked.

'Come in first. She's burning with fever and not speaking a word!'

'Fever? Since when? Where is your father?' Gojen followed Hasina into the house. Once his eyes got used to the dimness inside, he saw that Nerisa lay still on an old bamboo platform, one worn-out quilt under her and one covering her gaunt form. Her half-open eyes stared fixedly into space—as though she didn't recognize him.

'It's been four days since the fever began, but she's been worse since yesterday. She keeps mumbling something and doesn't recognize me. Abbajaan left this morning to get medicines from the doctor. She kept babbling for a while after he left. And now she seems to have lost her voice.'

Gojen noticed that her eyes were beginning to close. 'She's falling asleep—good for her.' He moved closer and saw that there was still some movement in her nostrils and colour in her face. Her hot breath came slowly. 'Which doctor has he gone to? The one in the tea estate or the government one?'

'I have no idea,' replied Hasina, a helpless look in her moist eyes.

'Come out—it's too dark in here.' Hasina followed Gojen outside. He sat on the stool and stared into space, deep in thought. 'Get me a glass of water, please. I'm thirsty.'

Hasina brought out the glass kept apart for Gojen and was about to pour when she saw that the pitcher was empty. Then she remembered that she had forgotten to fetch water that morning. 'Please wait. We've run out of drinking water—I'll quickly get some,' she said, picking up a pot and running towards the Kuroi. On the sandbank was a well-like pit from where they drew their water—it was clean and cool.

While he waited for her to return, Gojen calculated that whichever doctor Mansoor had gone to was at least eight to ten miles away. This meant that it would be evening by the time he returned. It would be good if the doctor could see the patient personally— her ailment seemed serious. But would a doctor come on a poor man's request alone? Maybe if I tried...? But how can the doctor be brought here—perhaps by boat, via the Kuroi? Nay, that would take the whole day and no estate doctor could come except on a Sunday. A government doctor could be brought to a port by bullock cart and ferried in through the Brahmaputra. But would he plod through the muddy pre-monsoon shores to come here? Even if he did, he would charge a fat fee! Never mind; that could be arranged. If Mansoor couldn't arrange for it, he would do something himself—there was half a barnful of paddy that he hadn't sold yet because the pre-monsoon rates were still low. He didn't want the traders to make extra profits and besides, every once in a while, a couple of very poor families from the village came asking for a little grain. Anyway, the paddy could be converted to cash if necessary.

The other alternative was to take the patient to the doctor by boat and bullock cart; but it was impossible to make her rough out the ten to twelve miles in her present state. What could be done?

Suddenly Gojen thought of Dharmananda kabiraj—he was only about five miles away. The man's diagnostic powers were legendary and he had cured a number of people in the village of what seemed like incurable diseases. Of course, Gojen still had certain reservations about the man himself. Many a time, there seemed to be too much jaggery in the intoxicants he sold. Gojen also disapproved of the fact that he associated with the likes of Jadob Bora in the evening newspaper-reading assembly. But would the kabiraj decline his request just because of these trivial issues?

Let him dare! Of course, being the staunch Brahmin that he was, he might object to touching a Muslim woman. But once Gojen set his mind on something, it was only very rarely that he failed to achieve his goal—and he had made his decision.

'Here's your water.' The words jolted him back to the present.

'Hm, okay.' Gojen drained the glass in a single gulp and said, 'Hasina, I'm off to fetch the kabiraj. It'll be two to three hours before I'm back. In the meantime, if your father returns with the medicine, give it to her by all means. But how effective it will be, I don't know—after all, the doctor hasn't seen the patient.' He rose and walked inside, Hasina behind him.

'I'm afraid to be here on my own. Look at how Ma-jaan is behaving.' She gripped Gojen's hand. The patient suddenly opened her eyes wide and fixed a stony look on her daughter. Gojen eased his hand from the soft grip and walked towards her.

'Don't worry,' he told Hasina. 'I'll ask one of the neighbours—Rahim or somebody—to be here until I'm back. But get a doctor we must.' He stepped outside, and moved his fishing gear to the backyard. Then, walking across to Rahim, who was weeding his chilli patch in the distance, he said something, gesturing towards the house. Hasina watched all this from the veranda until Gojen was out of sight.

◆

It must be around noon, mused Gojen. The sun was blazing hot. Two faces—one pale and hot with vacant eyes and the other misty-eyed and anxious—prompted him to walk faster when, suddenly, he realized that he was in the vicinity of Sarbai Pandit's school. And right there, just as it stood years ago, was the teacher's bicycle. Pausing for just a moment at the gate, he walked into the school compound and called from the veranda, 'Excuse me, Sir, I need to have a word with you.'

The teacher looked up from checking his dictation and seeing Gojen, came out to the veranda. 'So, Gojen—I thought you were out fishing?'

'Sir, there's been a problem.' Gojen informed Pandit of Nerisa's critical condition and asked if he could borrow the bicycle. 'It'll save a lot of time if I could ride to the kabiraj. I'll be right back and return your bicycle before school breaks up. That's the only way we may be able to save the woman.'

The desperation and sincerity in Gojen's voice left the teacher with no hesitation in lending him his cycle. He was well aware of the young man's nature of rushing to help anyone in need. He consented readily, watched Gojen hop on and kept staring until he was out of sight.

Leaning the cycle by the kabiraj's wall, Gojen rushed directly to the inner chamber, where the older man was busy grinding some sticky ointment in a large china bowl. Taken aback by the sudden intrusion, he barked, 'Why did you have to come in here? Couldn't you have called from outside?'

Ignoring the scathing tone, Gojen moved right up to the kabiraj. Gently pushing away the ointment bowl, he said, 'Deu, there's a very serious patient you need to look at. Please come along.'

'Who is this serious patient? At this time of day…?' The kabiraj asked, drawing the bowl up as he spoke.

Once again, Gojen pushed it away. 'This can wait,' he said. 'But you need to come with me to Kuroiguri right away. Mansoor's wife is in a critical state.'

The kabiraj knitted his brows and looked directly at Gojen, totally flabbergasted. 'What? To Kuroiguri? I have only heard of the place—never stepped there. And now, to trek all that way…'

'I've got a bicycle that will take us part of the way. The rest is not a very long walk,' said Gojen.

'I don't know how to ride a bicycle.'

'I'll ride—you just need to sit.'

'Hah! To break my bones in my old age! Don't I have anything better to do? Also, I can't enter a Muslim home just to see a patient. So get lost and let me do my work.' The kabiraj drew the bowl to him once again and picked up the pestle. This time, Gojen thrust it to the end of the table and, gripping the old man's arms, asked threateningly, 'Are you coming or not?'

The look in Gojen's eyes made the kabiraj feel like a helpless infant. His attitude mellowed, his fist eased and the pestle rolled on to the table.

◆

Forcing the kabiraj out of his clinic and onto the cycle, Gojen pedalled hard along the pebbled road of the local board which gave way to a sandy, grassy path. He carefully steered along the tracks left by bullock carts. The faces of the two women continued to haunt him. The kabiraj sat rigidly on the bar, worrying about what the local people would have to say about this later.

As they approached the school, Gojen asked the kabiraj to alight and start walking. 'You carry on—I'll join you as soon as I return the bicycle. And also, you needn't tell Pandit anything about this ride when you see him.'

'Big deal! The whole village has seen me ride with you and must be wondering whether I've lost my sanity or shared your intoxicants. As if he won't find out anyway!'

'We'll see about that later. Now just keep walking—no more talk.'

Gojen left the cycle at its usual place and went up to a window to indicate to the Pandit that he was back. The latter, busy with teaching his students some mathematical problem, simply nodded his head in acknowledgement and continued with his lesson. Gojen heaved a sigh of relief—at least for the moment, there was no danger of the teacher finding out that he had given the kabiraj a lift on his bicycle!

The road ahead was not fit for cycling anyway, and the two men continued to walk until they reached the forested hillock. Suddenly, the kabiraj remembered that this was where wild animals used to roam, and he stopped in his tracks. He called out to Gojen, who was slightly ahead of him and said, 'Hey, Gojen! There are lions in this forest. I'm not coming any further.'

Gojen retraced his steps and once again gripped the kabiraj by his arm. In a menacing tone, he said, 'Are you or aren't you coming with me? If I were to throttle you right here, nobody would ever find out.'

The kabiraj freed his arm and started to walk in silence. When Gojen was about to overtake him, he pleaded, 'Don't walk ahead without me.'

Just as they were approaching the peak of the hillock, Gojen thought he heard the sound of a woman crying. He rushed up and when he reached the top, he saw a few people milling around in front of Mansoor's hut in the distance. That was where the wails seemed to be coming from. He stopped short. 'That's their house,' he mumbled to himself.

The kabiraj, who had by then reached the peak, stood by Gojen and surveyed the scene before him. 'So she's gone?' he asked.

'Looks like it. Come on—let's get there quick.' Gojen started running down the slope.

'Er, maybe I won't come after all. Why do I need to see the dead and unnecessarily go through all the purification rites later?'

A sharp scream—perhaps Hasina's—rent the air. Gojen ran faster. The kabiraj took one look at the distant scene and slowly turned back homewards. The wailing sounds—both male and female—got more intense.

◆

'Aai! Open the door!' Gojen woke his grandmother around ten at night, standing in the courtyard near the veranda. He had already put away his fishing gear by the barn.

The old lady lifted the latch, opened the door and stepped out. 'Were you fishing so late into the night?' she asked.

Gojen ignored the question. Taking off his shirt, he said, 'Keep a dhoti and gamosa ready. I'll have a dip before I come in.' He tossed the shirt on his shoulder and moved towards the stream that flowed by their backyard. His grandmother went in to get his clothes, without giving it a thought.

In the lamplight, she noticed that Gojen returned from his untimely dip with a wet shirt which he had rinsed out and left to dry on the clothes horse. He was still dripping wet when he collected the clothes she handed him. Sensing something amiss, she asked, 'What got into you—why did you need to bathe at this late hour?'

'There's some terrible news, Aai. Mansoor bhai's wife is dead,' said Gojen as he wiped himself dry.

'What did you say?! Mansoor's wife? How did it happen?' asked his shocked grandmother.

'The fever got to her head.' Gojen told her everything as he changed.

'The poor thing! Their daughter will now be all alone—what a problem for the father!' Then, about to enter the house, she turned around and asked, 'Should I serve your meal in the living room? After all, it was a death in a Muslim home and you must have meddled with them. Go to the temple tomorrow and get the priest to purify you.'

'We'll worry about that later. Now you go sleep—I don't want any dinner.' The old lady had never heard him speak so seriously before. She could understand perfectly. He was so close to Mansoor's family, the death must have come as a real blow. She sighed deeply, turned down the lamp and got into bed.

Gojen went into the room, combed his hair by the dim lamplight, picked up a bundle of beedis and a matchbox and came out to sit in the old chair on the veranda. Lighting up a joint, he took stock of the events of the day. They appeared before his eyes as a sequence until he came to a stop on the last—the scene of Hasina embracing her dead mother and crying. The heart-rending sound still rang in his ears. Then the thoughts got all muddled up—a sick woman's glazed look, a soft grip on his hands, the helplessness in Hasina's face, his trip to the kabiraj, the desperate attempt to save a life, the difficulty in finding a doctor....

Many years ago, when he had gone to see Modon off at Kuroiguri, the latter had told him that once the country was independent, no one would need to trek through forests and grasslands to get from one place to another. There would be good roads, good transport, lots of doctors, engineers, schools and colleges, medical facilities in every village... There was talk of this independence coming soon. From what he had read himself or heard Jadob Bora read out at the kabiraj's clinic, he gathered that leaders like Gandhi, Jinnah and Nehru were in talks with the British for this purpose. Once the country was free, people like Hasina's mother need not die for want of medical attention.

Gojen thought of Modon again—if only he could meet him once more! The man spoke so well about the country! It would be good to hear him say those nice things again—about good roads and doctors who would cure the sick. He tried to imagine what an independent country would feel like.

9

Khargi mauzadar's estate. From the main road of the local board, a straight path of about one-and-a-half furlongs stretches out like a ruler to his door. This is a private road maintained by the estate. Every now and then, charcoal from the nearby tea estates is brought in to line its two edges, so that the mauzadar's Ford and the vehicles of the occasional white visitors can ply smoothly.

The mauzadar also owns two horses, which he rides on his rounds, just as he owns the land on either side of the path on which he has settled some fisherfolk and Nepali families. The pathway is neatly lined with evenly spaced trees which, despite their age, retain their beauty. There is a gate-house where the path meets the compound, and behind it is the sprawling bungalow.

To the left of the compound is the rectangular office of the mauza, a part of which is open and has wooden railings on three sides. Of the two rooms inside, one is the mauzadar's private office; the other is occupied by the clerks and peons. The open area has a huge mahogany-and-cane armchair and, a little farther, a few wooden chairs and three long benches. This area serves as a conference hall and can accommodate around twenty-five people. This is where the village folk wait to pay their taxes; it is also the area where the mauzadar holds court with the common people or their representatives whenever the need arises.

It is a routine practice for the higher district and police officials or the civil surgeon, or the OC of the Nihali police station to drop by if they are in the area and have a hearty meal with the mauzadar. They, too, use this open space for discussions with people they need to meet. Whenever the OC catches a petty thief, this is where he winds up the case. He beats the man until he confesses to the felony and returns the stolen goods—walking him the fourteen miles to the police outpost in handcuffs and then transferring him to the district headquarters is too much of an effort.

A few tough cases are also cracked with the mauzadar's assistance. This 'assistance' is in the form of serving as a middleman for financial negotiations—fixing the amounts that need to be paid to the police officials to close the files.

The drawing room in the main bungalow is unique in its décor. It houses expensive wooden furniture, some inlaid with brass, copper or even silver. On the walls hang priceless paintings, photographs, animal horns and antlers, and tiger skins. On one side are elephant legs and two massive, shiny tusks, standing tall. Khargi mauzadar's father, Gargi Singh, was a prolific hunter. Khargi too was a regular at this sport but gave it up a long time ago, after the death of his adopted son.

The deep bond he shares with the gaonburha—the village chief—Betharam Handique, aka Bethai, remains as strong as ever, though they both maintain their social distance where public matters are concerned. Their friendship dates back to the days when the two were classmates in primary school. And although Bethai dropped out right after while Khargi continued being tutored at home by his Oriya teacher, the two continued to be the best of friends. No one from the village ever dared enter the mauzadar's bungalow. But during their childhood, Bethai had often been invited by Khargi to visit his home and listen to music on the wound-up gramophone.

◆

The modern, cultured lifestyle within the mauzadar's estate made it taboo for young Khargi to go see the Bihu dance under the banyan tree in the field—it was too coarse and plebeian. But with Bethai's help, he managed to witness the dance as soon as he entered manhood. Worse still, he fell in love with one of the pretty young dancers. It was again through Bethai's connivance

that Khargi kissed the girl in the bushes as they returned home—
his first kiss. A number of firsts followed—seeing a young woman's
bare round breasts, touching them with his fingers and lips... These
experiences took over his body and mind and awakened in him a
lust to make this girl his very own.

The girl's name was Chandraprabha, but everyone called her
Chandra. She, too, began to lose herself in her fantasies. Many a
time, the shuttle fell from her hands and she made mistakes at the
loom; in the kitchen, she forgot to season the heated oil in the wok,
spent a lot of time by herself and was unusually eager to step out of
the house at a particular time each day. The Khargi-Chandra love
story provided juicy fodder for the gossip mills and the news soon
reached both sets of parents.

The waves of their passion hit walls of opposition. Chandra's
father called her a dwarf trying to reach for the moon. It wasn't
just the financial disparity that mattered—there was also the caste
factor. Who knew the background of Khargaram's ancestors in
Bihar? As for Khargi's father, tainting their aristocracy by making
a common village girl the mistress of the mauzadar's estate was an
unthinkable proposition.

A whole year passed. Khargi was morose and tense, and
Chandra, heavy-hearted and silently tearful. By the third year, their
minds were made up. One day, during that April Bihu, Chandra
feigned dizziness and broke away from the group of dancers.

'What's the matter, Chandra?' asked Betharam, coming
forward.

'My head is reeling and I'm feeling giddy. I won't dance any
more. Maybe I should go home.'

'Come, I'll see you home. You shouldn't go alone.'

Their companions heard the exchange and saw nothing
irregular in the situation. Besides, at that point, they were engrossed
in a competition to determine who were the better dancers—
the men or the women—so all eyes were focused on them. The
atmosphere was charged and everyone was rapt in watching the
dancers' supple waists, heaving breasts, swaying hips and tapping

feet. The drummers too got their share of attention, thanks to their nimble fingers and the beats they tapped out. Nobody realized that Bethai and Chandra's act was simply a ruse.

◆

Chandraprabha, Betharam and Khargaram went missing for a week. Betharam's father, Gunaram gaonburha, owned an old single-barrelled gun, which he loaded anew. Khargaram's father loaded his double-barrelled gun. Both lay in wait—whoever's son turned up with the girl would face his father's bullets; and they wouldn't spare the girl either.

A week passed. It was the middle of the night. Most households had turned out their lamps and gone to bed. The velvety darkness was broken only by the light of fireflies and a star-studded sky. Except for the faint strains of a bhaona being enacted in some distant village, all was still. Two men and two women landed up at Gunaram gaonburha's home. One of the women entered the bamboo gate, crossed the large courtyard and stepped onto the veranda. Seeing a flicker of a lamp in a room through the window slats, she went up to it and, in a suppressed voice, called, 'Kokaiti—are you asleep? Hey, Kokaiti!'

Gunaram called from inside, 'Who is it?'

'I'm Damayanti, Kokaiti. Do get up and open the door,' she said softly.

The sound of clogs was heard from within. Gunaram opened the door, held the lamp high and looked at his sister in amazement. 'Damayanti! Alone at this hour?'

'I'm not alone. I've got them with me.'

'Them? Who's them?' asked Gunaram, even more perplexed. Then, realizing the situation, he spoke as if to himself, 'So they have come! They landed up at your place, did they? But they won't enter this house. Hey, don't you move a step forward. I'll shoot you down—the gun's loaded.'

'Wait, Kokaiti! Don't shout—I beg of you. Please go inside. I knew you'd behave like this; which is why I'm here. Now please let them in. Anyway, the girl hasn't gone with your son—it's the mauzadar's son she's with.'

'That makes the situation all the more complicated. If my son had eloped with the girl, I would have just got them home and kept them here. But why did the bastard have to meddle with the mauzadar's son? Will the mauzadar leave me alone after what has happened?'

'Be quiet for now, Kokaiti. I'm telling you—please go in. They won't dare to enter the house as long as you stand in the doorway. Now, get inside.' The lady took the lamp from Gunaram and gently pushed him in. Then she looked towards the gateway and called, 'Why don't you all come in now?'

Meanwhile, Gunaram's wife got out of bed. 'Oh, Damayanti!' she exclaimed as she came to stand by the other lady. Just then, Betharam, followed by Chandraprabha and then Khargaram walked into the compound, stepping lightly, almost as though they were trying not to hurt the ground under their feet. To avoid facing them, Gunaram stomped inside, his clogs resounding loudly.

'Nobou, please take them in and make arrangements for their beds. Let them spend the night here. Matters can be sorted out later.'

Hearing Damayanti's instructions to her sister-in-law, Gunaram reappeared and interrupted, 'Nothing will wait until later. Matters will be sorted out right now.' Blocking the way for Khargi, who was about to enter the house, he said, 'Wait, Khargi, my son. You don't go in. Come with me to your home.' He had already tossed a gamosa over his shoulder and equipped himself with a five-battery torchlight.

'Should we go now? I wonder what my father will say,' said Khargi, his trembling voice betraying his intense fear.

'I don't know what he'll say. But my son, you have to come with me right away. If the girl had come with my son, I would have handled the case. But I can't risk the blame of letting you enter my home with her. Come—I'm with you. If your father attempts to shoot you, I'll save you. Come—there's nothing to fear.' He spoke with authority, stepped out of his clogs and into the courtyard.

'Come, my son.' Gunaram shone his torch as he walked ahead. Khargaram followed meekly.

◆

The judgement happened that very night.

Khargaram's head hung low as he sat in his chair in a special room in the bungalow. Beside the inside door stood his mother Haimawanti—Hema for short. Gunaram sat on a stool by the main door. On one side, on a mahogany shelf, was the double-barrelled gun, Gargaram running his fingers over the trigger like a tabla player readying himself to accompany a fellow musician. He stood unmoving, like a tree, and fixed his shamed son with a steady glare.

The atmosphere was akin to the dampness after a storm— Gargaram had gone through his share of thundering, flailing and bemoaning his lot. He reproached his son in no uncertain terms for tainting his dignity and his ancestry, and at times, got violent enough to pick up his gun and threaten to shoot him. Now, spent from his exertions, he tried to cool-headedly ponder over the judgement he should deliver. An eerie silence filled the room as everyone waited with bated breath.

Finally, Gargaram spoke. Very seriously, and seemingly with a total lack of feeling, he said, 'Well, what has happened has happened. Now tell me the truth. Your answer will decide my next step.'

Khargaram raised his eyes to his father's and awaited the question he was expected to answer honestly.

'In all these days, did you sleep with the girl?' asked Gargaram. Getting no response, he asked, 'Do you hear me? I asked you something.'

Khargi hung his head low and replied, 'Not as long as we were at Bethai's aunt's place.'

'So when did you sleep together?'

'The first night, when we couldn't cross the Kuroi, we slept on the sands...'

'That I know. But did you do anything to her?'

Haimawanti cast a sidelong glance at her husband and slowly retreated inside. Khargaram's head remained lowered.

'Hey! Why don't you speak up? Did you do anything to her? If yes, I'll get you married tomorrow and bring her home. But if nothing has happened, she goes back to her own home. That's final. Now tell me—truthfully—did anything happen?'

In a tiny voice, his eyes still lowered, Khargaram replied, 'It did.'

'Enough! It's decided. Since you've sowed the seeds of my race in her body, she has to be accepted—never mind whether she is a goddess or a demoness, beautiful or ugly. Who knows what her time is now? If the seed happens to sprout in her womb, no branch of our tree can be allowed to grow in somebody else's garden.'

Having passed the judgement as if in court, Gargaram once again addressed his son. 'Your Highness, please go inside now. Your elopement will make you go down in history. Just my luck! Now get lost, will you?'

Khargaram floundered out of his chair and made his way inside, feeling that a great weight had been lifted from his mind and body. As he was about to enter the inner chamber, his father noticed that Hema, who had been waiting behind the door, caressed her son's back, as if in welcome.

'So what do I do about Pitmal's daughter now? Do I take her back to her parents?' asked Gunaram, getting ready to leave.

'Sit, Gunaram. This evening, Burton sahib from the Bishnujan tea estate came calling. He got back from his six-month vacation in England just the day before yesterday, and has brought me a big one this time. I haven't opened it yet, but let me do that now. It's right here.' Saying this, Gargaram pulled out a huge bottle of scotch from a cabinet in the room.

'At this time of night...' Gunaram wondered about the propriety of Gargaram's proposal.

'The lateness of the hour doesn't matter. What does matter is the storm that's brewing in my head. I'll have to call that beggarly Pitmal's daughter my daughter-in-law! It would have been all too easy to give the man plenty of money and some land and hush things up. But since my son has feasted on the girl, it has become an issue of conserving the seeds of my race!'

And so it was that on the mauzadar's estate, in the middle of the night, with a glass of foreign liquor in hand, Gargaram reiterated the unexpected pronouncement that would preserve the pride of his family.

◆

The wedding, with all its pomp and ceremony, was organized in a day. It was arranged that the bride would depart from Gunaram's home—hers was too small to set up the canopy and leave room for the groom's elephant and accompanying musicians. In fact, her compound could barely accommodate a couple of people! So in less than half a day, Gunaram's home ground was covered with a huge canopy, and a ceremonial gate erected at the entrance. The tailor Ganesh personally supervised the decoration of the pandal with floral cutouts in red, blue, green, purple and yellow paper. Two day-lights and five Petromax lamps were also brought in.

The mauzadar directed Gunaram to take care of all expenses without skimping, on the promise that he would be reimbursed later. Pitmal shouldn't have to spend a single paisa. Whatever bamboo, tarpaulins, metal sheets or utensils were needed could be brought from the mauza estate. Bethai busied himself supervising the arrangements. All the curd that the Nepali milkmen of Kuroiguri had set for the Saturday market were bought up; so were tins of jaggery at the Marwari store and entire stocks of beaten rice wherever they were available. Those who had doubted that arrangements could be made in a day were proved wrong. There was plenty of food—and plenty of people to relish it. The servers served, the diners dined, and the festivities continued...

The father-son duo of Gunaram and Betharam played host to the hilt. The ladies of the house ensured that the invited ladies were well looked after. And when the guests left, it was Gunaram they took leave of. Amidst the flurry of activity, everyone failed to notice one couple—the bride's parents. Pitmal, the father, sat in a corner wiping the banana-bark dishes dry while the mother sat at one end of the veranda peeling and cutting tamul until she had blisters on her hands.

The jurun ceremony, in which the groom's family sent gifts for the bride did not happen. However, in the early evening, Haimawanti put some of her expensive silk mekhela-sadors in an imported leather suitcase. To these, she added some of her jewellery—a strung pendant, bangles, earrings and a necklace, all packed in a box inlaid with silver. She had this suitcase put in their Ford and, making a stop at the Marwari store to buy some musk perfume and vermilion—which she transferred from its packet to the silver case she had taken along—she arrived at Gunaram's door. She had also taken a tray of tamul-paan covered with a crocheted doily, but the mauzadar had this offloaded, saying, 'You don't need to show Pitmal these formal respects just because his daughter's going to be our daughter-in-law.'

The Ford came to a halt at Gunaram's gate and Haimawanti alighted. Children crowded around the car in awe, and Gunaram and Bethai rushed up to clear the way for the lady. The driver, Budhram, took out the suitcase, and Gunaram took it from him, carrying it carefully on his shoulder. They all moved towards the house.

When they reached the canopy, Haimawanti asked, 'Where is the bride?'

'In the living room; with some of her friends.'

'Take me to her.'

'Of course. Do come along.'

Haimawanti walked towards the room where the bride sat on a floral cane mat, surrounded by her friends. The commotion and excited chatter that pervaded the house a little while ago ebbed down to curious murmurs as all eyes were fixed on the lady. Dressed in expensive clothes and fancy footwear, gold ornaments adorning her fingers, wrists, ears and neck, the slightly plump, wheatish-complexioned lady with the large red dot on her forehead sallied gracefully into the room.

The bride's friends stood up, fascinated—they had never seen Haimawanti up close. The only times they had seen her were when she drove past in her Ford, or at the couple of brief appearances she made when invited to see a bhaona. Betharam rushed to summon his mother and aunt. The aunt spread out another mat beside the bride's. Without wasting any time, Haimawanti opened the suitcase and carefully transferred its contents to the mat. The clothes were fancy. A few of the sets were sparingly used, but one was brand new. She stole a look at the bride's outfit—it was silk all right, but rather old. It surely belonged to either Gunaram's wife or daughter. The people crowded around her as though something strange was happening.

'Betharam, please ask these people to leave us alone for a bit. You also step out for a while—and shut the door after you. The bride needs to change.'

Betharam ushered everybody out and personally stood guard at the closed door to ensure that nobody tried to enter the room.

With a couple of young girls assisting her, Haimawanti dressed the bride. She made her wear the new mekhela-sador and pinned it in place with an ornate silver brooch which she unpinned from her own shoulder. She sprinkled some musk perfume on her and decked her out in an array of exquisite ornaments. Some cream, a dusting of Cuticura talcum powder, a dab of rouge, and the bride's toilette was complete. She picked up the silver vermilion box, applied a dot on the bride's forehead and a dab in her parting.

When Betharam opened the door on Haimawanti's orders, a horde of women rushed in, and some started long ululations to ward off the evil spirits. Haimawanti adjusted Chandra's veil and gently lifted her chin to take a good look at her. The girl was really beautiful—her eyes, nose, and her smooth skin. She planted a soft kiss on each of her cheeks.

Suddenly, somebody from among the ladies started sobbing loudly. Looking towards her, Haimawanti asked, 'Who is she? And what's the matter with her?'

'Who else? Your relative now—the bride's mother! She's crying because her daughter is leaving.'

Haimawanti looked at the woman from top to toe. The words 'your relative' kept resounding in her ears. Just then, Bethai's aunt rushed in with a tray of whole tamul-paan. Placing it beside the bride, she said, 'Come, get up, Chandra. Touch your mother-in-law's feet.'

A friend helped Chandra up and assisted her in the feet-touching. Haimawanti tried to gauge the women around her. Was it just her imagination, or had Bethai's aunt made the term 'mother-in-law' sound slightly flippant? 'That'll do,' she said, raising Chandra to her feet. She was about to take off another ring from her finger and place it on Chandra's, but she suddenly met Bethai's aunt's eyes, and noticing a meaningful smile in them, decided against it.

'Okay, then. I'll leave now. You can bring your things in this suitcase itself.' A sobered Haimawanti hurried out of the door, paced up further on reaching the courtyard and moved towards her car, Gunaram and Betharam rushing after her.

'Aaideu, I had arranged for some curd and a baan-baati...' said Gunaram.

Haimawanti looked straight ahead and got into the car through the door that the driver held open for her. The father-son duo were left wringing their hands as the driver turned the handle and brought the car engine to life. Through the loud sounds of the running engine and the children's gleeful observation of the car, just two words kept ringing clear in her head—she now had a new 'relative' to whose daughter she was a 'mother-in-law'.

10

There was no evidence of a family wedding in the mauzadar's house—not even an extra cup of tea. The day started like any other. At the breakfast table, the mauzadar held forth at length to his wife, 'We have to perform the sacred rites at the bride's home before we bring her here. Any ceremony calls for inviting people and feeding them well. I have made all arrangements at Gunaram's place. There is nothing sacred happening here in my yard; so I'm not about to invite the entire village, okay? Let them stuff themselves at the bride's place. I've asked Gunaram to spend with a free hand—I'll reimburse him later. The bottom line is: there is no wedding in this house—no canopy, no drums, no band, no mantle lights, no food or sweetmeats. And listen—the temple priest, Bapudeu, will conduct the ceremony. Eight o'clock is the auspicious hour; so I'll leave home with the groom and the priest at seven-thirty.'

In the evening, when he saw his wife depart in the Ford with the suitcase, he realized that she had been making her own plans.

A female elephant was decked out in the mauzadar's yard for the groom to travel on. The entourage left at seven-thirty sharp. Ramu Sardar led the way, mantle-lamp in one hand, lathi in the other. Behind him was the elephant carrying the mahout, Bapudeu, Khargaram and the servant boy, Ponaram, who held an open umbrella over the groom's head. Bringing up the rear was the Ford. Gargaram mauzadar rode in the back. Next to the driver was his trusted personal attendant, Moniram, whose duties ranged from laying out the Kashmiri carpet for the groom and taking care of his needs to keeping enough money available to pay the priest and assisting with whatever was asked of him.

Khargi got off the elephant and was carried into the pandal in Betharam's arms. The mauzadar, still in his car, summoned Gunaram and said, 'I'll leave now—there's nothing for me to do here. I'll take the elephant—the car can stay; and when the wedding is over, the bride and groom can ride back in it. And listen—nobody else needs to come with the bride. You make sure of that. Oh, wait. Take this bag. There's something in it for you. I don't know how much is left—I uncorked it this evening. But it's imported and will help you relax after the wedding is over. Here...' Gargaram handed the bag containing a half-empty bottle of foreign liquor to Gunaram, got out of the car and went up to the elephant. As he rode through the night, he mused at all that he had done to preserve the seeds of the Singh family. He laughed out loud.

◆

But alas! One day, the truth came to light—Khargaram was impotent; he couldn't sire a baby. When Chandra remained childless for years after their marriage, Khargaram took another wife. And after years of waiting, her hopes too were shattered. So they adopted Chandra's nephew while he was still an infant and named him Swargaram—the lord of heaven. Contrary to his name, Swargaram led a wanton life, to the extent of a scandalous involvement with another man's wife. This probably incensed the gods; for, when he was barely twenty-six, he succumbed to consumption.

Khargaram was left childless once again. His estate, vast wealth and immeasurable landed assets now remained heirless. Whom would he bequeath them to? Not that this dampened his lust for other people's property. Right now, he was in the process of incorporating a public pond into his estate—so what if it was where the villagers fished and their livestock came to drink? He sat in the easy-chair in his open meeting hall as he awaited his partner-in-crime—none other than Jadob Bora.

A young boy sat on the veranda and pulled the deerskin punkha to and fro above Khargi's head. Its gentle breeze made golden memories of over thirty years ago—the lovelorn days of his youth—float before his eyes and brought him a sense of fulfilment.

Presently, Bora arrived. Leaning his cycle against the gate-house, he walked up to the hall, bowed his head to the mauzadar's knees in obeisance, and then pulled up a chair to sit by his side. 'Sorry I'm a little late. But I have made all arrangements. We had come up against a problem, but it's all solved now,' he said in a single breath.

'What was the problem? And how was it solved?' asked the mauzadar.

'Dino, the shopkeeper, can't ride a bicycle. But since he is an ace when it comes to walking, I have asked him to start early in the morning. It shouldn't be more than eight miles if he walks directly through the Kuroi sandbank; so he should be there before the lawyer's office opens.'

'Is the Pandit going with him?'

'I haven't told him anything. But the mahajan and Dino have been instructed to keep their mouths shut—like they met up only at the office!'

'You have to take overall responsibility—personally answer whatever questions the judge may ask. Robi and Dino might end up saying something when they mean something else. Of course, the lawyer knows the responses he needs to get out of each one.'

'Don't worry. I'll coach Dino beforehand. But how come you asked Sarbai Pandit to go? Wouldn't it be better if he didn't?'

'No. The Pandit is a sober man and everyone seconds his views. Once the people find out that he's there on my behalf, they will have nothing to say.'

'But I wonder what the Pandit will say? Even if you've not explained the issue in detail, have you at least given him a tip?'

'No, I haven't said anything. All I've told him is that the property lawyer in Nihali has summoned him.'

'What if he gives a contradictory statement?' Jadob Bora was worried.

'As long as you three speak in my favour, all will be fine.'

'And over here, we will let it be known that the Pandit has done the same. Don't worry—you want the pond for a good cause; so what have the people got to do with it? The pond is yours, and we shall explain that to the lawyer.'

'It's not what the pond is going to be used for. It's a matter of ownership. All I want to establish is that the ownership is mine.' Khargi deliberately stressed the word 'mine'. And then he added, 'What chance do those people have against me? Anyway, all that matters to them is their stomachs. But one of them—Gojen or whatever—tends to behave like a wild dog at times! Looks like he has his father's blood running in his veins all right. But the father ended up in jail, didn't he? The son will meet a similar fate, though he doesn't know it yet.'

'Don't worry, Deuta. Gojen will lower his tail. Leave that to me. I'll take my leave now.'

'Go, then. Tomorrow, come and see me once you are back from Nihali.'

◆

It was time for the newspaper reading at the kabiraj's clinic, but Jadob Bora hadn't arrived yet—he was late. The others were assembled already—young and old villagers, a couple of regulars who pedalled long distances to the session every day and Gojen's friends, Konloura and Rupai, who remained inconspicuous and left as soon as the reading was over. A small group of young men— ardent admirers of Jadob Bora—hung around until he was done with the reading and the discussions that followed, although they had no interest in the news.

On the rare occasions when Bora was absent or late, the kabiraj took it upon himself to read the paper to the audience. He was about to do just that when the man arrived, saying, 'I'm late today. The mauzadar summoned me for some important discussions. He won't do anything without consulting me first!' Although the comment was obviously an arrogant exaggeration and a stab at self-promotion, Bora uttered them so regularly in various contexts that people came to accept them as plain statements of fact.

He settled down in his regular chair and took the paper from the kabiraj. The routine they followed was that the headlines were first read out in Bengali, just as they were printed, and the news followed in order of importance or interest. After each item— or each column in case of a longer report—there was a recap, translated to Assamese.

That day's paper carried a very important piece of news: In Delhi, on Viceroy Wavell's directive to the Indian National Congress to set up a temporary government, it was decided to constitute a fourteen-member cabinet ministry led by Jawaharlal Nehru. Five of the fourteen members were to be Muslims and accordingly, Nehru inducted Asaf Ali and Abul Kalam Azad. The Muslim League, represented by Mohammad Ali Jinnah was to be given a fair representation, but differences arose with the Congress when Jinnah opposed the appointments and demanded that all five representatives should be chosen directly by the League. Nehru stood his ground, saying that if two of the five Muslim members were non-Muslim League, it didn't matter because the rest included non-Congress representatives too. Jinnah refused to accept the terms, announced the League's withdrawal from the cabinet and declared that 16th August 1946 should be observed as Direct Action Day throughout India to reopen the chapter of partitioning the country and carving out Pakistan. Meanwhile, Viceroy Wavell was holding independent talks with Gandhi and Nehru.

The long news item was read without a pause and discussed at great length, with Jadob Bora pointing out an imminent threat— that of Hindu-Muslim conflicts arising out of the League's stubborn stance. He also regretted that with all the sacrifices made in the course of the independence movement, now that the goal was in sight, the League was simply trying to get a free slice of the pie. It was a conveniently publicized fact that during the movement of 1942, Bora had led a Peace Corps volunteer group and been jailed for a month. What remained unknown was that it was a fake certificate from the mauzadar, stating that his mother was on her death-bed, that ensured his release. So he held forth on the current issue and the politics of partition with an all-knowing air.

Each of the listeners tried to figure out how the proposed Pakistan could be formed. How could a single country be divided in two? And, even if that were possible, what would become of the people? How could they be divided?

'All right, then. That's all for today.' Bora then turned to Robi mahajan who was sitting by him. 'Will you please come with me for a moment?'

Robi, following behind Bora, said, 'Let's go together tomorrow. Why don't you come by to my house?'

'May I ask what travel plans are brewing here?' asked the kabiraj.

Abruptly turning back, the mahajan explained, 'It's about the mauzadar's estate pond. Some of our men are all agitated and claiming it for themselves. So a few of us are going to the property lawyer...'

Bora spoke harshly to Robi. 'Yes, that's enough. You don't need to make an epic out of it. Now will you please come along?' Robi got the hint and hastily moved away.

•

Gojen was not among the day's newspaper audience. Not that he was a regular. He dropped by at any time of the day—sometimes every two or three days—picked up whatever papers he could find, quickly scanned the news and left. In the course of this exercise, he picked up some Bengali too.

By the time he came to collect his tablets from the kabiraj, the assembly had already dispersed. Dharmananda kabiraj was alone in his chamber, grinding something in a stone bowl. On the table, in an old biscuit box, were small vials of intoxicant priced at an anna each. Gojen bought two of these and asked, 'Have you seen Rupai or Konloura?'

'Maybe. They should be home by now,' replied the kabiraj gravely, without looking at him. He always felt a strange aversion to the young man, but couldn't deny that there was a degree of fondness too. The feeling was akin to what a sober man felt for his unruly younger brother.

A little further up from the kabiraj's clinic, near the bend in the road, a narrow lane to the left led to Moti mistry's home. The house was located in an isolated, abandoned plot on the edge of the fields. The land belonged to the Kanango family. A few years earlier, Kanango's son, Torun, had left home with a huge wad of notes to start a timber trade. However, lacking the enterprise and patience required, he quit almost before he started. Somewhere in the course of things, he happened to befriend Moti, a one-time mason, who was then the chief of the woodworking labourers. Moti introduced him to drinking and other pursuits which helped cement their friendship. It didn't take long before the money dwindled away. When he returned home, he brought Moti along, promising to set him up in a masonry business of his own. But Moti had other ideas—other business plans that would offer a more stable return than masonry could. On his first night in the new place, he got the saw-man Tikaram's wife to elope with him. The woman was an expert at brewing country liquor.

♦

The inside of Moti's house. As soon as Gojen entered, the mistry's wife greeted him with a smile and bade him sit. He ordered his usual half bottle. She stepped behind a screen and into the next room as he watched. She was wearing a red sari; her blouse-less back almost bare.

The regulars were engaged in an animated conversation in the next room. Even without looking, Gojen could tell who was among them. The hero of this gathering, as in the newspaper assembly, was Jadob Bora. But today, the excitement seemed to surpass earlier limits. Drawing the curtain to one side, he stood in the doorway to the other room, looking straight ahead.

The group, sitting on an assortment of stools and poufs, comprised youths of Gojen's age or younger, some holding glasses, others with their glasses beside them. On one side of the room was an untidy bed. Moti lay crouched on it by the wall and on the other edge sat Jadob Bora, legs tucked under him. Beside him was a table with a large bottle, glasses and enamel trays filled with roasted chickpeas, chillies and onions. Directly across from the doorway was a wooden shelf with bottles and glasses. The woman was using a funnel to pour some liquor from a large container into a half-size bottle. Once again, Gojen's eyes were drawn to her bare back. The light from the hurricane lamp was dim, but everything was clearly visible.

Gojen's appearance startled everyone to silence. Bora stopped in mid-sentence and said, 'Oh, Gojai! Come on in. But then, you never sit with us—do you consider us some sort of untouchables? Come, have a drink—on me.'

'No thanks, Kokaiti. I drew the curtain by mistake.'

'What mistake? Did you expect that no one would be around? Did you think Moti's wife was alone? Should we all leave this room?'

The younger men kept their heads lowered. One of them inadvertently let a sound escape his throat—the sound of stifled laughter.

Gojen, on the verge of letting loose a string of expletives, held himself in check. Turning to Moti's wife, he said, 'Hey, how long do you need to fill the bottle? Hurry up and give it to me,' and returned to the front room. He realized that his blood was boiling at what Bora had said. He clenched his teeth. Inside, Bora started a discourse.

'Hey! Why don't you get me the stuff?' yelled Gojen, kicking at a nearby stool. In an instant, the woman appeared and placed a half-bottle, a small ridged glass and a small paper parcel of roast chickpeas and chillies on a small wooden box. She then picked up the toppled stool and placed it beside him.

Gojen glugged half the contents directly from the bottle and then poured himself a glassful. In the next room, surrounded by his fans, Jadob Bora continued his oration. 'You—what will you guys understand? You, Ramchandra, are the son of the mahajan. And you, Torun—you are the son of the real estate king. You, Chandra—you are a distant nephew of the mauzadar, though I have my doubts because the mauzadar never calls your father his brother. You bastard, you come from Bihar and, showing the same regional roots, claim a relationship with the higher-ups here, do you? You bloody social climber...'

'No, Dada, we belong to the same clan.' interrupted Ramchandra.

'Shut up! Don't talk clan to me. And you Lalit—the son of contractor Kinaram—your father builds bamboo bridges and presents bills for wooden ones. And Moti—you are a crook of the first order; a bootlegger in the guise of a mason! You scoundrels—what do you know of sacrifice?'

'Dada, please explain it to us,' someone slurred.

Bora, encouraged anew, poured some liquor down his throat and resumed his discourse. 'Sacrifice is... Sacrifice is... you won't understand. We understand sacrifice. Jadob Bora understands it. We have made personal sacrifices, struggled hard, gone to jail and fought to earn this freedom. And you rascals, you want to enjoy it for free!'

Ramchandra asked, 'Freedom—this freedom—will it be ours?'

Bora's tongue was thick with liquor, but his eagerness to speak only grew stronger. 'What do you think? I read in the papers today that the British government will give us our independence. But in parts. They will divide the country. One part will be Pakistan and the other part, India. The Muslims will live in Pakistan and the Hindus in India. You know what? The other day, there was another news item in the papers.'

'What news?' asked many voices together.

'They tried to include our Assam in Pakistan. But our Bordoloi—you know, Gopinath Bordoloi?—he went straight to Mahatma Gandhi. Gandhi wrote a letter and it was stopped.'

'So we were almost gone!' piped in a voice from the group.

Bora got emotional once again. With a lot of difficulty, he spewed the words, 'How can we go, you rascals? This independence is a hard-earned thing. We have made sacrifices—and how! I have rebelled with Gandhiji—you all know I was a volunteer leader in the Peace Corps. I was a commander—did you know that? Bloody "do or die", bloody *"Luitor paarore aami deka loura*—we're the youth from the banks of the Brahmaputra", bloody…' Some of the youths tried to join Bora in his attempt to sing the anthem, creating a cacophony of atonal sounds.

Gojen finished his bottle, left an eight-anna piece on the table and slunk away.

•

Konloura and Rupai sat on their bridge railing as usual, the latter playing his flute. Dusk soon turned into the pitch darkness preceding the new moon. The golden sparkling stars were reflected in the stream. All was still, except for its rippling sound—as though it was playing a flute of its own. Rupai played a folk tune and then a movie melody, *Luitore paani jaabi o boi*—waters of the Luit, keep flowing, keep flowing…

Since the last few years, the workers in a nearby tea estate had been conducting a three-day theatre festival to coincide with the Durga Puja celebrations in a central location. Both the religious and the cultural festivals were big draws for people in that area. The entire surroundings took on the trappings of a huge fair, and there was a permanent Puja pandal and a stage coming up at the spot. But that is another long story.

One of the sweetmeat stalls at the fair played tunes from the plays of the time to attract buyers. On those days, Rupai hung around that stall at all hours, listening to the music with a keen ear to pick up the notes he now played on his flute.

The strains of the flute informed Gojen that his friends were at the bridge as usual. The music also soothed his nerves ruffled by Jadob Bora's taunts. When he reached the bridge, he hoisted himself onto its railing, between his two friends. Rupai stopped playing.

'Why did you stop? Play on—it's a lovely tune,' said Gojen.

'Play on indeed! Today you've drunk so much of that country stuff, it makes me want to throw up,' said Rupai with disgust.

Konloura added, 'All this while, we were enjoying the soothing breeze that carried the fragrance of flowers from distant gardens. And all we have now is your reeking breath!'

'Okay, then. Go ahead and smell the flowers. I'll carry on.' Gojen jumped off the railing and onto the path.

'Hey wait. You, always let your temper run away with you! We have lots of news for you,' said Konloura, gently restraining Gojen by his arm.

'What?' asked Gojen, perching on the railing once again.

'I believe Robi mahajan is going over to see the property lawyer in Nihali tomorrow. It's about the pond,' informed Konloura.

'About the pond? What about it?' asked Gojen, and then he lapsed into thought.

'Don't know—didn't quite understand. Jadob Bora changed the subject. But we gathered that he's going too.'

'Where did you hear all this?'

'At the newspaper assembly, as it was breaking up and the kabiraj asked where the mahajan was going tomorrow. Mahajan was about to speak, when Jadob Bora cut him off. I was right there.'

Gojen seemed to be lost in thought for a while. Then, turning to Rupai, he said, 'Hm! Come on, Rupai. Play your flute.'

Rupai played a folk tune. Then, suddenly, Gojen said, 'That's enough for today. Go home now—it's getting late.'

'How about you?' asked Rupai, lowering the flute from his lips.

'I'll go a little later. Jadob Bora will come this way shortly—I need to see him first.'

'Why get involved in all this? His goons will also be with him.'

'Have you ever seen me pay any heed to all that? Now you two run along; it's really late.'

'Well, okay. But don't get into a spat with those guys.'

Soon after Rupai and Konloura left, Jadob Bora came tottering towards the bridge, somehow pushing his cycle along. Though he was slurring, he kept up his attempt to sing—*Luitor paarore aami deka loura...*

Gojen was sitting alone at the bridge when Bora reached it. 'Oh, we have a bridge here,' said the latter to himself. When he was about halfway through, Gojen called, 'Jadob Kokaiti!'

'Who's that?' Bora stumbled over to Gojen and peered into his face.

'It's me, Gojen.'

'You—you scoundrel!' said Bora, trying to steady himself against his bicycle.

'I've been waiting for you, Kokaiti.'

'What for, pray? Do you have any specific reasons in your drunken state?'

'What takes you to the property lawyer in Nihali tomorrow?'

'Why do you need to know everything, you rascal?'

Gojen lifted the front wheel of the bicycle into the air, brought it thrashing to the ground and asked menacingly, 'Are you or aren't you telling me?'

Bora, who almost fell over in shock, straightened himself. 'What, eh? Do you plan to beat me up or something?'

Still holding on to the cycle, Gojen replied, 'I do all my beating up in broad daylight, in full public view. I don't touch lonely drunkards in the dark. Now tell me, why are you going to the property lawyer tomorrow?'

'Damn! Now my anger will ruin my intoxication! Yes, I'm going tomorrow—so what?'

'Never mind; please tell me,' said Gojen.

'Well then, listen. We are going to testify in favour of the pond being transferred to the mauzadar's name. What's wrong with that? He has already fenced it in and improved it.'

'Who else is going?'

'Robi mahajan, Dino the shopkeeper and Sarbai Pandit.'

'Sarbai Pandit? Don't tell me Sir is going too?' Gojen's fists, gripping the cycle, relaxed and he drew his hands away from it.

'Of course! You, bloody, keep finding fault with me alone. Who would refuse to help with a rightful cause? We, bloody, have always sacrificed everything—fought for what is right. Sacrifice, you see—sacrifice...'

Bora tottered off, hopping unstably on to the bicycle as soon as he had crossed the bridge. He resumed his singing—*Luitor paarore aami deka loura...*

Gojen was left totally cheerless. He wondered—should he visit Pandit's home? But the teacher went to bed early. This was the one man in whose presence he refrained from all vices and whom he took care never to meet in an inebriated state. No, he'd have to wait until morning to find out the truth.

◆

As soon as Gojen opened the bamboo gate to Sarbai Pandit's home, he noticed a set of footprints and cycle tracks on the freshly-swept sandy yard. He felt deflated—had the Pandit left already? Nevertheless, he walked in.

At the far end of the house, the teacher's wife, just through with her bath, was hanging up the washing on a clothes-horse. Her hair was tied in a gamosa and coiled into a large bun. Since she had her back turned to him, she did not notice Gojen's arrival. But when, after a few moments' hesitation, he called out to her, she turned around and said, 'Oh, it's you, Gojen. What brings you here so early?'

She moved out into the veranda and placed the brass clothes-basin she was carrying on one side. Gojen noticed that the veranda had been freshly swabbed, and the cycle tracks started right there. Hesitantly, he said, 'I'd come to meet Sir. But...'

'Oh, oh. He's already left. He's going to Nihali. I believe the property lawyer sent for him. He's cycling there and plans to drop by at his sister's on the way back—you know, she's married to the fitter at Tekela tea estate.'

'So he'll be late?'

'I suppose it'll be after dark. He'll rest a bit before he comes. Sit down, Gojen.'

'I'll come some other time. I shall leave now.'

He stomped homewards, his thoughts gloomy and restless. It was at moments like this that he needed to hew some wood and allow the physical exertion to put his mind at rest. He picked up his axe and hacked at the jackfruit stump in his backyard with all his might.

He landed up at Moti mistry's as soon as dusk fell and emptied a large bottle in no time. Moti's wife, noticing this, commented, 'You shouldn't drink so fast, Gojen. The booze will go to your head.'

'Why? Where else should it go? To my feet?'

'Do you realize you are beginning to drink every day? Earlier, you came in only once in ten-twelve days. But you were here yesterday, then again today… If you continue like this, you will end up like Jadob Bora and his ilk.'

'Wow—so now you can even lecture me, eh? Okay, pour me a glassful—I need to get going.'

Moti's wife got him a glass of liquor and stated, 'This is your last. It's getting too much.'

Hastily gulping down the contents, Gojen said, 'I know. But that's the only way I can handle the Pandit.' He rose, took out a shiny rupee from the fold of his dhoti, placed it by the glass and left.

◆

Gojen, Konloura and Rupai were perched on the wooden bridge railing. Gojen tried to convince the other two to go home, but they flatly refused, 'No way are we going to leave you alone tonight. God knows what you will do.'

They remained sitting in silence, except for the occasional break when Rupai or Konloura exchanged pleasantries with someone who happened to pass by. It was the lull before a storm—one that Gojen had been plotting, to his own disbelief, from the moment of the first hit of his axe on the stump this morning. Everyone in the area felt that the person who could confront Sarbai Pandit was yet to be born. But they were wrong. There *was* such a person—and his name was Gojen. In spite of his inebriated state, it took all his will power to prepare himself for the momentous task of taking on his teacher—the only man he had revered.

Suddenly, Konloura said, 'That's the sound of Sir's bicycle!'

All three got off the railing. Gojen said, 'Both of you keep quiet.'

Sarbai Pandit tinkled the cycle bell as he got on the bridge. It was a dark, cloudless night, with only a hint of light from the twinkling stars. He almost passed by the three young men when Gojen called out, 'What, eh, Pandit? Back from licking the mauzadar's leftovers?'

The teacher hopped off his bicycle and, turning towards the voice, asked, 'Who's that?'

Gojen took a couple of unsteady steps towards the older man, who was craning forward to get a better look. 'Oh, it's you, Gojen. You've gulped down quite a bit, right? Why—don't you have the courage to face me in your right senses? You've taken the last step to hell, haven't you?' He pushed the cycle and walked briskly ahead.

'Wait, Sir. I need to talk to you,' called Gojen, following him. He flailed his arms as he yelled, 'Sir, I never thought you would go fawning over the mauzadar like this. But remember, Pandit, the pond belongs to the people. It has been theirs since the kings ruled here. Never mind that the mauzadar pointed a gun at them and got it fenced—we will take it down. The lawyer can't make it over to the mauzadar on your word alone. We will bring down the fence, Pandit. Go ahead and lick whatever the mauzadar leaves behind on his plate; go with your tail between your legs. I'm telling you— we'll tear down the fence. And you know what? I *am* in my right senses—so what if I'm drunk? I'm telling you this in my perfectly right senses—we will tear down the fence, do you hear?'

Gojen kept shouting. Meanwhile, Pandit had reached quite a distance. Even the sound of the cycle cranks were heard no more.

11

The vast green stretch of land was where the villagers' livestock roamed free. On one end was the public pond, beyond which the mauzadar's estate stretched for about a mile to one side. Of the other three sides, two were bound by cultivated fields and one by the green plain. Livestock from the plain drank at the pond in the dry season, when the stream ran almost dry, leaving only patches of water here and there. Besides, the fish for the Magh Bihu feast was always taken from the pond, a practice that had prevailed for as long as anybody could remember. And now, not only had the mauzadar claimed this pond as his own and had it fenced with thick bamboo, but he was in the process of legally turning it into a part of his estate with the connivance of a property lawyer and a few prominent people testifying in his favour.

The plain was also a meeting place for villagers who came herding their livestock. It was like a soft green carpet and remained that way throughout the year. There was a huge solitary banyan tree to one side and around it, a few mounds—probably dead anthills—now covered by the grass.

It was the day of the new moon, a day of rest for the farmers. All the men from the village were gathered under the banyan tree to resolve the pond issue. No solution emerged—they were lost in silent thought.

Gojen sat on one of slopes of a mound, Rupai and Konloura at his feet. He had not come forth with his opinion yet, but looking down at the distraught crowd, he said, 'What's there to worry about? Let's go right now, pull out the stakes and remove the fencing.'

A hesitant voice said, 'But things are different now. What if the lawyer has actually made the pond over to the mauzadar?'

'How can a lawyer sitting in Nihali make this the mauzadar's property?' asked Gojen. He sounded harsh.

'No, wait. My second son-in-law works at the SDC's office and he told me yesterday that the papers have been processed in the mauzadar's name, based on statements by Jadob Bora and a couple of others,' informed a man named Pathak.

'Hah! As though a statement is enough!' mumbled Gojen.

'It was only Sarbai Pandit who created problems for them,' Pathak added.

Gojen was suddenly serious. 'How was that?'

'I believe he said that he had no idea if the pond belonged to the mauzadar. But as far as he knew, it was public property that provided water to animals and fish to the people.'

'Sir really said that?' asked Gojen thoughtfully.

'That's what my son-in-law said. Why would he make that up? But Jadob Bora and the others have given it in writing that the pond is a part of the mauzadar's property and has been that way for ever. So it was three against one, and the Pandit's statement was quashed.'

Gojen stood up, tightened the gamosa around his waist and said, 'All right—now who will come with me? The elders can stay here, but young men, let's go.'

The men looked at each other. Gojen once again called out sternly, 'Will the young men here come to pull down the fencing?'

A hesitant voice from the crowd called out, 'But if they've made the papers and so on, what if this becomes a police case?'

Another added, 'And what if the mauzadar comes with his gun—like he did the last time?'

Yet another man looked at his neighbour and said, 'Besides, the mauzadar has the support of those drunken goons—Jadob Bora's gang.'

Gojen looked sharply into each face before him. The young men turned to each other and hung their heads when they met his eyes. Rupai and Konloura looked inquiringly at him. Suddenly, he stomped off towards the pond. After a few steps, he stopped, turned around and yelled at the crowd—'Eunuchs! Spineless eunuchs— that's what you are. You call yourselves men? Go borrow your wife's—or if you don't have one, your sister's—clothes, wear those and stay home!'

The men lowered their eyes. Gojen continued forward. Then, turning again, he called, 'I don't plough my own fields; nor do I own any livestock. You need this pond much more than I do.' A few more steps, and then, 'But my point is, how can Khargi mauzadar wrest away something that rightfully belongs to the people? That's what makes me obstinate. But what good is my obstinacy if I'm on my own? I'll fight by myself and end up in jail like my father!' He went on his way.

The crowd dispersed and moved in the opposite direction. A few elders remained staring at Gojen's receding back.

Gojen was about to climb on to the pond's bank when he turned around and saw that Rupai and Konloura had followed him. When they were within earshot, he called, 'What made the two of you leave those eunuchs behind?'

In an uncertain tone, Konloura asked, 'How do you hope to pull down the fencing by yourself?'

'Why? Do you think I can't?' replied Gojen. He climbed up the bank to the fence, his two friends watching him from below and wondering what his next step would be. He ran his fingers over a bamboo and tried shaking it. The fence was sturdy—it wouldn't give. He kicked hard at it and pounded on it with his fists, grunting at the effort. Finally, beaten, he slunk down to the ground. 'I can't take it when I'm defeated in my purpose,' he said as Konloura and Rupai rushed up to join him. They noticed that his eyes were moist—he was running a hand across them. The three spent a few moments in silence.

Then, all of a sudden, Gojen got up and started walking. His friends followed. Rupai asked, 'Where are you off to now?'

'To see Sir,' Gojen replied.

◆

Sarbai Pandit's home. Gojen, Rupai and Konloura waited for him in the courtyard. As soon as the teacher appeared on the veranda, Gojen flung himself forward, fell at his feet and, holding them in an embrace, touched his head to them. 'Sir, please forgive me, Sir. Curse me, beat me, Sir,' he said passionately.

Yanking his feet free from Gojen's grip, Pandit said, 'What's wrong with this one now? Don't tell me you've swallowed that stuff at this time of day?'

Gojen stood up 'No, Sir. I'm fine. I haven't drunk a drop. But may maggots get my tongue. Why did I taunt you like I did last night, Sir? I knew nothing, Sir—I thought wrong. Jadob Bora led me to believe otherwise. Only today I came to know how you refused to attest in favour of the mauzadar at the lawyer's office.'

'And pray who gave you that news?'

'Pathak uncle. He got the information from his son-in-law.'

'Since you doubted what I might say, may I ask if you don't trust me at all?'

'Of course we do! You could have explained things last night itself.'

'Did you give me a chance? You relegated me to the company of scavenging dogs right away!'

'Please, Sir. Don't mention that ever again. May maggots get my tongue.' Once again, Gojen fell at his teacher's feet. 'Please, Sir. Tell me you won't think about this any more. I'll be cursed! Tell me you pardon me, Sir.'

'That's enough. Now let go of my feet. I won't hold your words against you. Now the three of you sit for a while and have some tea and tamul before you leave. I'm off to school.'

Gojen released Pandit's feet and said, 'You go get ready for school. We'll leave now and come some other time for the refreshments. But do forgive us all our transgressions.' He looked pleadingly at his teacher. Pandit smiled and said, 'Do I need to pull out the school cane and bring it down on your back to convince you that you are forgiven? Now listen. I've got a few new books, which I haven't finished reading yet. Come after a week or so and take them. Go now.'

A smile broke on Gojen's lips and his eyes filled with joy. He felt much lighter now that he knew his teacher had forgiven him. His respect for the man, which he had almost lost, grew manifold and filled his heart once again. On their way home, all three of them swam in the stream like cowherds, gamosas tied at their waists. Back on the bank and changed into their own clothes once again, Gojen realized that although he was still upset about the pond, the fire of suspicion regarding Pandit's motives had thankfully been doused. Only now was he at peace.

Bathing in the stream seemed to cleanse Gojen's mind too. He resolved to visit the temple of the goddess right away and propitiate her for having slandered his teacher. The goddess knew everything. Also, he hadn't met Bapudeu for quite some time now. The poor man was suffering from gastric problems. Right after Joba's incident, Gojen had visited regularly with medicines from the kabiraj. Yes, now that he had remembered, he better go there right away.

'Hey, Rupai, Konloura—the two of you carry on. I'll go visit the temple, and see Bapudeu. Please drop in at my place on your way home, tell Aai where I've gone, and ask her to have her lunch. Else the old woman will wait up, if only to share her milk-and-banana rice with me!' Gojen finished speaking and walked away.

As soon as he entered the temple, Gojen knelt down in front of the goddess and bowed low in repentance. Accepting that he had sinned by demeaning the Pandit and using swear words at him, he begged her forgiveness and prayed that no harm should befall anyone because of his act. After a long obeisance, he sat up and continued to meditate with his eyes closed. Then he slowly opened them.

A miraculous sight awaited him! Normally, the inside of the temple was always dim, the dark goddess' body gleaming in the light reflected from the oil lamps. Today, by her side, stood an unadorned young woman, dressed all in white. Her forehead was bare, as was the parting in her long jet-black tresses which extended below her waist. In her hand was a copper basket full of red hibiscus—the joba. Who was this goddess standing next to the goddess Chamundi?

'Gojen! What are you staring at?' Joba's voice jolted him back to his senses.

'Joba—it's you!' stuttered Gojen as he rose to his feet.

'The way you were staring at me, one would think you'd never seen me before.'

'You know, it's the first time I'm seeing you in this attire.'

'Oh, that! As for me, I recognized you as soon as I entered through the back door, wondering who it was that knelt before the goddess. I haven't forgotten your muscular arms and broad back as yet. I'd been waiting for you to rise. See—I was right.'

Gojen continued to stare in surprise.

'Wait a moment, Gojen. Let me bow to the goddess first. I cleaned up this place in the morning, but had to rush away. My father has just finished his worship.' As she spoke, Joba arranged the flowers around the goddess' feet. She poured some more oil into the tall brass lamp that was already lit, adjusted the wick and then slowly bowed to the ground.

All the while, Gojen stood in the doorway watching her intently. Her stark widow's attire was reduced to a farce by her youth, which was only too apparent throughout her body. There was no trace of widowhood in her looks, save her white outfit and bare forehead and parting. But her mind—had her mind been widowed too?

12

Joba had been married to a sickly middle-aged man, simply to keep up the tradition of getting a Brahmin girl married before she reached puberty. She had lived a cursed and oppressed life for a few years. Then, a few months ago, her husband had died. This was Joba's first visit to her paternal home as a widow; which was why Gojen had not seen her in her present state earlier.

Joba finished her obeisance, rose and walked towards the doorway where Gojen stood transfixed. He made way for her.

'What, Gojen—you are not to be seen these days? It's been over ten days since I've arrived. You are coming home, aren't you?'

'Of course I am. Did you expect me to leave without seeing Bapudeu?'

As they were walking towards the house, Joba said, 'Hey, Gojen, I almost forgot to tell you—Modon dada is here.'

'Modon Kokaiti? When did he come? And how come it took you so long to tell me this big news?'

'He arrived yesterday evening. He was asking about you.'

'Where is he now?'

'There, under the bokul tree. He's sitting on a rock, reading a book.'

'Wait, let me go greet him right there. You know, you are something else. You should have told me this first of all.'

'Go sit with him. I'm not making tea for you. Stay for lunch.'

◆

There were a few large trees that adorned the temple compound from years before Bapudeu's time. They provided the priest with the pancha pallav—the five different leaves he needed for his worship. Four of them were almost clustered together, but the bokul stood slightly apart, towards the river. It also happened to be younger than the rest, which meant that its branches were yet well-formed. It was like a beautiful young woman enjoying the gossip of her four male admirers and inspiring their lewd gestures. Just as she knew she was the object of their fantasy, the bokul was also aware of her powers. A sense of excitement ran through her in spite of her composed exterior. And it seemed like it was this tree's youth that ushered in the winter dew, the soft autumn sunshine, the damp monsoon breeze and the bright spring colours—as also the budding season—for the four others.

When Gojen reached Modon, the latter was leaning against the bokul and intently studying the trees around him. A large book lay open on his lap.

'Modon Kokaiti,' called Gojen softly.

Modon looked up and could not conceal his excitement when he saw Gojen. He spoke, as if in a single breath—'Hey, Gojen! Come, come. I asked Joba about you as soon as I arrived. I'd have gone looking for you today. Come, sit. It's cool here by the riverside. Where can we get such an environment in the city? Come, sit down.' Settling himself on a rock below Modon's, Gojen looked at the book that the former had just closed and put aside. 'This is a huge book, Kokaiti. What is it?'

'Jawaharlal Nehru's *The Discovery of India*—it's just been published.'

'Oh, but it's in English. We won't be able to read it.'

'I know—it's in English. But it's a great book. Panditji wrote it while he was in jail.' Modon summarized the book, and Nehru's viewpoint of Indian history, for Gojen. Then he asked, 'Do you read?'

'I do, sometimes. I've read most of the Assamese titles that Sir has in his house. I've read most of Lakshminath Bezbarua, Rajanikanta Bordoloi, Padmanath Gohain-barua, Jatin Duara and Ganesh Gogoi's works. I have some books at home too. And the

Kirtan, Ramayan, Mahabharat—these have been around since my father's time.'

'That's great. It doesn't matter if you can't read English. There are a lot of books in Assamese, and there are bound to be more. If you read those, that should be enough. Now tell me about yourself, about your village… I'm sure you've heard that we are now in the last phase of our struggle for independence?'

'We'll talk about all that later. Tell me about yourself first. I believe you are now a lawyer in the court?'

'Hey, how did you know?'

'Bapudeu told me when we went over to perform the last rites for Joba's husband.'

Modon used this opportunity to change the subject, choosing to dwell at length on Joba, rather than himself—her wedding, her married life, her husband's death and her widowhood. After his last visit, Modon had written a long letter to Bapudeu in which he explained the logic behind his response to his wedding proposal. Bapudeu had written back to say that bound by tradition as he was, there was no way he could accept such reasoning—in fact, if it weren't for a fondness for the younger man, he would have been quite offended by his suggestions, which were totally unacceptable under his circumstances. He had added his blessings and signed off formally. For some time after this letter, Modon had no news of Joba.

Meanwhile, Modon had spent some time in jail in the course of his efforts at liberating the country. One night, under the cover of darkness, he had entered the police station, pulled down the Union Jack, ripped it, tarred it and thrown it to the ground before hoisting the tricolour in its place. Seized by a fit of passionate patriotism, he turned around and cried out Vande Mataram, hail independent India, long live Mahatma Gandhi and so on in a totally unplanned move.

His companions, who had joined in the sloganeering from where they waited on the road, fled as soon as the torchlight-and-gun-wielding policemen fired in air. However, Modon was caught in the beam and told that he would be shot if he tried to escape. He surrendered to the armed police and took full responsibility for the contempt of the Union Jack and hoisting of the tricolour—'crimes' that earned him a year of imprisonment.

One day, when his mother came to visit him in prison, she showed him a postcard from Joba's father to his. It was an invitation to Joba's wedding; but there was no indication as to who the groom was. The next meeting between Modon and Joba was somewhat dramatic.

After his release, Modon resumed his studies and in due course, earned his BA and BL degrees. Immediately after his BL, he started practising law. This was about a year ago.

One afternoon about six months ago, Modon was getting a clerk to write out a document for him when he noticed a young woman, accompanied by a man about the same age, making inquiries at a typist's table. She looked really young, but the veil covering her head indicated that she was married. The typist, busy at work, paid her no heed. They probably didn't have a designated lawyer, mused Modon, and planned to take them to his senior as potential clients. Just then, the typist, still looking down, absently pointed them to a certain direction. The woman seemed slightly confused and Modon's hopes of getting a client rose. Then, when she turned around, he froze. His eyes opened wide and his blood pounded at his heart. The young woman, her forehead and parting bright with vermilion and a veil covering her head, was none other than Joba!

'Keep writing—I'll be right back,' Modon told the clerk, and he rushed towards Joba. She too hastened towards him in surprise.

'You... Joba!' said Modon, disbelievingly.

'I've been looking for you all morning,' said Joba. Then, either due to some unspoken ache within her or the relief of seeing Modon at long last, she burst into tears.

'Let's go sit somewhere else.'

Joba and her companion followed Modon until they reached an iron bench under a tree by the little pond that was part of a park adjoining the court compound.

'And who's this?' asked Modon.

'My youngest brother-in-law,' replied Joba.

'Come, sit. Let's talk.'

'I think I'll go take a look around the court,' the young man told Joba.

'Sure. But don't be too late, Bapukon. We need to leave soon,' she called after him.

They sat on the bench.

'Tell me, Joba—what's the problem? How come you are here?'

In the little time they had, Joba—sometimes placid, sometimes emotional—narrated her story

◆

Joba's wedding was arranged three months after the letter in which Modon proposed marrying her after she attained puberty. The groom was much older, but he belonged to a wealthy Brahmin family from Nihali. His father had retired from a tea estate job and now looked after his land and property. He had lost his wife a year ago. Of his children, the four girls were all married, as was the middle son. The youngest son was yet too young and the eldest, Joba's groom, had remained single all this while, thanks to his failing health. He suffered from asthma and epilepsy and spent most of his time in bed. Considering Joba's impending puberty and the man's secure financial background, the health factor was overlooked and the two were married.

Joba blossomed into a woman four months after the wedding, and was duly dispatched to her marital home. She had no illusions about married life; in fact, at her age, she had little idea what it implied. However, she knew she would now spend a lifetime with a man—one she would have to sleep with too—and hoped he would turn out to be nice, affectionate and pleasant-looking. However, on her very first night, she was exposed to an epileptic—and the frightful turn he took during an attack!

The expectancy and sweet togetherness that should have marked her nights were replaced by strange fears. The days were all right. But alone at night with her husband, Joba feared for what lay in store—what if he had another fit and took on that frightful stance once again? During his asthma attacks too, she needed to tend to him all night and little realized when the night had turned to day.

The other daughter-in-law of the household happened to come from a noveau riche family and, apart from flaunting her expensive possessions, spared no opportunity to make Joba realize that she was inferior to the rest. Thanks to her intervention, her two children were also not allowed to mingle freely with their new aunt. The only exception to this behaviour was her youngest brother-in-law.

As was her habit since childhood, Joba continued to bathe at dawn, go directly to the prayer room and sing hymns to the gods. This drew taunts from the sister-in-law and cold indifference from the others in the family, and made her contemplate changing her routine. But Bapukon urged her to keep at it.

Her sister-in-law got more abusive by the day. Everyone chose to ignore the fact that Joba was now the eldest daughter-in-law of the household—a position that commanded due respect. Instead, they heaped all chores on her, keeping her on her toes throughout the day. Thanks to her youth, she was none the worse for her toil physically. But emotionally, she started breaking down. As each night approached, her fears gnawed at her young mind, to be erased only by the dawn heralding a new day. She couldn't sleep; and when she did, she had nightmares that jolted her awake. She would notice her husband gasping for breath and rubbing his chest, so she would move over and massage it and, before long, the night had passed.

Then, one day, Joba's father-in-law suddenly died of a massive heart attack. Her husband, being the eldest son, had to go through all the rituals associated with the death ceremony—staying shirtless, sleeping on a mat on the floor, performing certain long-drawn rites in wet clothes everyday—and these took their toll on his health. Soon after the ceremony was over, he became completely bedridden and remained that way for over five months. During this time, they tried everything from consulting doctors from the tea estates and the local board to traditional healers and religious remedies. Joba had to slog through all this by herself because the other brother and his wife, who now ran the household, chose to turn a blind eye to her plight and did nothing apart from doling out a little money now and then.

Joba's trials awakened a new resolve within her—she would save her husband at any cost. She was suddenly free of her fears. Even when she saw one of his fits coming on, she didn't scream in terror as she did earlier or seek anybody's help. Rather, she saw him through it in a calm and efficient manner—gently wiping the froth from his mouth or prising it open with a spoon when it was clenched tight, easing his fists open, and sprinkling water on his eyes. When she absolutely needed a helping hand, she turned to Bapukon who, she knew, would assist her unconditionally.

But however hard she tried, her husband's condition continued to worsen. As a last resort, the local board doctor suggested moving him to the district headquarters and getting the civil surgeon's opinion. Joba informed her brother-in-law and his wife; but they seemed more irritated than concerned. Finally, she remembered that Modon was somewhere out there. And since his father taught Sanskrit in the high school, he shouldn't be difficult to find. She held lengthy discussions with Bapukon and drew up a plan.

And then they proceeded accordingly.

◆

The Brahmaputra had reopened for passenger traffic, which had been closed down for two years or so thanks to the war and its aftermath. Only cargo vessels plied the waters then. People had to use the bus—but there was only one every day, and so crowded that some needed to travel on the roof. The extra passengers were offloaded when the bus approached a police station—they walked across and waited for it some distance away. The bus made the requisite entries at the station, picked up the waiting passengers and moved on. The offloading and reloading process also happened every time the bus needed to cross a weak bridge.

The bigger rivers had no bridge during the monsoons. The bus and passengers were all ferried across in huge boats. In the dry season, they had to negotiate the weak 'cold weather' bamboo bridges. The main road belonged to the PWD, but was a pebbled track—there were no tarred roads yet. So, apart from the frequent alighting, passengers had to put up with a lot of dust and jerking around.

The only advantage of travelling by bus was that one could reach the district headquarters the same day—it took only five to six hours from Nihali. However, there were a lot of problems involved in taking someone as sick as Joba's husband. The ship took longer—and there was the five-mile bullock cart ride to the ghat—but that seemed more viable. Then came the question of raising the money. With Bapukon in tow, she visited an uncle-in-law in a nearby village who not only made a contribution, but also came over and convinced her other brother-in-law to sell some paddy.

They made the journey and arrived at the district headquarters early in the morning. Between the two of them, they carried the patient ashore and offloaded their luggage. They asked around—the school wasn't far, but there were yet a couple of hours before it would open. The hospital was much farther. Just as they were pondering on how to get there, they spied a horse-drawn buggy. The driver too saw them and solicited their fare. He knew the hospital well. He also realized that these people were new in town and, thereby, helpless. Their plight aroused his sympathy. He happened to know a compounder at the hospital, and with his help, he had the patient settled in a bed within the hour.

On their ride, Joba occasionally looked away from her husband and at the scene outside. The busy streets flanked by shops, markets and houses, people bustling around, cycles plying one after the other, the occasional motor-car, the bumpy ride, the busy hospital with its doctors, nurses and patients—they all fascinated her and left her breathless.

Joba thanked the buggy driver profusely—he was indeed a messiah! Then she and Bapukon settled down on a bench on the hospital veranda. This breather came after a long spell of hectic activity; but Joba's mind was still restless. How could she contact Modon? It had been quite a while since she set foot in this town, but she was no closer to finding him than when they just landed. The civil surgeon was due at noon and might ask to see someone from the patient's family. There were only a couple of hours left. Suddenly, she stood up and said, 'Bapukon, let's go look for Modon dada. His father should be in the school; all we have to do is find it.'

She went up to the senior nurse in the ward and asked if it was alright if she was out for some time. The nurse felt sorry for Joba— it wasn't fair that such a nice-looking, soft-spoken young girl should be married to this sickly middle-aged man! She assured her that she would take care of things until they returned, and gave them detailed directions to the school.

Joba and Bapukon walked the mile to the school in awe at all they saw along the main road. But once they got there, they learnt that Modon's father had retired a year ago and now lived some three miles away. It wasn't possible for either of them to grasp the directions to get there. Just as they were about to give up hope, the teacher informed them that they could meet up with the retired teacher's son Modon if they walked to the courthouse not too far away.

'He's the one we need to meet,' said Joba excitedly.

'The court is only about half a furlong from here. Look for him in the lawyers' chambers. That's where you should find him.'

Finally, after running from one department to another and much asking around, they had managed to find him and here they were.

'Now that I've found you, there's nothing more for me to do. I shall not worry either. From now on, you take care of things.' Joba finished her tale—and with it, ended her responsibility.

Bapukon returned soon after. Modon looked at his watch—'It's almost noon. We only have about twenty minutes. Let's get to the hospital.' He instructed the clerk to hand over the documents to his senior and to inform him that he had been called away on an important errand. Then the three of them walked to the hospital.

◆

The treatment continued for fifteen days. Modon ensured that the patient got the best of attention—medical and otherwise. He also arranged for Joba and Bapukon to stay in his house. His father welcomed Joba like a daughter, and the rest of the family followed suit. She spent the days by her husband and returned with Modon on his way back from the court. Bapukon stayed in the hospital at night, sleeping on a makeshift bed on a large bench. Later, when the patient got better, nobody needed to attend to him at night.

For Joba, every moment of those fifteen days held a sort of magical fascination. Her determination, plus her efforts, to heal her husband were finally bearing fruit. Modon's parents and siblings showered her with the affection that was denied her in her marital home. Besides, the very ways of the town and its people, the dazzling colours, the electric lighting—there was not a dull moment.

One other thing that made Joba's experience all the more special was her proximity to Modon. However short-lived it may be, it was something she never believed could be possible. For the first time in her life, she realized that there was a special man in every woman's life, and here was hers! It was him she had been waiting for all these years. How could anyone force her to think that the only man in her life should be her husband? That was impossible! Not for a moment had she failed in her duties towards the man she had married—she cared for him with true compassion and commitment, never ever letting his advancing years or failing health bother her. He was her husband all right, but he could never be her man. Only one person could, and that was Modon.

Fifteen days later, Joba boarded the ship to Nihali with her husband. The doctor assured her that things were much better— her husband had made a good recovery, though a total cure was not possible. As she was leaving, she buried her head in Modon's mother's bosom and wept her heart out.

Many times in the days after she was gone, Modon picked up paper and pen to write to Joba, but a strange inhibition held him back. However, he did receive two letters from her about six months apart. She couldn't write too well, but expressed herself adequately in her rounded childish handwriting. The first one bore bad news. Her husband's health had suddenly taken a turn for the worse and he had breathed his last after a week of suffering. All her untiring efforts could not save his life. The goddess did not answer her prayers in spite of the promise of a black goat sacrifice!

The second missive was much longer and ran into quite a few pages. Now that she was a widow, her life was being made miserable and her home was now a living hell. Someone had spread rumours that Joba had spent her time in town gleefully gallivanting with Modon while her husband lay sick and alone in the hospital. This made her the object of much ridicule and harassment at the hands of her sister-in-law and her companions. One day, the woman confronted her directly. Just as Joba was denying the accusations and trying to tell them the real story, her brother-in-law entered the room and raged about how everyone was talking about the 'scandal'. Could it be that Joba had deliberately removed the thorn in her path to happiness and done something to eliminate her husband...?

Bapukon, who heard the exchange from the adjoining room, stormed in and tried to defend his elder sister-in-law. But his brother's forceful assertions made him shut up and leave the room.

Joba spent an entire day and night crying in bed. Just before daybreak, she chose to write to Modon and serially recounted the events of the past few months. In the end, she wrote that she was leaving for good for her father's home by the temple. Would he come and visit her there if he could?

13

'I didn't waste a moment after I got the letter. I came here right away,' said Modon, winding up Joba's life story of the past year for Gojen.

'So that was the day she came away! I wonder how and with whom she got here,' said Gojen, mostly to himself.

'I haven't spoken much with her—just got here last evening. Bapudeu was quite surprised to see me. I've told him I'm here on some official work. Joba came and talked to me for a while when I was out in the courtyard after dinner. The morning she left, she had taken leave of her brother-in-law and sister-in-law, though no one but Bapukon knew that she did not intend to return. Bapukon had come to see her off at the bus stop and had told her, "Even if you hadn't said so, I'd have asked you not to come back to this home and to the demon couple."

'She couldn't tell me much more. Bapudeu called sternly from inside—"Go to bed, Joba. You don't need to chat at this time of night." She was reluctant to go, but I sent her on. As it is, I had sensed a sort of reserve in Bapudeu's attitude towards me from the moment I arrived. Joba has been busy all morning and I haven't been able to speak to her at all.' Modon sounded rather rueful as he spoke.

'Oh, my! So much has happened that I didn't know of! I did know some, of course. Everyone saw the groom go through an asthmatic attack even as the wedding ceremony was on. I also heard people sigh about the man being so old. Then I heard that he had passed away. I sort of guessed that Joba couldn't have been too happy—that was all. But I tell you, Modon Kokaiti, I'm stunned by what you have told me. I am extremely pained.' Gojen's heart overflowed with sympathy.

'I have no clue why Joba asked me to come here. I wonder what she needs to tell me? She hasn't had any opportunity so far; and I think her father's behaviour is making her hold back.'

'Dada,' called Joba from the distance. 'Come Dada, lunch is served. You come too, Gojen.'

◆

Then Modon did the unthinkable. He had been served in a plate and bowl laid out in Bapudeu's kitchen, so that he could eat with the priest. Gojen had been served on a banana leaf on the outside veranda. Seeing this, Modon stated that he too would dine outside—the open air and gentle breeze were quite soothing. Bapudeu objected at first, but the young man stood his ground as inoffensively as possible and got himself a peera and a pot of water. By the time Joba came out with the plate of rice in one hand and bowl of dal in the other, he had already spread a piece of banana leaf before him. 'It's been a long time since I've eaten off a leaf, Joba. So there's no need for those—serve me on this,' he said lightly.

'Gosh—look at what you have done. Pitadeu is really upset and is mumbling to himself.'

'Never mind—he's a priest and entitled to his tempers. You can take away the bowl. Pour out the dal on the rice itself.'

Joba did as she was told and said, 'There's no fish today. There is some meat from yesterday's sacrifice, but Pitadeu will serve you that. He has cooked it himself. Now that I can't eat any of those things, he has not let me handle them either.' She walked in with the empty plate and bowl, and Bapudeu came out carrying a big bowl and ladle.

'Modon, I am not at all happy at your behaviour. What is this about flouting all social norms?' he said, spooning mutton curry on to Modon's leaf and then pouring the remainder on to Gojen's. 'Gojen is aware of our traditions and has always upheld them. He wouldn't have minded.'

'It's true that he has upheld them so far. But only he will be able to say if he would have minded, Khura.'

Bapudeu ignored the comment and went in, disgruntled.

Modon turned to Gojen and said, 'Don't take offence at what Bapudeu said.'

'The thought of taking offence doesn't arise at all. We've been blindly following Bapudeu's traditions. But I'm wondering about one thing now—Joba's vegetarianism. You know, she would always pick the largest of my catch when I came fishing and would say, "Every time I have to eat the sacrificial meat two days or more in a row, I can't help thinking of you and your creel, Gojen. And you inevitably land up at the right time". Believe me, Kokaiti, I'd come fishing every two to three days just because of that girl. And now she can't eat any of those things. Look at us now—here we are feasting on mutton curry and she will have none. It's just not right.'

Modon, who had been listening intently to Gojen, suddenly pushed away the meat on his leaf to one side. Gojen too halted in the process of putting a piece in his mouth. Following Modon's example, he too put his meat away, eating only his dal, rice and vegetables. When Joba returned to serve them their curd, she saw that both men had finished the rest of their food, but the meat lay untouched. 'Can I serve you some more rice? You both have almost emptied your leaves.'

'No thanks—the little we have left will be enough for the curd,' said the two men almost at once. They lowered their eyes and toyed with their rice.

'Oh, oh! Did Pitadeu forget to salt the curry or something? He has finished eating!' asked Joba, a knowing suspicion in her voice. She looked in amazement from one face to the other and became suddenly serious.

'It's not an issue, Joba! What if we don't eat meat one day?' said Gojen.

Modon tried to lighten the situation. 'Here, serve me some of the curd you've brought. I love the sweetened curd you serve the goddess. What better way to end a meal, eh?'

'What's all this? I'm telling you, I'm really hurt.' Joba's voice faltered as she spoke. She hurriedly served the curd and rushed inside. As he watched her turn her back on them, Modon noticed that she carried the bowl of curd in one hand and wiped her eyes with the other.

On the third day, early in the morning, Gojen heard a voice calling out to him while he was yet in bed. Realizing it was Modon, he said, 'Wait a minute, Kokaiti. I'm coming.' Rubbing his eyes, he got out of bed and opened the door. 'You're leaving already? I thought you were staying a little longer?' he asked.

'Yes—I'll get going. I've already spent two days and three nights here. I'm still rather new in the court and it isn't right that I should be away for too long.'

'But it's too early for the bus! What's the time? Come, sit down,' said Gojen and blew on the chair on the veranda, to clean it.

Modon looked at his watch. 'It's just after five. But I'll set off slowly. It's about three miles to the crossroads where I can get a bus, right? I'll wait there.'

'Have you had tea or anything to eat? Of course, I know that Joba is an early riser.'

'No—they are all asleep. I decided not to bother them by waking them up. I've had a wash and come away. They don't know I've left.'

'How could you come away without taking their leave?'

'Never mind. They'll figure out when they don't see me,' smiled Modon.

For a moment, Gojen seemed lost in thought. Then he said, 'Wait, Kokaiti. I'll wake Aai and get her to make us some tea. I'll wash and be right back.' He went in.

Modon had his tea and left. Gojen saw him off at the bus stop. Instead of taking the stony road, they took a shortcut through the fields. It was autumn and the morning sun shone softly on the paddy fields, which hadn't borne seed yet. Occasionally, a gust of gentle breeze brought with it the scent of dew and xewali flowers, and of the fields that stretched as far as eye could see. It soothed Modon's agitated mind after the sleepless night he had spent.

'You know, Gojen, I came over to your place because I needed to tell you certain things. I'm glad you offered to come with me,' said Modon.

'I knew something was wrong the moment I saw you in our courtyard. And I used the excuse of seeing you off, so that I could ask you what it was. Tell me now, Kokaiti—what happened?'

Walking through the cattle tracks in the field, Gojen listened to Modon like he was listening to a sermon. That was the sort of gravity in his words.

◆

The very day he arrived at their house, Modon realized that Bapudeu was not very comfortable about him talking openly with Joba and indicated his displeasure, though covertly. Modon, however, was curious to learn the reason why Joba had summoned him and couldn't wait to speak to her. The opportunity presented itself the following evening.

After lunch, Modon lay on a mat in the temple area, alternating between reading *The Discovery of India* and dozing off. At one point, he was awakened by Joba, who had brought him a cup of tea. As she held out the tumbler towards him, she almost whispered, 'This evening, Pitadeu is going for a ritual in Khargi mauzadar's house. He'll invite you; but don't go.' She immediately moved away.

Sure enough, a little while later, Bapudeu, almanac in hand, came to Modon and said, 'You know, I'd almost forgotten that today is the full moon. Every full moon, I go to the mauzadar's in the evening and read the scriptures. The mauzadar's mother is very keen on this ritual, and some of the village elders come over too. I was thinking you could come with me today. You can also meet some new people.'

'I've heard the entire scriptures that you are about to read. When I was in prison in 1942, a priest would come and read to us jailbirds and we would listen intently. Now that you have asked me,

I would have loved to come, but my head has been aching for some time. My headaches, when they happen, tend to get really bad and I sometimes tend to throw up. The only medication is complete rest.'

'Oh! Now to leave this Joba... She doesn't want to come and I can't even force her in her present condition. Earlier—before she was married—I'd take her along wherever I went. But I wonder what can be done about today. To leave her alone at home...'

'Why? I'll be around! I can stay right here, light a lamp and read my book, and she can continue with her chores in the other house. It's just for the evening. So what's there to worry about, Khura?'

'I know I shouldn't be worrying. But you know...' Though not totally relieved of his concern, Bapudeu moved away in helpless resignation.

◆

It was the full moon of autumn. The sky was a sea of silver and the moonlight, bright as sunshine.

Joba and Modon sat in the courtyard—he in an old wooden chair, she on a cane stool. Joba was recounting the experiences she had written about in her letter. But the moonlight and the fragrance of flowers from a nearby bush were distracting—very distracting—for both of them.

'Let's go sit by the riverside, on the rock under the bokul. The moonlight will be even more beautiful when seen through the leaves,' suggested Modon.

The two sat on the rock with just as much space between them as propriety demanded. Before them flowed the river. The waters were low; the currents weren't too strong. The moonlight kissed the surface of the river and turned it into a ripple of silver. They had spent much time together when Joba had gone to town for her husband's treatment, but this was different. Never did they share a magical moment like this—so intimate, yet so distancing! They seemed like strangers to each other and were at a loss for words to express whatever needed to be said.

Finally, Modon spoke. 'Joba.' His voice echoed back to his ears.

'Hm?'

'You wanted to tell me something, right? Isn't that why you called me here?'

Joba was silent for some time. Then she said, 'I have no clue why I asked you to come. Perhaps there's no particular reason at all.'

'So you have nothing to say?'

'I do; and plenty at that. I have written and spoken about my trials, but that isn't it. There are some other things I need to tell you; only I don't know how. But you know what?'

'Tell me.'

'I know that whether I tell you or not, you know what it is that I want to say. You understand, right?' She turned to look at Modon and saw that he was staring unblinkingly at her. Their eyes locked and the moonlight radiated between them, bathing their faces in its soft glow. Suddenly, Joba buried her head in Modon's chest and started sobbing. In between, she said, 'Tell me if I'm right, Modon dada—you know all that's there in my heart. Not my problems and tribulations, but what lies deep within?'

Modon gathered Joba in a tender embrace. When she was done crying, she raised her wet face towards him. He cupped it between his palms and lowered his lips to taste the salt on hers.

A tempest brewed over the sea and hit a solitary isle. Modon retreated into the thick forest on the isle and discovered a new goldmine at every step. Then he felt the whistling winds heralding the storm. Modon and Joba held themselves in check for the final storm. Bapudeu would be back any moment now. Joba released herself from Modon's arms and they both stood up.

'Come, let's go. Pitadeu might come early today.' Modon was deeply touched by the closeness in her tone. They made to go their respective ways, but after a couple of steps, Joba suddenly turned around and said, 'Don't fall asleep tonight. And leave the back door unlatched.'

For this visit, Modon's sleeping arrangements had been made in the temple, to one side of the idol of the goddess. There were two beds in the two rooms of Bapudeu's house. Before she was

married, Joba slept with her father when they had a visitor. She was
a little girl then; so there was no problem. But now, for the first
time, after her return, they faced the problem of a guest bed. Where
would Modon sleep? A bed was made on the temple floor and after
a long debate as to who, of the three, should sleep there, Modon got
his way. There was a small door at the back.

After dinner, Modon made some short conversation with
Bapudeu and retired for the night. He first unlatched the back door
and then turned the lamp out. The room was bathed in moonlight
anyway. He lay on his back and stared unblinking into space. Joba
had asked him to stay awake.

◆

The following night too, Modon lay awake for a long time—and
he had left the back door unlatched once again. But the course
of events in the meantime erased all his hopes of ever seeing
Joba again. What happened was that at dinner, he spoke without
preamble to Bapudeu. 'Khura, I need to tell you something.'

'Go ahead.'

'I'd like to marry Joba.'

Joba was bringing a bowl of curry in case anyone wanted
second helpings and had just reached the threshold of the room.
She turned around and rushed back. Bapudeu stopped eating and
stared agape into Modon's eyes. Then he averted his gaze to stare
at a lizard on the wall.

Modon spoke in a single breath, 'I had proposed this marriage
once before, with but one condition. And you had refused. As a
result of the step you took, Joba is the widow she is today, though
she has barely stepped into womanhood. Her entire life lies before
her. Khura, please accept my proposal and absolve yourself of
your sin.'

Bapudeu picked up the pot of water by his plate, poured half
over his uneaten rice and stepped outside to wash. Modon ate a little
and then rose. After he had washed and stepped into the moonlit
courtyard, he noticed that Bapudeu was standing at the veranda.

The older man spoke sternly, determinedly. 'Listen, Modon. Leave this place first thing in the morning. This is a holy place and any sinful utterance bodes ill. You shall not try to see Joba again. And make sure you never return to our place in future. Joba's fate is not in your hands; it is determined by one's deeds in an unseen previous life. Go sleep now. But remember, you have hurt me very deeply.' He finished speaking and agitatedly entered the house.

The hours ticked by, but Modon could not sleep. Although the back door was unlatched, he entertained no hope that Joba would dare come to him tonight. Images of the many incidents they shared, from the time he first met her as a little girl right up to their recent tryst, floated before his eyes. At one point, he dozed off lightly.

Joba eased the door open and entered the temple. Just as she had done the previous night, she took off her freshly washed white sador and draped it over the image of the goddess to cover her, face and all. She knew that although Modon's bed was to one side, she would be embarrassed if the goddess saw what was going on. What if she took offence? She would certainly need to be covered.

Modon had been amused at Joba's 'precautions'. He had said, 'Don't worry about the goddess, Joba—she won't mind. What we are doing is sacred. When a man and woman become one, it is adoration of the highest order. This is what the Upanishads say. They state that, in their unadorned forms, the male and female genitalia are symbolic of all that is needed for a sacrificial fire. This goddess is herself naked; so why would she be offended by anybody else's nakedness? There's nothing to fear from her.'

But Joba covered the idol anyway. She knelt on the ground and offered her obeisance and then made her way to the bed. The light that entered through the window made everything clearly visible inside. Joba brought her face close to Modon's and whispered, 'Wake up—I'm here.'

Modon slowly opened his eyes and saw Joba's face almost touching his. He locked his lips to hers in a passionate kiss, raised his arms and drew her close. There was no sador covering her today either, and the buttons on the front of her thin blouse were open. He felt the storm in its full force. The blood in his veins pulsated like a galloping horse. Joba was overcome by waves of passionate longing too and they subsided only when they hit the rocky shores of Modon's body. The horse's hooves left her smeared with blood...

They knew not how long they lay blissfully spent. Oh, what pleasure, what divine bliss, what sweet headiness this togetherness was...

Suddenly, Modon said, 'Listen Joba.' She slowly opened her eyes. 'Let's go sit under the bokul like we did yesterday. All's quiet and peaceful—it'll be lovely by the riverside,' he said eagerly.

'Let's!' Joba got out of bed, adjusted her blouse, took the sador from the idol and draped it, and bowed long before the goddess to seek her pardon. Then she walked up to Modon who was waiting at the door.

'Is it morning already?'

'It will be in a while—must be about three now. We don't have much time—let's go.'

They sat in silence on the rock under the tree. Joba rested her head against Modon's chest. Everything was so beautiful! The sparkling moonlight, the peace and silence all around, the living ripples of the flowing river, the fragrant cool breeze—the very experience of being together in such an idyllic setting was new and exhilarating for both of them. They were entranced.

'Joba,' said Modon softly.

Joba raised a finger to his lips and said, 'Hush! Don't say a word. This feels so good.' More silence. There was only wordless intimate communication on their lips.

Modon spoke again. 'Joba, I'll leave at dawn.'

'That's easy!'

'Well, I wanted to do the difficult thing, right?'

'By marrying me?'

'Yes. By marrying you.'

'I thought the sky fell on my head when you suddenly brought up the subject at dinner. How could you say something so presumptuous?'

'You were surprised?'

'Of course! How could I think of getting married again—that too to you?'

'Why? Why do you think it's not possible?'

'I can't possibly think such thoughts. I'm already married. How can I marry again?'

'So you intend to spend a lifetime like this? In your white clothes, no vermilion, no non-vegetarian food? What about your brimming youth or the fires that burn in your body—will you let them waste away?'

'No—why would they? I've already surrendered them to you. They are all yours. Why will they be wasted?'

'Now, that's a strange statement.'

'Nothing strange about it. I am all yours, but I can't marry you. If that had to happen, it would have happened years ago, when my father proposed it before my puberty. You refused me then. How can it happen now?'

'It will. I've said I want to marry you now.'

'Didn't you see how my father reacted?'

'That's the only problem.'

'And what about your family?'

'They'll resist at first, but they'll come around.'

'But how can the wedding happen if Pitadeu doesn't agree?' Both were lost in thought for some time. Then Joba spoke again, 'Modon dada, I don't know about this marriage and stuff. But as a girl—and as a woman—you have always been my only man. This was true even when I was married and living with my husband, and that's the way it will always be. I may be a widow, but I still have my man. That is why I asked you to come here. I will be truly widowed only when you die. And listen—I will never see you again. You get married soon. You'll find plenty of girls—pretty town girls at that!'

'I don't think I'll ever get married. I'll remain this way.'

'As if that's possible! I'm telling you—get married soon. Just as I didn't think of you when I got married, I won't think of you when you are married either. If at all we meet again, whether you are married or not, it will be like our meetings of the last two nights and I will sleep with you—even if you have a wife. My body, my mind, my love are all yours and I will save them for you. You are mine, whether or not you can belong to me...' Joba started sobbing and Modon kissed away her tears.

Suddenly an owl flew hooting overhead. Modon and Joba were jerked out of their reverie. She got up to leave. 'I have to go now. Sometimes Pitadeu comes out in these early hours.' Without turning back, she walked hurriedly towards the house.

◆

'There's the bus! We're just in time,' said Gojen when he saw the bus from the fields.

'Let's hurry, Gojen. Else I might miss it.'

'Don't worry. It'll stop here for a while.'

Modon said, 'So now you know everything that happened between Joba and me. I haven't held back anything.'

'Yes, I've heard all. But I'm thoroughly confused. I too am extremely fond of that girl Joba. I've known her ever since we studied together in primary school. She's much younger than you or me. It would be ideal if you could marry her. This Bapudeu is so adamant! Imagine wanting to keep his young daughter like this! I just don't understand you Brahmins and your traditions!' He spoke in his typical blunt style.

'I'd like to ask something of you. Please look after Joba. If possible, I will keep in touch with her through you. And you know what? I still haven't given up hopes of marrying her. I'm sure we can find a way.'

The bus honked. Gojen and Modon rushed towards it, waving for it to stop.

14

The solution Modon desired did not take long to appear. And it all happened in the most unexpected way, about two months after he had left the temple grounds.

Gojen was fishing at his chosen spot one morning. The river had dried up in other places, but the water here was deep and full of fish. One had just pecked at the bait when Joba's voice called from behind, 'Hey, Gojen! Come here for a moment.'

'Wait, don't shout! I can see a fish biting on my line—a nice big specimen wagging her tail,' he replied without looking back.

Joba waited for a while and then called again, 'Please, Gojen—I need to talk to you.'

'Wait, I say! The fish is still nibbling. It'll swallow in a moment and I'll have it up in a jiffy.' His eyes remained on the float.

Joba waited some more time and seeing that Gojen was paying no attention to her, stomped up to him and yanked his fishing rod from his hands. 'I can't so much as sniff the fish, and that's all you can think about!' she scolded.

Gojen stood up, very slowly. There was an awkward silence between them. 'It's not that, Joba. The fish isn't for me. My aunt's daughter has come visiting and Aai asked me to arrange for some. Haven't you noticed that since Modon kokaiti left, I've been coming here to see you every day, but haven't fished once?' There was a perplexity in his voice and his face seemed drained of all colour.

His deferential tone made Joba smile. 'Aha! So someone's offended now, eh? Now come on up. Let's go sit under the bokul. I've got some really important things to tell you.'

Once they were under the tree, Joba turned around and scanned the area with a keen eye. Then she said, 'Pitadeu is at his worship. There aren't any pilgrims today, so he won't take long. I'll have to hurry.'

'Tell me now. Stop beating about the bush.'

Joba started, 'I haven't been feeling too good lately. I'm nauseous and get put off by food. Pitadeu noticed this a few days ago and demanded to know what was wrong with me. "Nothing," I said, and he kept quiet. Then last night, when I couldn't eat my dinner, he suddenly asked, "Joba, you don't seem to have taken your monthly bath ever since you arrived here two months ago. Have your periods stopped?" I said I didn't know. I also told him that I was pretty regular until I came here. Pitadeu was dumbstruck—he looked like he was about to scream, but someone was throttling him. He finally asked me, "Did anything happen between you and Modon while he was here?" I remained silent and hung my head. Suddenly Pitadeu grabbed me by my hair and pushed me to the ground. I hit my head against a corner of the bed and now have a big bump there. Pitadeu started screaming—"You cursed woman, you demoness! You have ruined me. I'll cleave you in two—sacrifice you to the goddess."

'Pitadeu kept scolding me well into the night. I poured some cold water on my head and went to bed, but I couldn't sleep. In the morning, I noticed that Pitadeu was writing a long letter. Every time I passed by, he tried to cover up. When he went for his bath, I rummaged through his things and found it inside a book. It was addressed to the religious head of an ashram near the Kamakhya temple in Guwahati. To cut a long story short, he wants to send me to the ashram. If possible, they will make me undergo an abortion and I will continue to live there.'

'Ever since that moment, I have been dying to see you. Thank god you are here today! Believe me, Gojen, I had no idea that something so momentous was happening within my body. I never once wondered why I missed my periods until Pitadeu asked me last night. Now I've read his letter and I'm afraid. My heart trembles and my head reels. What will become of me now, Gojen?' she sobbed, holding one of Gojen's hands in both of hers.

'Give me about three days' time. I'll go to the district tomorrow, meet Modon kokaiti and return the day after. By the following day, everything should fall into place. Now, now, don't you worry. And don't cry. Run along now—Deu will be out of the temple any moment.'

Joba felt much lighter at Gojen's assurance. She turned towards the house, wiping her eyes as she went.

◆

Four days later, Joba was nowhere to be seen around the house. Bapudeu searched the temple grounds. Finally, he found a letter that she had left for him in the brass basket he used to pick flowers. The text of the letter was this: 'O revered Pitadeu, I had never expected that I would ever be married to Modon. In fact, I knew nothing of his child in my womb until you broached the subject the other day. Now I have no choice but to leave you. I am sad that you will be left all alone. But think of it this way—if my husband were alive, I wouldn't have lived with you anyway. I implore you, don't grieve for me. Eat well and take care of yourself. Make sure you have your medicines regularly. Your ever trusty but unfortunate, Joba.'

Bapudeu finished reading the letter, prostrated himself before the goddess and cried loudly.

Four days later, when Gojen returned from the 'district', he went directly to see Bapudeu. The priest was busy winding a new sacred thread around his knees—the earlier one was about to fall apart. He saw the younger man, but continued with his task, feeling no need to acknowledge him. When he was done, he saved the freshly-wound thread by twining it around a brass pot and, still without looking up, asked, 'You want to say something?'

Gojen fell to his knees and touched the priest's feet. 'Forgive me, Bapudeu. There was no other way.'

'I won't forgive you—ever! The day before yesterday, I learnt from the villagers that you took Joba away in a bus. I came back and sacrificed an ash-gourd in your name to cleanse my sins. Even if I were to forgive you, the goddess will not. My daughter is innocent; her sins have been committed unknowingly. But you men are evil; you are demons. Now get out of my sight!'

Gojen took the rebuke with his head lowered. Then he slowly withdrew a letter from his pocket and placed it respectfully on the tray of tamul-paan near the priest. 'Deu, here's a letter from Modon kokaiti's father. Read it.' He spun around and left.

'Hey, Gojen! I don't need any letters from anybody. I refuse to read them. Take this back—I don't want to look at it!' Even as he shouted this, he picked up the letter and started reading it as soon as Gojen had left.

'Dear Rotnokanto', went the letter, 'I am writing this to you with all humility, repentance and prayers for forgiveness. Although he is my son and hence much younger than me, I have always had to pay heed to all that Modon says and does because of his courage, compassion and conviction in justice for all. We have differed on many issues, but eventually I have always conceded to his point of view. This time too, in spite of its violation of social norms, I have accepted the Modon-Joba marriage on humanitarian grounds.

I know that Joba has recently become an adult. So there is no problem from the legal angle either. They have had a court marriage, but I plan to take them to Kamakhya next week and make them go through the religious ceremony also.

Joba is your daughter. That makes her my kin too, except that she will be my daughter "in-law". But she will be a part of my family and will live here like a daughter. I hope you will try and accept the reality and bless the two of them from afar. With best wishes, Your friend, Tolon Sharma.'

The tears flowed freely from Bapudeu's eyes.

◆

After a long time, Gojen landed up in the Kuroiguri area. He made his way directly to Mansoor's house. He stooped as he entered the thatched shed fronting it. Just as he was straightening up, a soft cough escaped his throat and almost immediately, Hasina called from inside—'Gojen bhai!'

'Hasina!' said Gojen as she came out. 'How did you know it was me?'

'By your cough. The moment you coughed, I knew you had come.'

'You knew my by my cough? How can you identify anyone that way?'

'I don't know about others, but your cough, I know—khhr!' She smiled mischievously and winked at him.

'Isn't Mansoor bhai home?' asked Gojen, sitting down on the bench.

'No, he isn't. He's gone somewhere.'

'Where?'

'God knows! I don't understand all this.'

'Hey, wait a minute. I'm just asking you where your father has gone and you say you don't understand. What is it that you don't understand?'

'Two maulvis have come visiting from Sylhet or Mymensingh and are camping by the Brahmaputra. They have called all the Muslims from this area to their camp. They apparently have something to tell them. That's where Abbajaan has gone. They had come over last evening and talked to him for a long time.'

'Did you hear what they discussed?'

'I wasn't close enough. Abbajaan will tell you.'

'Okay. Now get me a glass of water,' Gojen said seriously.

Hasina walked in and fetched Gojen's glass and a pot of water. She rinsed out the glass, filled it and handed it to him saying, 'Abbajaan was quietly thinking about something long after the men had left. I asked, "Abbajaan, what did the maulvis say?" and he replied, "You won't understand all this—even I don't seem to understand." He said that and went off to the fields.'

'You don't understand, Mansoor doesn't understand—I wonder what all this is about,' said Gojen, trying to solve the puzzle.

Hasina continued, 'When we were about to sleep, Abbajaan said, "Hasina, we might need to leave this place." Suddenly I was wide awake and sat up. I said, "Why? What happened? Why will we leave this place? Where will we go?" He said, "They have made a separate country for us. All Muslims will live there." I said, "But why should we go to the new place? What's wrong with this one? This is our country too. Go tell the maulvis, Abbajaan—we won't go."

'Then Abbajaan said, "I don't understand anything of what they say. They have asked me to come to the riverside for a meeting tomorrow. But, Hasina, however much they try to convince us, we will not leave this place. Why should we? We have created these fields on this land. I don't understand—what is this about a new country being created?" Then I said, "Abba, go to Gojen bhai tomorrow. He will explain everything to you. But I know already—he won't allow us to leave. That I know for sure." Abbajaan said, "You are right, Hasina. I will ask Gojen about all this. He will be able to explain." You know, Bhai, neither Abba nor I could sleep a wink thinking about all this. And now you are here.'

Hasina said all this without a pause. Then she rose and raised her head to look at Gojen who, she saw, was sitting lost in thought, his head lowered.

'Did Mansoor bhai say anything about when he will be back?' he asked, raising his eyes to hers.

'No, nothing.'

'Where did you say they were having the meeting?'

'On the riverbank, at Kuroimukh.'

'I think I'll go there then and see what this meeting is all about.' Gojen rose and started to walk towards the river.

'You must drop by on your way back,' Hasina called out to him.

'I will. Keep a couple of roasted corn cobs ready. And cut a few cucumbers and set out the salt, chilli and onions. I'll also have a cup of your strong tea,' said Gojen as he walked away.

◆

The Kuroiguri sapori was home to about twenty-five Muslim labourers and their families. Between the two arms of the area—the Kuroi and the Brahmaputra—lay their destinies—their trials and tribulations, joys and sorrows, fortunes and misfortunes. Their homes were thatched huts; but each was surrounded by fields of various crops. Oh, what a beautiful sight!

Gojen had first come to this area about seventeen years ago, when he accompanied his uncle on a fishing expedition. He would never forget that day—or how they got here, making their way through thick forests and tall grasses until they reached the banks of the Kuroi. It was an exhilarating outing, the memories of which still made his skin tingle every time he saw the place. Today was no different, although the wilderness had now given way to fields that were green with some crop or the other throughout the year. In all the years he had been here, Gojen never saw any of the settlers involved in any kind of squabble or disorderly behaviour.

The peace among these hard workers was almost palpable, Gojen mused—it was as if he could touch it, see it and experience it deeply. But today, as he followed the cattle tracks towards the Brahmaputra, the shadow of an unknown fear rose within him like a dark cloud. There were certain ominous indications in what Hasina had just told him, though he couldn't quite put a finger on them. There seemed to be some danger looming ahead—a threat to disrupt the peace of the Kuroiguri inhabitants. He walked faster. Perhaps he would be able to gauge what was happening if he could get to the maulvis' meeting on time.

On reaching the steep dyke by the Brahmaputra, Gojen saw that the Kuroiguri Muslims were sitting huddled around a middle-aged man with a salt-and-pepper beard who stood addressing them—probably one of the maulvis. His loud speech, though in their own language, contained a generous smattering of Urdu words. Gojen also noticed that the other long-bearded maulavi was sitting next to him. The boat, moored to the shore, was probably their home. But what surprised Gojen the most was that in the middle of the gathering stood a tall bamboo post with a green flag flying atop it.

This flag had a crescent moon at its centre. Gojen had so far seen two flags—the Union Jack and the tricolour of the Indian National Congress. So what was this flag before him?

Just as he was about to make his way down the slope, Gojen noticed that the maulvi who had been addressing the people had suddenly stopped speaking and was fixing him with a keen stare. He seemed to be checking on the identity of their visitor with the assembly. The men turned around and saw him, and it seemed as though a couple of them told the maulvi who he was. But the information made no difference—the man stood sombrely transfixed in his spot and directed a look of deep suspicion at Gojen. Sensing danger, the latter halted in his tracks. The people he had known all this while suddenly felt like strangers. He carefully scanned all the faces before him, and then turned around and walked back up the slope. He could tell that his arrival was something that the maulvis neither expected nor appreciated.

Gojen made his way through the narrow lane amidst fields of pulses. Suddenly, he heard someone calling from behind—'Gojen bhai, wait!' He turned around, and seeing that Mansoor had followed him, he stopped.

Both started walking homewards, Mansoor narrating the proceedings of the meeting, which was still on—the maulvi had regained his composure and resumed speaking. Mansoor had walked away because he did not agree with anything the man had to say. And it wasn't just him—most of those present weren't convinced about what they were told.

Mansoor explained things to Gojen the way he had understood them: We have one country in which all people—Hindus and Muslims—live together. This country is now going to be free. The English government will go back and will let our own countrymen form a government. But the Muslims will have a separate government that will rule another country. This country will be carved out of the existing one. It will be called Pakistan. All Muslims will live in Pakistan. Some people don't want this new country and want Hindus and Muslims to live together as brothers in one country. But the Muslim leaders haven't accepted that. Pakistan must happen. And to achieve that end, the Muslims have to resort to jihad if necessary—that's what the maulvis are saying. The two maulvis who have come here are saying that too—that we Muslims must be united in our demand for Pakistan. Once this country is free and Pakistan is formed, we will have to move there; because if we continue to live here, we will always be at the mercy of the Hindus.

By the time he finished speaking, they had reached Mansoor's home.

◆

Gojen picked the corn kernels from the cob and chewed on them. 'So what have you decided?' he asked. 'Once this country is free and a separate state created for you, will you go away from here?'

Meanwhile four or five more of the Kuroiguri Muslims had left the maulvis' meeting halfway and come to sit under the thatched canopy of Mansoor's home. From them, Gojen got to know that most of the people at the meeting had abandoned it halfway and walked into the fields.

It was an elderly person in the small assembly who chose to answer Gojen's question to Mansoor. 'The question doesn't arise. Why should we leave just because there is a Pakistan? Is it there that we have created these stretches of cultivable land, built our homes, attended weddings and pujas in the homes of our Assamese brothers or gone to see the Bihu functions and what not? How can we leave this place, Gojen bhai?'

'You are right, Rehmat miyan. There is no question of our leaving this place—never mind if there is a Pakistan or not,' another added.

'That's right. This is the truth. We are not about to leave this land, this country,' they all agreed.

Hasina served the assembly some black tea in an assortment of aluminium, stoneware and glass tumblers. As she handed

Gojen's special tumbler to him, she said, 'Rahmat chacha, I had told Abbajaan yesterday that whatever you do, consult Gojen bhai first.'

'There's nothing to consult me on. How can I advise you? You Muslims are trying to decide something for yourselves and it is not right that I should interfere. The only thing I can tell you is that if you people decide to remain here in Kuroiguri, there will be no danger from people of other religions. I know the maulvis have planted such a fear in your heads, but I can assure you that here at least, your people are safe. We will not let them come to any harm. We are certain of that.' The words had an impact on the small audience and they seemed reassured.

'Did you hear what Gojen bhai said? Nothing will happen to us. There is no fear. Even if there is a Pakistan, we will remain in this country. This is our country. Am I right?' Rehmat asked the others.

'Yes, it is. You are right,' the others chorused.

◆

Gojen looked up at the waning sun and wondered why he had come to Kuroiguri today. He wasn't carrying his fishing gear and had no important errand in the area. It was just that he had thought of Hasina this morning, and that too, for no apparent reason. He had woken up very early and was planning on getting back into bed after relieving himself. But mesmerized by the soft light and the cool breeze following the gentle early-morning shower, he lost all inclination to go inside. Lighting a beedi, he settled down on the chair on the veranda. Some birds had settled on the branches of the gooseberry and rose-apple trees—shrikes, mynahs, wagtails, a couple of sparrows and a pair of doves—and they were hopping about all over the courtyard. That was when he remembered Hasina. She couldn't resist running after a bird whenever she saw one, as if to catch it, and had not outgrown this habit yet. In Kuroiguri, whenever she came to watch Gojen fishing, she ran after the cranes and egrets by the river.

He kept looking at the birds and thinking of Hasina. And then it struck him that he hadn't visited them in a long time. He set off

immediately after breakfast. He would spend the day in Kuroiguri—
first at Mansoor's place and then at Chaila's. It would be nice to call
on them and see how they were doing. And now he was embroiled
in this serious situation!

From the regular newspaper readings at the kabiraj's, Gojen
knew that the country would soon be liberated. But lately, another
name was beginning to feature alongside those of Gandhi, Nehru,
Patel and Azad—that of Mohammad Ali Jinnah. The man seemed
to be creating a number of hurdles on the path to freedom. It was
almost as if he was trying to reverse the flow of a river. The entire
country was caught in the currents; and the waves were being felt
here in Kuroiguri too.

These days, the picture of free India in Gojen's mind seemed
rather blurry. From what he heard from Modon and the meetings
held in his neighbourhood, and from all that he read in the papers,
he had imagined what his free country would be like. But would
it ever become a reality? Would people like these maulvis and
Jadob Bora allow things to take the right course? Bora was always
puffed up, boasting about the 'sacrifices' he had made in this quest
for freedom. But if that man's deeds were indeed sacrifice, his own
were no less, mused Gojen. His back tingled as he recalled the
lashings at the hands of a police constable five years ago. He had
never bragged about it, but he was indeed proud of what he had
done—what Modon had inspired him to do.

Gojen remembered those days. It was about a year since he
had quit going to school; but he happened to hear of a peace corps
for the independence movement being mobilized in the middle
school premises. One group comprised older men and the other,
younger people like Gojen. When he landed up there, they were
being paraded in the fields behind his school. For some time,
he remained a mere spectator from the sidelines. Then the parade
passed by him—girls marching in twos and pairs of boys bringing
up the rear. Every now and then, the commander yelled 'Left, right,
one-two, turn right...' Suddenly, Gojen noticed that the boy at the
tail end had no partner. A tall ruddy man, dressed in khadi shorts,

shirt, white canvas shoes and socks and a Gandhi cap who, he later learnt, was the district head of the corps, marched beside the boy as he commanded the group, whistle in pocket and baton in hand. His eyes caught Gojen's and he called, 'Hey boy! Why don't you fall in line?' And before he knew it, Gojen had fallen into step and was marching alongside the last boy.

The group was trained in various aspects of the movement over the course of a week. Apart from physical fitness, the focus was on first aid and self-protection in the event of the police resorting to lathi charge, tear gassing or even firing upon protestors. They were taught how to identify secret signals and informed—in simple terms and great detail—about facts relating to their purpose.

It wasn't long before Gojen caught the commandant's eye. The boy was smart, brave, alert, willing and quick to voice his fearless opinions on issues discussed, and would be the ideal person to head group B. And so it was that Gojen Keunt was nominated group in-charge—a person bound by oath and willing to take on any challenge for the cause. And it wasn't long before the revolutionary committee placed that heavy responsibility on his young shoulders.

It wasn't easy to carry the secret commands of the underground revolutionaries from one place to another. One of the major items on their agenda was to hoist the tricolour at all local police stations. People from all the villages under the police station would march to it, with the peace corps leading—the men from group B in front, followed by the youth from the group A death squad, and the regular men and women behind them. A young girl would enter the compound carrying the tricolour, flanked by the heads of the two groups to assist her. Some of the youngsters in the gathering would be equipped with first-aid kits.

The day for the flag hoisting was declared—the 20th of September. The local Congress wings supervised all arrangements. Modon served as the link between the local and central secret wings—he had been deputed to carry the commands from the district central committee to the local branches and to assist in their implementation.

15

All was set for the 20th September agenda, and members of the revolutionary committee stayed up late on the preceding night, going over the plans in minute detail. Gojen was not expected to participate in these discussions; but eager as he was, he sat on the side and listened to everything. At one point, one of the seniors saw him and said, 'Gojen, you should go home now. It's rather late. Everyone will assemble near the school at six in the morning and you will have to arrive a little earlier to take charge of your group. So go now.'

As he tried to fall asleep, Gojen visualized the next day's procession and prayed that he would be able to carry out his duties diligently. It was his first experience of serious responsibility, and he realized how exhilarating that could be. He fell into a deep slumber. Suddenly, he heard a faint voice calling out to him—'Gojen, o Gojen bhai, please wake up…'

Gojen stepped outside. In the faint moonlight, he saw two men waiting in the courtyard. One looked like the Nepali, Maila, from Kuroiguri. 'Is that you, Maila?' Gojen asked.

'Hm, it's me. I've brought Bhodaram too.'

'What's up—so late…?' Gojen stepped into the courtyard.

'Here's a letter. A person from Nihali brought it to me and said I should hand it over to you right away.' Seating the two men at the veranda, Gojen carried the letter into the house, lit a lamp and read the short missive: 'As soon as you receive this letter, make haste to Kuroiguri in the night itself, cross the river by boat and await a special command from the central committee. It is on the basis of this command that tomorrow's procession and flag-hoisting will be carried out. If time permits, also inform the local heads about this, and ask them to hold on until further orders from the central committee. Yours—MS.'

Gojen pulled on a shirt, roused his grandmother and said, 'Aai, I need to step out on an important errand. You go back to bed. If someone asks you where I am, tell them you don't know.'

'God knows what you are up to—neither eating nor sleeping on time!' The old lady carried the lamp to the door and watched her grandson leave with the two men.

At the gate, Gojen suddenly looked skywards. 'It's pretty late, right Maila?'

'Yes, it's past midnight,' the man replied.

Gojen calculated that if he had to inform the local members, he would have to walk two miles to the first of their homes—the others were even further. He would then need to return and walk the four miles to Kuroiguri. By the time he was through, it would be morning. The orders would be waiting. And they would have to be delivered to the rest before six! No, there wasn't enough time— he should go directly to Kuroiguri, he decided, and set off resolutely in that direction.

It was almost daybreak by the time Gojen got to the other side of the river in Maila's little boat. He had hoped that his messenger would be waiting, but peering through the faintness, he saw no trace of anyone on either horizon. Returning to the boat, he sat at one end and fixed his gaze upon the cattle track while Maila sat at the other end, humming a Nepali tune. This humming, the rippling music of the flowing river and the cool autumn breeze soothed Gojen's restlessness to some degree.

The day dawned. He started pacing the sands and moved some distance down the cattle track. Nobody there. The eastern sky got redder. And then the red sun rose from the waters of the distant Brahmaputra.

Gojen was getting impatient. There was no news yet—and he needed to carry those special orders to the seniors before six, when the procession was scheduled to begin. It was at least six miles to the school across the river. The sun seemed to soar high in the sky over the water, like a white egret on the wing. At this rate, it would be past six before he got out of here. He wondered what he should do—should he wait for the missive or go ahead without it? He held prime responsibility where the procession was concerned. What should he do now?

His neck ached from craning out at the path. Pulling at his hair in exasperation, he asked Maila for a beedi and lit up. On his commander's orders, he had given up all intoxicants ever since he joined the peace corps over a month ago, but he chose to forget all about that. As he puffed, he realized that both the peace and death squads would have assembled in the school compound by now and that their chiefs must be puzzled by his absence.

Still puffing on the beedi, he scanned the cattle track once again. Then suddenly, in the distance, he saw a man hurrying towards them. There was no doubt about it—this was the messenger he had been waiting for. They sprinted towards each other and once within earshot, he called, 'Vande Mataram!'

'Vande Mataram!' Gojen replied.

'Are you Gojen Keunt?' asked the man.

'Yes, I am. Have you brought my orders?'

'Here, take this letter and give it to Bhuyan.' The man pulled out a letter from the folds of cloth at his waistline and handed it to Gojen.

'Let's talk as we proceed towards the ghat—there's no time to wait and listen,' said Gojen as they both rushed towards the boat. 'How come you were so late? Weren't you supposed to be here before daybreak?'

'The person coming from Jotiya to Nihali was held up. He was supposed to take the bus to Nihali and arrive there by evening so that he could come to Kuroiguri at night. But the bus didn't come yesterday, so he had to cycle all the way and reached Nihali only after midnight. We did take note of the delay and arrange for a bicycle, but the chain broke after a short distance; so I had to leave it in somebody's house and walk the rest of the way. What should have taken an hour and a half took four hours! But will you be able to carry this message to the assembly on time? It's quite a distance from here, isn't it?'

'What's in the letter?' asked Gojen, still running.

'The procession needs to be stopped. If at all they have to go, they may parade peacefully by the police station, but plans for the flag hoisting have been aborted.'

'What? No flag hoisting?' Gojen stopped short.

'Right. That plan had to be abandoned because the government has made heavy deployment of armed police at all the outposts. There will be unnecessary loss of lives.'

'Oh, god! But the procession would have already started!' Gojen rushed towards the boat once again, both men calling out 'Vande Mataram!' as they parted. He jumped in and ordered Maila to row as hard as he could.

◆

By the time Gojen covered the six miles from Kuroiguri to the school compound, it was already two hours since the procession had left. It was four miles to the police station and before long, it would arrive there. For a moment, Gojen felt the letter in his pocket and wondered what to do. Then he started running in the direction of the police station, hitching pillion rides on bicycle carriers a couple of times. But thanks to the pebbled roads and under-inflated tyres, they made slow progress. It was faster to run, and run he did.

He was about a mile from his destination and there was no sign of the procession. Had it reached already? He ran faster. In the distance, he heard a medley of voices—'Vande Mataram!', 'Hail Mahatma Gandhi', 'Do or die'…

'Vande Mataram!' Gojen shouted, and charged forward. The procession was almost at the station gate and he was trailing. He sped up.

Reaching the assembly at last, he rushed forward, hand protectively on his pocket, looking for the seniors to whom he could hand over the letter. Strains of patriotic songs rent the air and resonated in the sky.

He was somewhere around the middle of the assembly when Gojen heard the boom of gunshots drowning the voices. The people went berserk, running in all directions, crying, screaming... By the time he reached the front, he saw that the police were aiming their guns at the people and the youngsters in front were trying to beat a hasty retreat. A girl of about fifteen was just turning back after dropping the tricolour she carried when the bullets hit her and brought her bleeding to the ground. Suddenly, out of nowhere, Commander Kakati appeared and picked up the flag. Three more gunshots—then he too fell to the ground, blood spurting from his chest and spilling over the flag.

Gojen looked on, stupefied, at the commotion around him— people running for their lives, shouting and wailing. Turning towards the station, he saw the armed police move forward and cordon off the area with the two bodies. He had gone unnoticed so far and wondered if he should charge forward and retrieve the now blood-red flag from the ground. Just then, one of the policemen spotted him and, pointing his gun at him, shouted, 'Hey boy! Hands up!' He raised his arms and fixed a keen gaze on the man. Would he shoot him now?

After a while, he turned around and slowly made his way back, arms still raised. A constable who had been bustling around suddenly hit Gojen on the back with his cane and yelled, 'Run— scoot.' But instead of doing that, Gojen slowly brought his arms down and stopped short. He wondered—why did the man need to hit him? The constable too, puzzled by the boy's reaction, tried to figure out what was on his mind.

'Hey! I asked you to run and now you stand there like a prince. I say, scoot! Come on, run, run...' And the constable lashed Gojen's back several times with his cane. Seeing no response even then, he shouted once again, 'Run, I say!'

Gojen stumbled forward and moved slowly ahead. The deserted main street before him was strewn with cloth and paper flags and a few first-aid kits. Suddenly his legs felt leaden—he couldn't move further. His throat was parched and he was exhausted. Somehow, he plodded on until he reached the riverbank. He drank his fill, wrung out his shirt in the water and wiped his now swollen and aching back. He dragged himself to the shade of a large tree by the nearby bridge and sat down on the grass, leaning against its trunk. The important missive he carried in his pocket remained unread. There was no point in reading it now—things would have turned out differently if he could have delivered it on time. His eyelids turned heavy and he knew not when he fell asleep.

◆

Next morning, Gojen woke early and even as he was in bed, planned to go see Bhuyan, tell him all that had happened and inquire about what happened to the two who fell to the policemen's bullets. His back was hurting badly, but he dragged himself out of bed and, after a cup of tea, set off on his errand.

From the crowd that was engaged in animated conversation in front of the kabiraj's shop, he learnt that the police had arrested some of the local Congress workers, including Bhuyan, and had taken them away in Kanubabu's bus. Some claimed they also saw Jadob Bora in the bus, though they were not sure whether it was the police who had nabbed him or if he had voluntarily courted arrest.

At any rate, whatever Gojen had planned to tell Bhuyan remained untold. And no one heard the saga of what had happened to him apart from his grandmother who gathered bits and pieces of the story as she massaged his back with medicated oil. The sight of his back initially drove the old lady to tears. But once she gathered how he had acquired the welts, she was overcome with a sense of pride. 'Never mind, my son,' she said. 'You have hurt yourself following Mahatma Gandhi's words. The country is about to earn its independence. That Kakati and the young girl have died—so let bygones be bygones and bear this the best you can.'

◆

Today, five years later, Gojen once again felt the biting pain of those lashings on his back. Hasina, Mansoor, the Muslims of Kuroiguri, the maulvis' speeches, Pakistan, the partition of one country into two, the talk of freedom, independence....

The freedom movement, his role in it—once again he recalled the stimulus of those days in a steady sequence. And before he realized it, he was back home.

16

'Dharmadeu!' called Jadob Bora from a distance. The kabiraj and his audience at his newspaper reading turned back in unison and saw Bora parking his cycle on the stand. He took off the Gandhi cap that he had recently started donning and busily made his way towards the group. The kabiraj put down the paper and vacated his chair for the new arrival.

'Gosh—I haven't had a moment's respite since morning,' said Bora, pulling out a handkerchief from his pocket and wiping the sweat from his face and neck as he settled into his chair.

'There is no end to Bora's work,' said the kabiraj, seating himself on a cane murha. 'There are so many social commitments! But did anything new crop up today?'

'Why? Haven't you heard? There is going to be a huge public meeting in the middle school grounds tomorrow. You all have to go there carrying the tricolour flags.'

'Of course we know of that—why wouldn't we? I already have my clothes washed and ready for tomorrow and have bought a flag for four annas.'

'That's it. Arrangements for that meeting took up the entire day. Bhuyan and the others simply can't do without me. I've just come from the mauzadar's place—he's going to preside. Then there's Mahendra Singh—sickly, no doubt, but an old Congressman. He'll be the chief guest. And we will all deliver the speeches.'

'What do you plan to say in your speech, Kokaideu?'

Bora turned in the direction of the voice and tried to determine the identity of the questioner. The voice was familiar—and it belonged to Gojen! He looked straight at him and their eyes locked.

'You are right, Gojen. I suppose I'll have to learn the content of my speech from you, since we have someone so enlightened amongst us. Tell me, Gojen, what should I speak about tomorrow?' But Bora's barbs missed their target. Unperturbed by the taunts, Gojen replied, 'Just tell them all about all the difficulties you faced, all the sacrifices you made in this quest for freedom—about how you spent twenty days and nights in jail. And how, with Khargi mauzadar's influence, you managed to…'

'Hey, Gojen, will you shut up?' the kabiraj interrupted. Gojen shut up and lowered his head, a smile of satisfaction playing on his lips. Bora saw the sarcasm in his smile. He directed a venomous look at the young man, but Gojen didn't look up.

The kabiraj turned to Bora. 'Let's not waste time on all this trivia. Let's concentrate on more serious things. Let the reading begin.'

Bora tore away his gaze from Gojen and picked up the newspaper. 'There's no use reading this now,' he said. 'This news is a week old. I have brought fresh hot news.'

'What news?'

'Where did you get it from?'

'Who told you?'

These and other questions immediately cropped up from among those present. Pleased at the response, Jadob Bora started his detailed discourse. 'We had gone to the mauzadar's place to request him to preside over tomorrow's meeting. He had just returned from Burton sahib's bungalow in Salem tea estate. Burton sahib owns a radio, and they had just heard the news—the cabinet of ministers of free India have been sitting in the Delhi parliament since evening. At the stroke of midnight, the moment the 15th of August starts, the country's power will be handed over to them. Jawaharlal Nehru and Lord Mountbatten will assume office as the first Prime Minister and the first Governor General respectively. The Union Jack of the British government will be lowered and our tricolour flag hoisted in its place. Then tomorrow morning, there will be massive public rallies at the Red Fort and other places in Delhi and the leaders will make their speeches.

But there is one other thing. Pakistan assumed independent power last midnight itself—that is, on the 14th of August. They already conducted their country's flag-hoisting ceremony in Lahore last night.'

'So Pakistan has been created after all,' someone commented.

'Why else would so many people have died? So many people lost their lives in the Hindu-Muslim clashes in Delhi, Kolkata and elsewhere. Mahatma Gandhi, Nehru, Patel and all the people in their Congress could not hold the country together. Jinnah appropriated Pakistan all by himself. We have been reading about all this in the papers for a year now. Partitioning one country into two…'

It was Gojen who had spoken. He wasn't a regular at this forum and even when he did attend, he kept his opinions to himself. Today, for some reason, he decided to speak up. But even as he was speaking, Bora rose from his chair. 'Dharmadeu, I'll take my leave. There are other people here who can give you the information.' He cast a sideways glance at Gojen and took a couple of steps. Then, turning to him, he said, 'So now, Gojen, what will you call the Kuroiguri farmers now—Pakistanis or something else? Almost twenty five families there—so on an average of five bighas of land, they occupy no less than'—he paused to multiply—'a hundred and twenty five bighas. Now that the Muslims have their own Pakistan, that's where they ought to be. Well, I'll be off now. We'll take care of that at the opportune time.'

Bora placed the Gandhi cap on his head and hurried towards his bicycle. Soon after, one by one, the others left too. It had been decided that they would all go to the following day's meeting together.

◆

Gojen woke early and went directly to the bamboo grove behind the house. He cut a tall, erect piece of bamboo and scraped it smooth at the joints. Then he carried it to the front courtyard and dug a hole in which he could plant it. Just then, his grandmother returned from picking her forbidden paan. Standing at one end of the courtyard, she directed a sharp look at Gojen, wondering what he was up to.

'Hey, I keep this courtyard neatly swept and swabbed in spite of my backache and you go messing it up. Why on earth are you digging it now?' she asked sternly.

'Just you watch, Aai. I'm about to do something great. Now don't fuss—just watch,' said Gojen, still too busy to look up. The old lady went up to the veranda and, between stacking her leaves, stole a look at her grandson.

Once the hole was dug, Gojen wiped his hands clean on the gamosa around his waist and pulled out a piece of cloth from his vest pocket—the tricolour flag. On his last visit to his teacher, Sarbai Pandit had given him one of the two he had bought at the district headquarters and Gojen had carefully folded and stored it in a suitcase.

When he was with the peace corps in 1942, Gojen had learnt how to tie a flag for hoisting on a high pole. He now used his know-how and planted the bamboo vertically in the hole he had dug. Then he called his grandmother and asked her to tug at the free end of the cord. The old lady followed his bidding, and the flag fluttered in the breeze. Gojen saluted it as he had done during his corps training and uttered the words, 'Jai Hind! Vande Mataram!'

Aai too raised her hand to her temple in an imitation of a salute. Then she said, 'You could have simply explained to me that you wanted to raise Gandhi's flag. But son, why today? Is it because our country is free as of today?'

'You're right, Aai—it's because our country is now independent. But this isn't Gandhi's flag. That one—meaning the one used by the Congress—had a spinning wheel in its centre, whereas this one has a chakra instead. This is the flag of our independent country—it's our national flag,' explained Gojen. 'Now come, let's get some tea and something to eat.'

'Wait; let me swab this area first.' The old lady smoothened the hump of earth at the base of the flag-post with wet hands, placed a lit earthen lamp on a piece of banana leaf near it and covered the rest of the hump with rose petals and jasmine. Then she knelt before the flag and bowed her head to the ground.

Some time later, Rupai and Konloura came by, so that they could all go to the public meeting-cum-flag-hoisting together. Gojen announced that he had no intention of going; he had made up his mind the previous evening. 'You go ahead and see how things are conducted,' he told his friends. 'And listen—come over tonight. We shall have a feast in our home to celebrate our self-governance.'

As soon as the two had left, Aai berated Gojen, 'It's such a big event; why don't you go? People are flocking there in droves. Last night, when Rupai and the others came looking for you, they told me all about it. If only my back was stronger, I too would have gone and listened to the speeches.'

'Come on, then. If you are that keen, I'll carry you piggyback and take you there.'

'Hah! I'm not going—not even on piggyback. But when all the people do something together, the least you should do is support them,' she said angrily.

'I will certainly lend my support if the people do something. But if antisocial elements get people to do things, I am not with them. When the flag of independent India flies high in the sky for the first time, I will not be able to tolerate the likes of Khargi mauzadar and Jadob Bora sitting around to mar that beautiful and respectful sight. It is the mauzadar who is going to preside over this meeting—that parasite who fleeces the public, the demon who licks the feet of the British government! Why couldn't they opt for someone like Sarbai Sir instead? Bhuyan and the others are voiceless—they are overpowered by fiends like Jadob Bora.'

Suddenly, the flag fluttered loudly as the breeze grew stronger. Gojen looked up at it and spoke softly, 'Go, Aai, get me some tamul. I'll go see which household has a duck to spare. We'll need to catch a couple of pigeons too; maybe you should set the snaring basket out. We have the bamboo shoots which can be fried. And put out some bait in the pond—I'll come back and catch the fish. Else I can go to the ghat in the evening and see what big fish I can get. My friends are coming and we'll have a feast—the feast of swaraj!'

'The feast of swaraj'—Gojen's own words echoed in his ears. The mental picture of this independence that he had drawn up with whatever he had heard from Modon seemed to be held up by two men before him—the mauzadar at one corner and Jadob Bora at the other. Would this really be a feast?

A flock of cackling ducks waddled down to the river from a house on the bank. Gojen walked up the path to the house to see if he could buy one.

◆

One evening, about a month later, Gojen went to the kabiraj's clinic. He had taken to reading the paper in the daytime itself and had not attended the evening assembly for a while.

The paper that arrived that day was being read by lamplight. When Gojen appeared, everyone turned to look, then returned to listening to the news. Even Jadob Bora acknowledged him with 'O, Gojen—come, sit,' and went back to his reading. What they gathered that day was this:

In the few weeks since independence, citizens were facing a grave crisis. Many areas were in the grip of communal riots involving Hindus and Muslims, as a result of which Pakistan's minority Hindus and India's minority Muslims were moving into the other country, leaving all their movable and immovable assets behind. The mindless violence—unspeakable torture, inhuman murder, looting, rape, arson and what not—affected the fleeing innocents and claimed thousands of lives.

The headlines in that newspaper had to do with Jawaharlal Nehru and Liaqat Ali Khan flying to Lahore and Lyallpore in West Pakistan and holding talks to find a solution to the refugee problem. A reporter who had interviewed some of the two-lakh-seventy-thousand Sikh and Hindu refugees from Pakistan, now camping in

Kurukshetra near Delhi, recounted their travails. There were many more of these refugee camps in other towns, and the Muslims from India were now refugees in Pakistan. Lakhs had died on either side.

The reading continued for quite some time and it was only after lengthy comments, questions and discussions that the audience dispersed. After a while, Gojen entered the clinic and came out carrying two paper pouches. In the sparkling moonlight, he saw that Bora's cronies were huddled around him and his cycle, discussing something in suppressed tones. Things seemed serious, and Gojen wondered if he should go join them. He would have to go that way in any case, so he moved ahead and walked past them.

A little later, he realized that Jadob Bora was walking right behind him, pulling his bike along the side of the pebbled tracks. When he turned around and confirmed this, he stepped aside. 'You go ahead, Kokaideu.'

Bora moved forward but did not get on the cycle. 'It's a nice moonlit night and it feels nicer to walk. Come, Gojen, let's go together. I'm sure you'll want to stop at the bridge.' They moved on in silence. Then Bora said, 'So, Gojen, what do you propose to do about us?'

Gojen did not get the import of the question. 'What are you talking about, Kokaideu?'

'Those Muslim farmers of Kuroiguri.'

'The Kuroiguri farmers...' Gojen was still puzzled.

'I mean those Muslim settlers,' Bora said derisively.

'You mean Mansoor bhai and his ilk?'

'Right—I mean those ones.'

'What's the matter with them, Kokaideu?' Gojen's voice faltered slightly.

'Nothing. But shouldn't something be done about them? The fires are burning all around us—haven't you read the papers? Shouldn't we also be feeling the heat of those fires? That too with a hero like you around—a strong young man...'

'A hero like me? What hero? What do I do? And fire—what fire? I don't understand a thing, Kokaideu!'

'Oh god! You have a brain that works only when it is convenient. Why—aren't those people Muslims? Don't they have a country of their own now? East Pakistan? Shouldn't they return to their own place? Let them go to their country, and let our land be ours. Isn't that right?' Bora turned to look at Gojen.

'Kokaideu...what are you saying...' Gojen was at a loss for words. But even before he could speak, Bora butted in, 'Oh I'd forgotten. But you are on extremely cordial terms with those folks, aren't you? Right—I was beginning to wonder why this villainous mind of yours wasn't opening up. I've figured out now. Anyway, you carry on, Gojen.' Bora hopped on to his cycle and pedalled away, whistling his trademark tune, *Luitor paarore...*

The whistling faded into the distance. Gojen had raised his hand to protect his face from the dust that Bora had stirred up while alighting the cycle. As he slowly brought it down, the moonlit night seemed as dark as the moments before a thunderstorm, and he felt suffocated by the heavy clouds looming over him. He had felt uneasy as he listened to the news being read out at the clinic. And then Bora had spoken—Mansoor Ali and the rest of the Muslims must go to their own Pakistan. But what if they refused to move? And if they did, who would own or live in the acres of land that they had converted from impenetrable jungle to lush greenery? They didn't want to move—they were happy living in peace with their neighbours here. They had even attended the flag-hoisting ceremony. Gojen knew this—Rupai had told him.

In fact, Mansoor had carried home a paper flag distributed by the volunteers and Hasina had carefully hung it with thread on the front wall of their house. Later, one day when Gojen went visiting, she learnt from him the symbolism of the colours and the chakra. What the maulvis had preached had gone over their heads. For them, this place provided them the scope to work for a living, their peace and contentment and their meals, and allowed them to perform their namaaz for their Allah. This country was their very own.

So why had Bora asked, 'What do you propose to do about us?' What was there for him to do? The facts were all tangled inside his head. He had meanwhile consumed the contents of the two paper pouches—were they too heady today? No, Gojen decided. This wouldn't do. He would go to Jadob Bora right away and directly ask him what he meant when he called Gojen a hero. Only then would he understand.

Gojen knew that once Bora left the kabiraj's clinic, he headed straight for Moti mistry's and then spent some time at another special place before he returned home. By that calculation, Bora should now be at Moti's, drinking with his supporters. But once he reached the courtyard, he saw no signs of the cycle. All seemed to be quiet inside too. Was nobody home? Just then, Moti's wife called out, 'Come, come, Gojen. Come right in.'

In the moonlight, he noticed that she had risen from a stool on the veranda, holding a glass of liquor in her hands. As he was about to enter the house, he asked, 'Hasn't Jadob Bora come by as yet?'

The woman followed him in. 'Jadob Bora is all you care about! You don't take any notice of us. Just sit down. You'll meet Bora by and by.' Smiling at Gojen, she drained the glass in one long gulp and tossed it away.

'How about the rest of them? Bora's cronies?'

'They'll all come. Why do you need them anyway? Just make yourself comfortable.' The woman took his hand and forced him to sit on a large chest. 'You haven't come here in a long time. I keep thinking of you. Can I get you a half?' She continued to smile as she spoke to Gojen in her Nepali-accented Assamese.

'I won't drink today. I've come here only to see Bora. I have something important to discuss with him. Isn't your husband home either?'

'He's gone somewhere—the sick man!' After a short pause, she added, 'There's nobody home. I'm all alone.'

Gojen turned grave. He had been feeling uneasy ever since the woman had taken his hand and made him sit down. Her grip had felt like a clamp.

The woman scanned his face. Then she said, 'I have some really fresh stuff today. Try it—you'll like it. It'll also soften you up in your head.'

'I'm telling you I don't want any. Now stop nagging!' said Gojen, irritated but still composed.

'You are such a hothead!' The woman lifted the curtain and went into the inner chamber.

Gojen, sitting all by himself, wondered aloud if the people he was waiting for would come at all. Then he turned towards the inner room and called, 'Hey, aren't these guys coming today? Do you have any idea?'

'They'll all turn up. You just wait—what's the hurry? Tell you what—come on here. There's no one around and you can sit more comfortably on the bed,' she replied from inside.

'Never mind; I'm fine. But what are you up to in there?'

'It's so warm, I'm readjusting my clothes.' Then, moments later, 'You had nothing to drink today—have something to eat instead.'

'No thanks. I could do with a glass of water, though. All this drinking makes you thirsty.'

'Ha! So you've already had your drinks. How can my local stuff even compare? Once you are married, remember to have a dose of liquor before you get into bed. It increases your stamina, do you understand? I'm glad you have drunk today—you don't need my local brew now.'

'Shut up and get me a glass of water, will you?' said Gojen, rising angrily.

'Wait, Gojen. Don't go yet. I'm getting you the water.' She parted the curtains and stepped out carrying a glass. She was wearing a red petticoat and her blouse was barely buttoned in the front, exposing all that lay within. Her eyes were bloodshot. Gojen drank and returned the empty glass to her. Fixing him with a come-hither look, she said, 'You know, Gojen, Jadob Bora came by some time ago, had two quick ones and left carrying a half with him. And the gang was here even before him—they've taken four bottles with them. Moti has gone with them. They are planning a feast somewhere tonight. It'll be late night before they return.'

'How come you didn't tell me all this before? I'll be off now.' He rose to leave.

'Wait, Gojen; don't go.' The woman blocked his way. 'Stay with me tonight, Gojen. Please spend the night with me,' she pleaded and suddenly gathered him in a tight embrace.

Gojen released himself from her grip and pushed her away. The woman stumbled backwards, almost falling, and steadied herself against the wall. For some time, she stood stonily against it, her eyes bloodshot, her bare breasts heaving. Then, slowly, she buttoned up her blouse.

Gojen wanted to throttle her, but was soon able to control his anger. His clenched fists eased open and the fire in his eyes died down. 'Don't try this on me ever again. Live like a good woman. Just because you are poor doesn't mean you need to be bad, you know,' he explained patiently, as though nothing had happened. As he was leaving, he turned around and asked, 'Do you have any idea where Bora and the rest are having their feast?'

'No. But Moti did say they would be late coming back.' The woman's voice quivered as she spoke.

Gojen stepped out of the house and erased the unpleasant episode with the woman from his mind. His main mission was yet to be accomplished—confronting Bora with his question. He knew that the man was in the habit of visiting one other place on a daily basis. It was also possible that that was the venue of the feast. However, it was doubtful that Bora would wish to have a noisy party at a place with which his association was so secret and personal.

17

Jadob Bora's evening visits to Moti mistry's home were a prelude to his next stop, and they provided him with the physical and mental preparedness for that one. This second stopover was at a house in a village on the far side from Gojen's. Bora needed to cross this village on his way home, and had made it his moral responsibility to check on a lonely lady who lived there.

Soon after the birth of their first child, clerk Nareshwar had returned his wife Bimola and the infant to his father-in-law, declaring that the baby wasn't his. Bimola was a distant cousin of Jadob Bora's wife—so it became his social obligation to reunite her with her husband. All efforts were in vain, and soon Nareshwar ended the possibility of reconciliation by marrying a young girl. To top it all, Bimola's father suddenly passed away due to some unknown ailment, and the orphaned mother-child duo became Bora's responsibility.

Much as Bora tried to keep the association secret, it soon became known to all, except that everyone chose to turn a blind eye to it. Even when the news seeped into his own home, his wife railed for a few days and then accepted the arrangement, explaining it away saying, 'All men are like that. One woman is never enough to quench their thirst.' And for her part, she received full cooperation of her husband in keeping her lap constantly full by getting her pregnant every year or two.

Apart from his public duties, this was one indulgence Bora allowed himself. And he optimized the time spent at his two stopovers on his way home each evening—first at Moti's, and then at Nareshwar's estranged wife Bimola's.

◆

Gojen wondered—would Bora really want to host the revelry at this secret getaway of his? No, perhaps not. He had probably arranged for it somewhere else. And if he did happen to be at Bimola's, it wouldn't be the right place to ask him his question. They would all be drunk crazy by now. Gojen decided to give up his quest for the day. It would have to wait.

◆

'Baap. Oh, Baap,' Gojen's grandmother called from the other room. 'Hm?' he replied, and without opening his eyes, rolled over in bed.

'Has somebody died or something? I thought I heard bamboos popping.'

'Just go to sleep, will you?' Gojen mumbled. Even through his opium-induced drowsiness, he gathered that the old lady had opened the door and stepped outside.

'The sky is red over there. Looks like there's a fire in someone's home or something,' he heard her say from the courtyard.

Gojen jumped out of bed and rushed out. True—the south-western sky was red. But... He rubbed his eyes. But that was where Kuroiguri was—beyond the forest, where the sky was aglow! His hair stood on end and his skin tingled. He rushed inside, pulled on a vest and hastened out again.

'Aai, you go back to bed. There's a fire in Kuroiguri. I'm off.'

'At this time of night...'

Gojen didn't hear what his grandmother had to say. He jumped over the stile and into the street and started running. A few people from other houses had also stepped out and were gazing in the direction of the fire. Some shouted out questions to him. But there was no time to acknowledge anyone and even less to answer them.

◆

The shortcut to Kuroiguri led past the temple of the goddess, through the fields and the forest. Each time Gojen looked up, the vermilion sky over Kuroiguri met his eyes. Beneath that very sky lay about twenty hutments, twenty families in them. The faces of those people floated before him—Mansoor, Hasina and a few more. How would they look now, in this light, in these circumstances? Then he recalled the faces of Jadob Bora and his cronies as they sat drinking at Moti mistry's place—and that of the semi-clad woman who served them their onions, chickpeas and fried fish. Oh, how extremely repulsive they were!

Gojen suddenly realized that he had reached the temple entrance. He rushed in. Next door, Deu was in a deep slumber induced by the kabiraj's drugs and wouldn't hear him. He unlatched the temple door, bowed with his head to the ground, groped at a place where he presumed the sacrificial machete was kept and, finding it, picked it up and rushed out towards the path.

As soon as he was atop the hillock, Gojen saw that all the hutments in the Muslim settlement had been reduced to ashes. The fire had died down, and except for a few posts that were still aflame, there was no trace of any house anywhere. The Nepali settlement, however, remained intact, and near it, he spied a small group of people. Raising his machete, he ran in that direction.

In the faint light of the dying fires, he saw that the group comprised Kaila, Maila and a few others from their community. They were unable to recognize Gojen in the distance and looked distinctly perturbed when he approached. They were soon reassured when they figured out who he was, although a couple of them were still disturbed by the machete he carried. Even before he reached them, Gojen called out, 'What, Kaila? How did the fire happen?'

And excitedly, Kaila, assisted by a couple of his companions, narrated the events of the night.

◆

About three hours ago, Kaila's sleep had been disturbed by screams from the Muslim settlement. He and a couple of others rushed that way. The moonlight was faint and in the distance they saw ten to fifteen torchlights shining all around. When they got caught in the beams, two men, faces masked up to the eyes, moved up to them. Shifting the beams directly to their eyes, they ordered them to return to their homes and remain inside. Else, they threatened to impale them with a spear one of them held. The other menacingly showed them the double-barrelled gun he carried. The two men escorted the Nepali men to their respective homes and threatened to kill them if they dared open their doors.

Thus intimidated, the Nepali men did remain inside, but through the gaps in their reed walls, they peered at the scene that unfolded not too far away. Although they could not identify the men from where they were, they did notice that the thugs as well as the occupants of the huts were running helter-skelter. Most of the Muslims seemed to be running towards the river. Then a chorus of screams and wailing rent the air—something terrible must be going on out there; people must be getting killed.

An hour or so later, when the screams had faded away and all was quiet once again, they noticed that the Muslim hutments were systematically catching fire. In the reddish light, they thought they saw a few Muslims being chased towards the river by spear-wielding men. Then, some time later, presuming that the thugs had left, Kaila and the other Nepali men slowly emerged from their huts. And now, as they huddled together as a group, they could see that nothing remained of the Muslim settlement—neither the huts, nor the people.

◆

The entire episode was narrated almost in a single breath, and it left Gojen stunned. Then, gathering his wits, he asked Kaila, 'Where have the Muslims gone? And their families?'

'I have a feeling that the thugs have killed them and thrown the bodies into the river. However, some may have taken shelter in the forest or across the river.'

Gojen swung the heavy machete on to his other shoulder and rushed towards what remained of the once-flourishing settlement— burnt-down hutments, scorched wood, clothing and utensils, the heavy smell of smoke, cows mooing and dogs baying in the distance... Hastening his pace to a fast trot, he finally arrived at a place where he ascertained Mansoor's hut would have stood. Nothing there. Only smoke and ashes, except for one collapsed wall which remained half-burnt. Gojen looked around. There was no sign of life. Only an eerie silence pervaded the atmosphere.

Suddenly, in the dim firelight, Gojen noticed a large amount of blood in the courtyard. It had spread far and seemed to lead in a particular direction. He shuddered—and in spite of the fires around him, felt a chill run through his entire being. Gripping tightly on the handle of the machete, he slowly followed the trail of blood towards the field behind the burnt-down hut. Some distance later, the light gave way to faint darkness. Gojen stood helplessly and shouted out, 'Mansoor bhai!'

His voice echoed and faded into the distance. But there was no response. There were no villages for quite some distance on the other bank. One side was bare, but the other was thick with forests and grasslands. Once again, he called, 'Mansoor bhai!'

Gojen heard his voice penetrate the darkness and reach far into the distance. But once again, there was no response.

◆

The day dawned. Slowly, the sky lit up and the trees, fields, the Kuroi and the forests beyond it, the Brahmaputra and the blue vegetation on its far bank—all became visible. Along with Kaila and his companions, Gojen moved to the banks of the Kuroi, where they saw numerous footprints and scattered pools of blood. In many places, there were bloody indications of something—or someone— having been dragged along. But they were yet to find anybody.

Gojen was tired. He asked Kaila and the others to return home and made his way back to what remained of Mansoor's hut. He had trodden the trail that led from the hut to the river hundreds of times, Hasina skipping along behind him, a folk tune on her lips. Now he stood facing the devastation before him. All was now clear in the morning light. Among the ashes lay a metal trunk, utensils, earthen pots, clothes, Hasina's saris and burqa, piles of lentils and chillies—all half-burnt, and exuding a strange mix of burning smells.

Gojen stared at the scene before him. Suddenly, he noticed that one end of the collapsed earthen wall was slightly higher than the other. Could someone be under it? He sprang forward and lifted it. No—it was the wooden chest he always sat on. He flipped the wall over and saw the half-burnt paper tricolour—the one that Hasina had hung up. Carefully, he picked it up, folded it and put it in his pocket.

A little further lay the metal trunk with its floral pattern. The colours had been obliterated by the fire. He opened it—nothing inside. But just below it lay two books—Lakshminath Bezborua's *Grandmother's Tales*, which Gojen had got her, and a school textbook, open at the poem *How beautiful is my village*, the pages all yellowed by the heat. Next to them lay a pencil and a notebook in which Hasina had written a few sentences in Assamese—among them, 'Gojen Keunt keeps fishing'.

Gojen sank to the ground. Sobs racked his body and he wept his heart out. Then he gathered the books and put them in his pocket. He slowly made his way homewards, the machete on his shoulders glistening in the sunlight. But he didn't go home directly. Instead, he took a shortcut to Jadob Bora's village.

Those who did not know him looked at him in puzzlement. Those who did, rained questions about him, but he chose to ignore all of them, plodding on with head bowed low. His eyes were bloodshot.

Calmly, he entered Jadob Bora's courtyard and asked one of his daughters who was on the veranda if her father was home. She replied in the affirmative and went in. As he waited, many of the other children looked fearfully at him from behind the curtains. Some time later, an older boy came out, said, 'Father isn't home,' and went back inside.

Gojen stared at the drawn curtains for a few moments before he turned back towards the gate. Then, suddenly, he swung the machete over his head and yelled, 'Hey, Jadob! If you're the son of a human, why don't you come out? What did you do to those people?

Will you bring them back or not? Or have you massacred each one of them? Come out, you bastard—let me sacrifice you!' His language grew viler by the minute. A group of people had assembled, but ignorant of what had triggered his outburst, they simply stood around and stared at Gojen. After a while, he left the place.

He went home via the temple, changing into his gamosa and taking a dip in the river before he entered. He dipped the machete in the waters too. Then, holding it above his head, he walked up, all wet, to the idol. Placing the machete a little away from the goddess' feet, he prostrated himself before her and said, 'Oh, goddess, please forgive me. I had decided to bring you a few human heads, but I have failed.'

Deu had panicked when he had found the sacrificial machete missing. Now, as Gojen raised himself from the ground and turned around, he saw the old man framed in the temple door. Falling at his feet, Gojen said, 'I have committed a grievous sin, Deu. Please forgive me.'

But instead of berating him, Deu began wondering where this proud young man had taken the machete and why. Without waiting to see the old man's reaction, Gojen walked past him and stomped out of the compound. Changing back into his clothes, which he had left to dry by the riverside, he dragged his feet homewards. He felt totally drained.

As he approached the house, even from a distance, he could see that his grandmother was waiting for him at the entrance, hands on her hips. As soon as she saw him, she moved forward and accosted him. 'Where on earth were you? You've been away so long, I was dying with worry. And that Mansoor's daughter is sitting behind the house.'

'Mansoor's daughter? Hasina?' Gojen rushed into the house.

His grandmother followed behind him, saying, 'She landed up here through the fields. Her clothes were all wet and are now drying on her. She won't speak a word—she's just sitting by the wall and has been crying ever since she arrived.'

'Hasina!' called Gojen as he came up to her. She looked up and, seeing him, grabbed his legs, buried her head in his knees and cried loudly, speaking a few words in her own dialect in between.

'Come on, now. Get up. Enough of this,' said Gojen, releasing himself from Hasina's grip and lifting her to her feet. He saw that the thin cotton sari she wore was still wet and she was muddy right up to her knees. Her hair was dishevelled and eyes red and swollen, probably from crying. Gojen felt as though his blood had clotted around his chest and knocked at his heart, making it ache.

Turning to his grandmother, who stood by uncomprehendingly, he said, 'Aai, give her a set of your clothes—let her go bathe.' Then, he looked at Hasina and said, 'Hey, listen. No more crying. Go have a bath and change out of these wet clothes. You can tell me everything later. Aai, show her where she should go. I, too, need to go bathe now.' And he walked off towards the well.

'You can go to the river ghat—it's right behind the backyard. I'll get you a set of clothes,' said the old lady to Hasina. But she saw that the girl showed no inclination to move. 'What's up? Why do you just stand there? Go—it's right behind the garden. Isn't that the way you came?'

'Aai, I'm afraid,' said Hasina, her voice trembling.

'Come on, then. Follow me,' said the old lady as she led her to the ghat.

18

Hasina, dressed in a clean set of Gojen's grandmother's clothes, sat on an empty sack laid out like a mat on the veranda. Gojen sat in the wooden chair and Aai on the wooden peera, the tray of tamul before her.

It had taken a lot of coaxing and cajoling before Hasina had a few sips of tea. Then she had burst into tears again, and it was with much difficulty that they could comfort her. And then, she told them her story.

The previous night, some men had landed up at their house and had woken them up by beating on their doors and walls with rods. Even before Mansoor could light the lamp and open the door, one of the men crashed it open with a kick and stood before them, holding a large spear. She rushed into the kitchen as soon as she saw their visitor. Through the reed walls she saw a few more men enter the house. They were armed with spears and long machetes and their faces were masked. They addressed Mansoor, 'Hand over whatever money, gold or silver you have here and leave this house right away.'

Mansoor fell at the man's feet, and they overpowered him and dragged him out while two of them rifled through whatever was in the house. Then one of the machete-bearers turned towards the kitchen. She realized that he would soon enter it; so she ran out through the back door. After a while, she saw that the man was in hot pursuit, shining a torchlight on her. She ran faster. Then she heard a voice crying out, 'God! I'm dying!' She knew that it was her Abbajaan's voice. But the man was yet chasing her; so she simply rushed ahead and jumped into the Kuroi.

The torch beam was no longer on her. She stood in neck-deep water, diving below and swimming underwater for a distance every time she heard a sound. At one point, she heard loud screams and wailing from across her village. Her Abbajaan's voice kept echoing in her heart and seemed to remain stuck there. Swimming and wading in turn, she moved upstream until she came to a high sandbank. She was barely onto it when she suddenly noticed that there was a fire. Climbing up and craning her head, she saw her entire village go up in flames.

She had waited until dawn. Then, making a rough estimate of the direction to take, she had run through the fields and arrived at Gojen's home.

Hasina broke down once again. When Aai's assurances failed to calm her, Gojen barked, 'Stop crying, I say! I'm yet there for you.' Then, looking at his grandmother, he slowly added, 'So is Aai.'

Hasina stopped crying. She covered her face and sat with lowered head, and without realizing it, fell into a deep sleep on the sack.

◆

Gojen realized that he would now have to summon all the courage he could and face up to some serious problems—the first among them being Hasina. Where would she live now, with whom and how? It was decided that for the moment, she could stay them, sleeping in the front room, on a sheet-covered reed mat. But his grandmother was averse to the idea of having a young Muslim girl living under the same roof for long.

The shed on the eastern side of the barn was open on two sides and held the loom and a hearth for boiling paddy. The loom had lain idle for a while—Aai's backache made it impossible for her to sit for long—so it was folded and put away. The hearth was moved to the timber-shed and the open sides were strongly walled up so that Hasina could live there.

There were many other problems concerning the girl. But at least the issue of her accommodation had been addressed, if somewhat temporarily.

The other problem was of Gojen's own creation—the fate of the burnt settlement of Kuroiguri and its missing people. What would become of them? And, more importantly, who were the perpetrators of this devastation, and why?

Meanwhile, a swift series of events took place. Two or three days after the Kuroiguri fire, the news of fishermen in the Brahmaputra finding a number of human bodies floating by became the talk of the village. Gojen felt that in all likelihood, one of those was that of Mansoor bhai.

Gojen wondered who he could discuss these things with, and the name that cropped up in his mind as the most natural choice was Sarbai Pandit. He was familiar with Pandit's afternoon routine. After school, he returned home and had a snack before settling down to his gardening. His back garden was lush with seasonal vegetables throughout the year and the front garden, impeccably maintained, boasted flowers of all kinds. Fruit trees bordered the compound of his house and remained heavy with seasonal fruits all year round. Beyond the back garden was the pond that served as a fishery. Tending to the gardens, trees and pond kept the Pandit busy from the moment he returned from school until late evening.

Once he was through with these, he went to the cowshed, patted his cows and checked that the mosquitoes had been smoked out all right. Then he had a bath, after which he relaxed on the recliner at the veranda for an hour or so. Sometimes, his wife and their three children joined him and they talked about various things. From around six-thirty to nine or so, Pandit read his books and assisted his children with their studies if necessary. He had a small library and it held a number of Assamese books.

Gojen decided that, in view of this routine, the best time for him to see the Pandit was when he was relaxing on the veranda.

The first four days after the incident, Gojen had been tied up with making arrangements for Hasina's shelter. Today was day five. It was late; but something had to be done. What that was had to be determined in consultation with Pandit.

When he arrived at the teacher's house, he found the older man at the veranda as expected, cupping a brass tumbler of tea in his hands. Gojen narrated the entire story—what he had seen for himself and what he had heard from Kaila and later, from Hasina. He added that Jadob Bora and his gang were at the root of all this and that he believed that Khargi mauzadar was also party to it, because no one except he possessed a double-barrelled gun around this area. Gojen also told Pandit about how he had arrived at Bora's courtyard with the machete on his shoulder and all he had done there.

In the last two days, on his way back from school, Pandit had heard various versions of how miscreants had burnt down the Kuroiguri farmers' settlement. He had also heard about Gojen setting off to slay people with the sacrificial machete. The stories had passed from one person to another several times, getting embellished and altered at every stage. But now, from Gojen, he learnt the true course of events and realized the brutal mentality and disgusting selfishness of the people behind them.

'Sir, what do we do now? What do you suggest?' asked Gojen at the end of his narration.

The Pandit remained silent as he stared into the open sky before him.

Gojen continued, 'I don't know what you are thinking, Sir. But I cannot keep quiet. That day, if I had come across any of them, I would have hacked them to pieces. I'm not that worked up any more—which is why I have come to discuss this with you, calmly and thoughtfully. How can we slay these animals—I mean legally?'

'I see what you mean. But the legal and police networks are rather treacherous. It was these that threw your father into prison. Telling the truth can often be dangerous; especially when you stand up to a bunch of demons like these. We have to weigh all aspects before making any move.'

'But I'm afflicted with the habit of speaking the truth, Sir.'

'It's no affliction—it's a great human quality. Not everybody possesses it—most lack the courage. You are blessed with it and you are a brave man.'

'Yes, Sir, I know I am brave. I don't want to sound boastful, but I know that I am made of sterner stuff than most. I alone will be able to fight these monsters according to your directions.'

'But Lord Krishna always took on the demons by himself.'

'I am no Lord Krishna, Sir. He is a god—I am a man of flesh and blood. But I will fight as a man—alone like Krishna if need be.'

'I understand. But let me warn you—if you go ahead and fight, courage alone will not be enough. There will be many hurdles you will have to overcome along the way—all by yourself.'

'I understand that I will have to proceed alone, Sir. I won't involve anyone else. But I will keep consulting you every now and then. And in case I need to go to court, Modon Kokaiti is there at the headquarters. Now tell me, Sir, what do I start with and how?' Gojen stressed the words 'what' and 'how'.

'You first need to file a petition and, with the help of the law, prove the crimes of the criminals. The court will do the necessary investigation and recommend due punishment for the guilty. This is the basic rule. But in order to achieve that, you have to face up to various agencies—the police, the courts, lawyers, witnesses...'

'I'll do it, Sir. I'll face up to anyone I need to. Just tell me how to get started.'

'A first information report needs to be filed at the police station. In that, you have to tell them the gist of what you have told me. You also need to state that you seek the aid of the esteemed court to find the perpetrators of the arson and massacre and mete out due punishment to them. You can also name the people whose involvement you suspect—but you wouldn't want to, right? Let the police do their own investigation...'

'Of course I'll name them—why shouldn't I? I'll name each one of them. I'll also mention how Khargi mauzadar and his double-barrelled gun were a part of the crime.'

'Think about it—should you name them right away? They are such a dangerous gang.'

'No, Sir. There's nothing to think about.'

'There's also the question of witnesses. You'll need to prove your allegations in court. If you fail to do that, they'll shift the blame to you.'

'If something as clear as the afternoon sunshine cannot be proved, if the court fails to do that and decides to punish me instead, I'll gladly take the punishment. But I've got to write all that I know, Sir.'

'Fine, then. Make a draft copy of the report you want to write and show it to me tomorrow. I'll check it for you.'

'Why tomorrow, Sir? I can make out the initial—and the final—drafts right now, right here. Just give me the essentials—some paper and a pen.'

Gojen pulled his stool up to a nearby bench and, in the lamplight, started penning his report in a long notebook Pandit had provided. He was soon done. Pandit was surprised. 'You continue to be a fast writer, Gojen. And your writing is as neat as it used to be. Now let's see what you've written.'

The report didn't need much editing, except for deleting a couple of sentences, substituting milder alternatives for a few strong words and modifying the title. Gojen instantly started off on making a fair copy.

◆

As Gojen walked homewards with the copy of the report in his pocket, he decided—why wait until tomorrow? If he could submit it at the beat office right now, by morning the police could have the criminals all roped up and transported to their outpost at Nihali. Jadob Bora would probably escape the trussing, but he would have to be handcuffed anyway. And what about the mauzadar? Would the constables at the beat office dare lay their hands on him? Also, he shared such a close acquaintance with all the police and administrative officials, it would make his capture difficult. What would the police do about him? Gojen failed to find an answer.

Lost in thought, he was proceeding on his way when he heard a woman's voice calling surreptitiously, 'Hey, Gojen, come here for a moment, will you?' All was darkness, intensified by the bamboo grove bordering the path. Nothing was visible except for a host of fireflies. Gojen gauged that he was somewhere in the vicinity of Moti mistry's house.

He plodded along the narrow pathway when he heard the voice again. 'Gojen! Do come here for a moment.' He now figured that it was the voice of Moti's wife. What was she up to this time? Hesitantly, he walked towards her.

'What's up? What are you doing here, alone in this darkness?' he asked calmly.

'I've been waiting for you. Not just today—I've been slinking out and trying to meet you these last three evenings. There's something very important that I need to tell you in secret. Let's move towards the house. There may be other passers-by coming along.' The woman spoke without a pause, and she sounded shaken.

Gojen wondered what this vile woman needed to tell him in secret. Offended by the lack of any response from him, she said, 'Gojen, you are still upset with me, aren't you? Never mind. But I can't keep quiet if I know that you are in danger. Come, let's move over there.' She dragged him by the hand and led him towards the house. In his confused state, he followed unquestioningly behind her. The darkness seemed deeper by the large tree some distance from the house, and they both stopped there.

'Move into the shade of the tree if you hear anyone coming,' the woman warned Gojen.

'That'll do. Now tell me. What danger am I in? I have important things to attend to.' Gojen sounded impatient.

In a hushed voice, Moti's wife said, 'First of all, don't come to our house for liquor in the evening or night. That's when Jadob Bora's party is there. They may beat you up or, in this sort of pitch darkness, even kill you.'

'It isn't that easy,' Gojen interrupted.

'I'm scared.'

'You needn't be. Nothing's about to happen to me.'

'These are villains in the guise of gentlemen. They can go to any length to further their ends. It's they who burnt down the village in Kuroiguri, massacred its people and threw them into the river.'

'How do you know?'

'Moti blurted out everything when he was drunk. They have taken all the money, gold and silver the Muslims had. They've been drinking and talking about all this in my house ever since. They are scared of you and have contemplated doing away with you. I've been so afraid—that's why I've been lying in wait, so that I could warn you.'

'Look, if I wished, I could beat up each one of them until they saw stars.'

'No, Gojen! I beg of you, don't do anything of the sort. Don't come to my house at all, Gojen—please keep away. If liquor is all you want, go somewhere else.' Moti's wife was on the verge of tears as she pleaded.

'Okay, I won't come. What else did you wish to say?' asked Gojen blandly.

'There's a Muslim girl in your house, the daughter of one of the Kuroiguri Muslims, right? A girl who somehow escaped with her life?'

'Yes.'

'They have been talking about her. If the police were to come and conduct investigations, she will tell them everything. But what they are saying is that she doesn't know any of the men here. Anyway, they keep talking of her, and I thought I should let you know. Be careful.'

Just then, someone stepped out of the house, shining a torch into the darkness. He shouted, 'Hey, you harlot! Where are you preying for your men? You need to serve the stuff out here—why don't you come? You bitch, you slave, you whore...' Moti stumbled forward as he kept calling out to his wife in the foulest of language. As he neared the tree, his wife dragged Gojen into its shade. Gojen seemed reluctant to hide at first, but the woman's insistence and physical pressure made him yield and they both stood in silence, their bodies close together.

Moti started urinating in the pathway, still shining his torch. He slurred as he talked to himself. 'This whore, where has she been off to these last few evenings? She's never home and I need to serve the booze. If you've found yourself a new man, why don't you just bring him home? This bloke Gojen hasn't come in to drink for some time now. Could the bitch be chasing him? The bastard, Gojen! Flaunting your bravery, are you? Walking into Jadob Bora's compound and slandering him—I should have been around! The bastard!'

At one point, Gojen clenched his teeth and was about to emerge from their hiding place. But the woman hugged him tight and held him back.

After some time, Moti stumbled back homewards, still swearing drunkenly, his lungi almost slipping off his waist.

Gojen and Moti's wife emerged from the shadows. 'Go home now. Else, you will lose your temper and god knows what you will do,' said the woman.

Gojen suddenly put a hand to his chest pocket and checked that the report was safe there. After a few steps, he turned back and said, 'Now you don't go around telling anyone that you met me.'

'Why would I risk telling anyone? I won't say a word. You don't either. If they get to know, they won't leave me alive. Don't get me into trouble.'

'Don't worry—I won't tell.'

Moments later, he heard the woman caution him again, 'Be careful. Don't come here.'

'Sure. Now you go home,' said Gojen without turning back. He hastened his pace and reached the main street. The walk to the beat office and back would take about an hour-and-a-half. It would be rather late and Aai would worry. Hasina would be sleepy. But he decided that it was imperative for him to submit his report to the beat office immediately. He felt his chest pocket once again. The papers were safe there. Once again, in his mind, he went over

184 * Arun Sarma

what he had written. Pandit had said his handwriting was still beautiful...

Gojen wondered... What if, on the basis of the report, the police were to actually handcuff the culprits and lead them away on leashes roped around their waists? If Jadob Bora were really handcuffed! And the mauzadar?

19

It was rather late by the time Gojen got home from the beat office. Just as he had guessed, his grandmother was sitting, lamp by her side, in the wooden chair on the veranda, looking out towards the lane and worried that he had not returned yet. Hasina was fast asleep on the reed mat in the sitting room. Gojen decided there was no point in waking her up and asking her to move to her newly readied room. Anyway he had been worrying about her ever since he heard what Moti's wife had to say. He sat outside for a long time and even after he went to bed, his worries kept him awake until the wee hours.

Since he had slept so late, Gojen remained in a deep slumber long after the sun was up. Suddenly, he heard his grandmother's agitated voice and woke up. She was trying to shake him awake saying, 'Hey, Baap, wake up! A police officer and a few of his men have come looking for you.'

'Officer? Policemen? Looking for me?' Gojen jumped out of bed, picked up a small pot of water, hastily washed up and stepped out, still wiping his face on his gamosa. It was true. The ASI from the beat office and four constables were waiting.

'What happened, Sir? How come you are here so early in the morning? Have you started attending to my report already?' asked Gojen excitedly.

'That will happen, by and by—now that the report has reached the police station. But right now, I'm here because of another report,' replied the ASI. Then, abruptly turning to his men, he said, 'What are you waiting for? Handcuff him now.'

'Handcuff? Me? Sir, what have I done? Why am I...?' Gojen was taken utterly by surprise and stood stunned in place. Two constables moved forward and handcuffed him.

'Gojen, we are arresting you under IPC Section 307. The charges levelled against you include attempting to murder innocents with a sacrificial machete, threatening to kill a gentleman in his own compound, using foul language to insult a gentleman's family and spreading terror in the village through antisocial acts,' said the ASI with a dramatic flourish. The constables, in the meantime, were tying a rope around Gojen's waist.

'But, Sir, I spent so much time with you last night when I came to submit my report—how come you didn't let me know that there were so many charges against me?' asked Gojen, puzzled.

'The report came in after you had left.'

'After I left? That late?' Gojen's brows furrowed. He was even more amazed.

'If you can come and submit a report that late in the night, so can others. The police station registers FIRs any time of the night.'

'But...'

'Come on, now. Get the convict. We have a bus to catch. I'll have problems if we can't get him to Nihali today,' said the ASI to his men.

Men, women and children had meanwhile crowded in and around Gojen's courtyard. As he was led away through them, he walked straight, looking forward. He had hoped to see Jadob Bora in handcuffs this morning, but by a strange quirk, it was he who was wearing them! He suddenly wondered how Bora must be feeling right now. Did he wish to have his morning tea extra-sweet today and ask his wife to put in some extra sugar? Gojen smiled at the thought.

As for his grandmother, she stood transfixed, staring stonily at him as he moved away. It wasn't him she was seeing right now. Years ago, another proud young man bearing the same look, the same voice and the same gait had been handcuffed and taken away by the police—Gojen's father, her son Holodhor. That day, she had cried her heart out. But now she held back her tears. Suddenly, she heard sobbing from inside the house and stepped in. Hasina was kneeling on the ground and peering through a patch in the reed wall where the plaster had peeled off, her body racked by sobs.

◆

It was the morning after Gojen had been taken into police custody, and at the station in Nihali, they were taking his statement on the charges framed against him. He immediately conceded that yes, it was true—he did go to Jadob Bora's house with the sacrificial machete and raise hell there. He added that if he had come across Bora or any of his cronies then, he would have, in all likelihood, hewn them in two. But his anger had now been transformed—he would use the law to get back at them.

As he started to elaborate upon the reason behind his anger, the officer brought down his cane sharply upon him and roared, 'Shut up! We don't want those details. Now, it is true that you had intended to kill Jadob Bora with the machete, isn't it?'

Still flinching with the pain of the caning, Gojen replied, 'Of course. I've already told you so!'

'So can't you repeat it one more time?' yelled the officer.

With a huge effort, Gojen controlled his fit of temper and stood with his head lowered.

The officer cradled the cane in his armpit and started rolling a cigarette. With full concentration, he held the paper between his lips as he kneaded the tobacco on his palm with his other thumb. Then, carefully transferring it to the paper, he rolled it, tapering it slightly, sealed it with a lick, placed the narrow end in his mouth and lit up. The aroma of the tobacco mixture filled the room and made Gojen, who had been watching the process intently, crave a smoke. He waited for the officer to release the smoke he had inhaled in a long draught, but somehow it didn't emerge. Instead, with a distorted smile playing on his lips, he asked, 'Now tell me— haven't you violated the modesty of the wife of Moti mistry alias Moti Rai, by raping her? This allegation too features in the FIR.'

Gojen heard the question and comprehended it all right. But he couldn't believe that such an allegation had been levelled against him and stood staring at the officer in silence.

'Hey! Why don't you speak up?' roared the officer. He jabbed his cane into Gojen's belly and rained slaps, punches, kicks and blows on him. But Gojen refused to plead guilty to the rape charges.

The officer began to roll another cigarette. 'Fine—don't confess if you won't. Your uncles at the police headquarters will make you open your mouth anyway. They know how to get you to speak up. You have already admitted to attempted manslaughter. That confessional statement is enough for me to send you off to the headquarters.' He turned to the red-capped constables and said, 'It's time for the bus. Get him ready to be transported to the headquarters right away—I'll go write out his statement.' And he stomped off to his own chambers.

Soon after, the bus came to a stop in front of the Nihali police station. As he was led out of the lock-up to the bus in handcuffs, Gojen saw Jadob Bora and the mauzadar's accountant engaged in serious discussion with the officer who had interrogated him. The two men looked out. As soon as their eyes met Gojen's, they averted them and looked away, concentrating on the cane lying on the officer's table.

In those days, the two benches immediately behind the bus driver's comprised the upper class. This was separated from the lower classes in the back by a brass-topped wooden railing. The policemen led Gojen in through the rear door. Once seated in the corner of the last seat, he looked up and saw that Bora's entire gang was sitting on the lower class bench and staring at him. Gojen, shocked and disturbed at the sight, turned to stare out of the window as their comments and laughter occasionally fell on his ears.

Soon after, Jadob Bora and the accountant, accompanied by the police officer, boarded the bus and it started moving. Were Bora and his men going to the headquarters too? And if so, why?

Gojen got to know the reason for their trip a few days later, and also what had transpired between the men in the officer's chamber.

But that story started quite some time ago.

•

Rupai and Konloura had rushed to meet Gojen when they heard that he was being taken away by the police. They walked with him up to the beat office and remained with him until he was put on the bus to Nihali. During this time, it was decided that the two of them, plus a couple of the Nepali men from Kuroiguri should take turns to guard Gojen's home in groups of three or four. This was imperative due to Hasina's presence in the house. Gojen also instructed them to make Hasina sleep in the main house itself—his grandmother would not object if she knew he wished so. In case of any problems, they should contact Sarbai Pandit right away—only he would know how to go about things now that Gojen was arrested. He added that in these matters, the teacher was the only god who could lead them to deliverance.

If there were matters of the court, the person to consult was Modon at the district headquarters. Gojen was certain of his assistance in every possible way. He didn't know how long it would be before he could return. It would probably be after a term in jail. He knew there was a system of bailing people out, but had no idea how these things actually happened. That was best left to Modon.

There was no need to worry about the running expenses for the household. The barn was still half full of grain. That could be taken out and used whenever necessary. Rupai and Konloura should look after his home, his grandmother and Hasina just as he would. They should be especially careful about Hasina—the dangers looming over her had not passed yet.

His two friends assured Gojen that he didn't need to worry about domestic matters—his home was as good as theirs and they would take full responsibility for it. Then, as soon as the bus was gone, they hurried to see Sarbai Pandit, ignoring all the questions people asked them along their way.

The Pandit had already heard the news. Several people had come to him and personally narrated their own interpretation of the events. He had been getting ready for school—in fact, if he were not slightly delayed, he would already have been on his way. However, today he was sitting in his reclining chair at the veranda and musing over all that had happened. He knew he was getting late for school; but the thought of Gojen in trouble made him unable to stir.

Just then, Rupai and Konloura came rushing in and narrated all that Gojen had told them. They also mentioned that he said that Pandit was the only god who could save them now.

All worry was suddenly erased from the teacher's face as he blushed and smiled slightly. 'I'm a man of flesh and blood—why should I aspire to be a god? You two carry on. I'll do what I need to do.'

He got his younger son, a sixth-standard student in the ME school, to speak to his head master and take two days' leave, so that he could monitor and coach Pandit's students during his absence. It was very rare for the Pandit to stay away from his school, but this was a special situation.

•

Sarbai Pandit went to the district headquarters, managed to find Modon and tell him Gojen's story in complete detail—from the night in Kuroiguri right up to the time he was arrested. After a patient hearing, Modon said, 'Sir, there is nothing more that you need to do here. I take on the responsibility from now on. You only need to stay here until the bail is granted. Stay with us tonight. You can leave tomorrow. Now come along with me and don't worry—I will do whatever needs to be done.'

Modon figured that Gojen would be kept in a lock-up either at the police station or within the jail premises. After a few inquiries, they finally found him in the jail lock-up. At the sight of Modon and Pandit, Gojen broke down and cried.

After a casual conversation with him, Modon went back to the court to process the bail papers, Pandit by his side. They discussed who could bail Gojen out. Pandit volunteered—that was why he was here, wasn't he? But Modon cautioned him. That act could put him in the bad books of Bora and his ilk, the consequences of which would be less than desirable.

'Do you mean to say that nobody will bail him then? Of course, it is true that apart from me, there may not be anyone else from our area who would be willing. Bora's ire cannot be disregarded altogether; but I have to do this, Modon. We'll see about what comes later. Now just go ahead with the official procedures.'

◆

Jadob Bora and his gang members, along with the mauzadar's accountant, two lawyers and a few unknown men, emerged gleefully from the chamber of the judge to whom Gojen's bail petition had been submitted. All of them directed taunting looks and smiles at him as they passed. Once again, the question that had occurred to Gojen when he saw them in the bus resurfaced—why were they here?

The judge exchanged a few words with Modon and accepted Sarbai Pandit's bail plea. Once free of the handcuffs, Gojen followed the two men out of the court, rubbing his wrists. He then asked Modon the question that was tormenting him all this while, and learnt that Bora and his cronies had come to the headquarters seeking anticipatory bail, just in case any action was taken on Gojen's FIR.

Gojen's question was answered; but he was as puzzled as ever. What machinations people resorted to, to protect their selfish interests!

◆

Modon insisted that Sarbai Pandit and Gojen should spend the night at his home. Pandit was initially reluctant—he stayed at the local school boarding house on his rare visits to town—but finally yielded to Modon's persuasion. Gojen, on the other hand, was intimately acquainted with his host's family and was more than eager to accept the offer. He hadn't seen Joba for quite some time.

As they approached the house in the twilight, from a distance they saw Joba waiting with an infant in her arms. For her part, she tried to figure who the two men accompanying her husband could be, but gave up after a while. Must be some clients as usual!

When they were within hearing distance, Modon called out, 'Joba, look who's here.'

Joba moved forward eagerly. The baby reached out for Modon and she handed it over to him. The Pandit spoke. 'Joba, my child, how are you?'

'Oh, Sir! When did you come?' Joba exclaimed with joy. Then she looked at the other man.

'What are you staring at? Having trouble recognizing a hardened criminal, eh?'

'Oh my god! Gojen!' Joba playfully punched him on the chest and asked, 'When did you land up here?' Without waiting for an answer, she said, 'Come on in—please come in, Sir' and warmly ushered the two men from the gate to the house.

Joba was shocked when she saw Gojen in the lamplight. He sported a stubble of four or five days, had dark bruises near his eyes and lips, his hair was dishevelled and dusty and his clothes shabby and dirty. 'Gojen, what have you done to yourself? You look a sight!' she said, her brows furrowed.

'How much better can I look after the police have had their fill of hitting, punching and kicking me? Thankfully, my muscles are tight and strong thanks to all the wood-chopping.' Even as he recalled his trials, Gojen could not help a proud smile.

'Well, we can talk later. Joba, go show Sir where he can freshen up and see if there is soap and oil in the bathroom. Gojen will feel much better after he's bathed. Give him a set of my clothes from the chest,' Modon instructed.

◆

Modon had enclosed the wide kitchen veranda with bamboo matting to accommodate a dining table and chairs. He often needed to dine with his clients and non-Brahmin friends, sometimes in his formal clothes and footwear, and this arrangement not just made things convenient, it also left the kitchen unsullied. His mother continued to dine on the kitchen floor, on the plate her husband had eaten from. Joba ate with her mother-in-law, but right from the beginning, Modon had prevented her from using his plate, so she had one of her own. When her in-laws were away, Joba dined at the table with her husband.

At the table at dinnertime, Modon declared, 'Sir, we have two cultures operating in our house—the eastern and the western. One group follows one and the other follows the other. Joba is somewhere in between—she needs to oscillate between the two as circumstances demand. For example, she normally eats on the kitchen floor, but sometimes she also sits at the table.' He picked up a bowl of fish curry, poured half on to the rice on his plate, split the fish-head in two and transferred half on to the rice, leaving the rest in the bowl. Joba carried the bowl inside.

The import of the act did not escape Gojen's notice. He realized that although Modon forbade Joba to eat his leftovers, she derived some kind of emotional fulfilment, a sense of well-being, by eating a share of his food.

Joba and her mother-in-law fussed over their visitors as they served them at the table, piling various gravies and vegetables on their plates. Suddenly, Modon asked, 'Gojen, do you remember the time we dined off plantain leaves on the veranda of Joba's parental home?'

'Of course I remember,' Gojen replied.

Joba intervened. 'Enough—you don't need to go into all that now. Just eat well, Gojen. Sir, you too.'

'Sure, sure—of course I'll eat well. The thought of what they fed me these last four days makes me want to throw up! My stomach's nice and empty.' The atmosphere became heavy on Gojen's words.

After dinner, the three men sat at the veranda discussing Gojen's case, Modon explaining the legal aspects in detail. His father joined them for a while and then retired to bed. Joba stood by and listened to the goings-on. By the time they were done, it was rather late in the night. Modon led Pandit to the bed they had made for him in the living room and Joba took Gojen to his bed in the office room. He sat on its edge as she settled into the wooden chair beside it, her infant daughter asleep in her lap. They had named her Amrita, Ami for short.

Once again, Joba heard Gojen's story, this time in every minute detail. When he was narrating it in the evening, she had heard bits of it, moving away occasionally to help her mother-in-law in the kitchen. But now that she was the sole audience, the words left a deep imprint on her mind. Her eyes filled with tears when she heard of Hasina's plight.

Gojen finished his narration and said, 'Now tell me about you.'

And Joba eagerly told him all about her new life with her husband and in-laws, about the infant daughter who had come into their lives, and the love she had found in this new home of hers.

Gojen peered at the face of the beautiful child in Joba's arms. She had her father's skin colour and her mother's features. And the eyes… He looked carefully, and then exclaimed, 'Your daughter's eyes are exactly like those of the goddess, Joba!'

'Really? That isn't surprising. You know, the goddess was watching us when she was being conceived. In spite of covering her eyes with a cloth, she's a goddess, you see—she saw everything. So I suppose the goddess' look somehow got imprinted in my womb and became Ami's eyes,' Joba explained.

'No one needs to be told that you have found happiness—it's there for all to see. You look like a pot brimming with happiness. But you're putting on weight, you know.'

'Hey—don't you dare look at me greedily like that! My body now has an owner. And you are no longer the Gojen of yore. You are a man now—a young man.'

'You're getting shameless, aren't you?'

'What's there to be shameless about—and that too with you? Modon has told me that he had told you everything right then. You are so much younger than him, I wonder why he had to confide in you.' Joba paused briefly, and then said, 'Hey, get married.'

'Get married? Me? With a lawsuit looming over my head?'

'That one you will win. Modon is gaining a reputation as a good lawyer. His senior is rather well known anyway. They'll ensure that you win. So get married.'

'Hah—now you don't need to become my marriage guidance counsellor! It's getting late—go sleep. The little one looks uncomfortable sleeping in your lap. Even I haven't slept these last few nights. The prison cell was so filthy—I wonder how I survived there. I've been on a trip to hell and back.'

'You're right. I'd forgotten. Meeting you after such a long time, it felt like we were chatting at the riverside by the temple. Go to sleep, Gojen. You must be really tired. I'll leave for now.' Joba lifted her daughter's head to her shoulder and stood up. At the doorway, she turned around and asked, 'This girl, Hasina—what is she like to look at?'

'Hasina? She's rather nice looking. She's slim—not thin. Her skin colour is like yours and her face is sweet. Why do you ask?'

'For no particular reason. Anyway, sleep now. It really is late. The husband of mine is snoring already. Good night, Gojen.' Joba left the room, gently pulling the door shut after her.

20

The case went to court, dates were scheduled and the proceedings continued. In the midst of all this, Gojen did the unthinkable. But that is another long story.

Hasina had been housed in the room by the barn, which had been walled up securely, but Gojen found it difficult to come to terms with the arrangement, although that was what his grandmother desired. He worried more during the nights. Many a time, he imagined he heard her crying. Whenever he sensed that she was awake, or noticed her lighting a lamp, he would step outside and call out to her, and in a weepy voice, she would tell him that she thought there was someone outside. One night, Gojen too thought he heard someone. The moment he called out, there was the sound of running footsteps. He circled his compound before going back to his room.

Two days later, Gojen was woken by Hasina frantically calling out to him late in the night. He rushed out of bed and towards her door, followed by his grandmother, who had also woken up. 'What's wrong, Hasina? Open the door,' he called agitatedly.

Hasina opened the door and, still crying and terrified, rushed into his arms.

'What's the matter, Hasina?' Aai asked.

'Aai, someone had come—and was trying to cut the wall to enter the room.'

A lamp, with its flame lowered, remained lit in the room every night. Gojen entered, picked it up, raised the wick and scanned the surroundings in the now brighter light. It was true—one corner of the rear reed wall had been cut out. Whoever it was must have attempted to enter that way.

Gojen returned to his grandmother and the still sobbing Hasina. 'Aai, there's no way we can leave her alone here. Let's take her to the sitting room again,' he said.

'Go get your bedclothes,' the old lady instructed the girl.

Hasina hesitantly entered her room. Gojen held up the lamp so that everything was clearly visible. Rolling up her bed, she followed Gojen and his grandmother into the main house. She made her bed on the sitting-room floor and the old lady returned to hers after a few reassuring words.

That night, Gojen spent a lot of time sitting out at the veranda, lost in thought. He figured that the goons could be after Hasina for two reasons. One was her young, now orphaned, body and the other was the fact that she was the prime witness in the case he had lodged against Jadob Bora and his men. The outcome of the case depended largely on her testimony since she was the sole eyewitness to the events.

Gojen realized that it would be dangerous to leave the girl alone at night. Yet, it was impossible to keep her in their house. She belonged to a totally different community—one which was deemed almost untouchable. What to do?

As he sat with his arms folded, Gojen suddenly felt a strange tingling in his veins. He recalled Hasina's grip on his arms on the day of her mother's death. Also, the day she had arrived here escaping the murder and arson in Kuroiguri, she had stopped crying only when he had declared, 'I am there for you.' Yes—at the moment, there was no other person who was genuinely concerned about her security and welfare. In future, there could be another—her husband—who would need to ensure that she was free from any threat to her life and well-being, even if it was only for the selfish reason of setting up home with her.

Gojen decided that his immediate duty would be to find this other man. Hasina was a Muslim, so it was natural that the groom he sought for her should be from that community. The problem was—where could he find such a man? The Kuroiguri settlers, the only Muslims he knew, had either died or disappeared without a trace…

Suddenly, he remembered another Muslim man he knew—the maulvi peer who vended local medicines at the Saturday market. He could surely help. Gojen felt relieved. He would go meet him this Saturday. Then he realized that Saturday was tomorrow—nay, today. He looked up at the sky. From the positions of the stars, he could tell that it was almost dawn. He would have to set off soon. Deciding to catch a short nap until then, Gojen went into the house.

◆

Peer Mohammad Suleiman Rasool sat in a specific place in the marketplace—on a mound. The man was over seventy. His long hair and beard were silver and he always wore a long alb-like garment and a black cap. His eyes were keen and his bearing tall and remarkable. On his shoulders, he carried an assortment of cloth bags which held his medicinal herbs and amulets.

Gojen had planned to reach the market early, before the crowds gathered. But having gone to bed so late, he failed to rise early and by the time he reached, the medicine man was already surrounded by a horde of people. Gojen managed to catch his eye and said that he would come back later—he needed to speak to him in private.

The old man smiled suspiciously, assuming that Gojen had caught some secret malady. 'Don't worry—we'll take care of that right now,' he said. Then, addressing the group around him, he said, 'Go away, all of you. Come back in five minutes. This guy has important matters to discuss—let me hear him first.'

The men moved away. Gojen looked at them and edged closer to the old man.

'What, eh, Gojen? Have you got married? Or are you in trouble with some girl? Any problem?' asked the medicine man, amused. Gojen informed the man that his assumptions were wrong and told him, as briefly as possible, why he had sought his audience.

He requested the old man to somehow find a suitable match for Hasina at the earliest.

The maulvi peer, who gave Gojen a patient hearing, sat dazed for a while and then said, 'Gojen, I see your point. But I need some time. There are people waiting right now. Meet me again just before the market winds up.'

That meant a four to five hour wait. What would he do until then? Gojen wondered impatiently. He was here with a mission and he had to accomplish it at any rate. Then he remembered. He walked to a far end of the marketplace, checking his pockets as he went—yes, there was some money in them.

The dice games were already in progress. His old mates were elated to see him after such a long time and welcomed him wholeheartedly. Some of them asked him about the events in Kuroiguri and his subsequent stint in jail. He answered in monosyllables, donned a detached air and sat down to the game.

A little later, Gojen felt a strange sense of exhilaration when one of the dice kingpins left on some errand, leaving him in charge of the proceedings. He, too, had been a kingpin for about two years, but things had turned ugly with a couple of unscrupulous players. When things came to a head, requiring him to come to blows with them, he tossed away his gear in disgust and rarely played the game afterwards. When he did, it was at someone else's board, where he placed his bets like all other players. But he soon tired of that and stopped visiting the den altogether. Today, after such a long time, he felt the excitement return as he tossed the dice around in the leather cup. He was still pretty adept at it—no, he hadn't lost his touch yet. The hours that flew by, but he was oblivious to it.

'Hey, Gojen bhai, I'm leaving now.'

He looked up and saw the medicine man. Quickly gathering the money he had stacked under the board and handing it to the game owner, he said, 'Count this. I have to leave.' He rose. The game owner clutched some money and handed it to him—'Here, take this. I don't need to count.'

'I wasn't here to earn money. I just needed to pass some time. Keep it—it's of no use to me. I'm off. Come, Baba, let's go.' He walked up to the older man and the two of them left the marketplace.

They found an empty bench by a stall selling fruity beverages in various colours and sat down on it. A little further was a tea stall with a couple of jalebis growing cold on the large plate next to the paraphernalia for frying them, now that it was almost closing time. Gojen recalled that this was where he had brought Hasina one day. She was so fascinated by the sight of the loopy jalebis frying in the hot ghee that she had been reluctant to move away.

Gojen bought himself a glass of the brightly coloured 'juice'. The older man did not eat or drink at random joints. Looking at the glass, he said, 'Gojen, I understand your problem. It is imperative that you get the girl married. I have someone in mind—she will have a comfortable life with him. She is parentless, but will get enough affection from his family.'

'That's exactly what I want, Baba. That is exactly the sort of person and household I would like to see her entrusted to. With Mansoor bhai gone, I will have to take that responsibility. Now that you have somebody in mind, tell me, Baba, how do I go about things? When and where can I see the man?' Gojen spoke excitedly, not even pausing to breathe.

'It'll all happen, Gojen. You don't need to get so excited.'

'I do need to, Baba. We need to visit the man's family with the proposal, they need to accept it and the wedding needs to happen soon. We don't have much time,' said Gojen, still sounding impatient.

The medicine man smiled mysteriously. 'Look, Gojen,' he said, 'you don't need to visit the man or ask him to accept your proposal.'

'Why? How come?' asked Gojen, puzzled.

'Because you have met the man, you have spoken to him and he has accepted already.' The smile remained on the old man's lips.

'I don't understand, Baba.' Gojen looked bewildered.

'Why don't you understand, you fool? I myself will marry the girl.'

'You—you mean you will marry the girl?' asked Gojen, his voice shaking with shock.

'I have two other wives. But this one is so young, I will give her all the love I can. You don't need to worry.'

Gojen was speechless. What was the man saying? He was old enough to be Hasina's grandfather! He already had two wives. And now he wanted a third! Gojen sat with his head bowed low.

'What's the matter? Why have you fallen silent?' asked the old man, realizing that Gojen was not very happy with his proposal. 'You don't need to worry about anything. Just bring the girl over to my place tomorrow. I'll read the nikaah. The bride-price will also be arranged. You can be her guardian—never mind that you are a Hindu. We will need two men as witnesses for the nikaah—I will arrange for that too. You don't worry. Just get the girl and reach my home by afternoon.'

The words fell on Gojen's ears all right, but he had no inclination to grasp their import. His thoughts were in a turmoil. First of all, there was no question of getting Hasina married to such an old man. But if this wedding didn't happen, would the man help in finding her a groom? It wouldn't be easy for him to find an eligible Muslim man on his own.

Suddenly, a momentous thought occurred to him. The inside of his head felt like a whirlpool created by a large fish biting his line. He waited until he could think clearly once again and, in a low voice, asked, 'Baba, what if I marry Hasina?'

The old man laughed hard, as though he would never stop. A few people turned to look in his direction and Gojen wondered what he had said that was so funny. Finally, his laughter dying down, the man said, 'Gojen, you should have told me at the very outset that this was your intention all along'

'No, no, Baba. I honestly hadn't thought about it earlier, I swear. I was really thinking in terms of finding a nice Muslim youth. But it suddenly struck me that if Hasina is under threat in my own house, how will any other man protect her in her present circumstances? And I have come to the conclusion that I alone can deliver her from the dangers she is facing.'

'So now you want to marry her and keep her with you,' said the old man. After a pause, he continued, 'Sounds fine. Maybe you should marry her. Your age will also be perfect. However, there is a catch.'

Gojen looked uncomprehendingly at him. The man said, 'If you have to wed her, you will have to convert to Islam. You will have to read the kaalima, swear on the Koran and adopt a Muslim name.'

'Oh, really?' Gojen wondered how such a thing would be possible. He sat, lost in thought. Then, suddenly getting to his feet, he said, 'Okay, Baba, I will take my leave now. I'll let you know what I decide.' As though speaking to himself, he mumbled, 'It would be nice if we could find a nice young Muslim man for her,' and walked away, his head still lowered.

◆

Hasina had already retired for the night by the time Gojen sat down to his dinner. While he was eating, he told his grandmother about his decision—how he had resolved to marry the girl and put an end to all the threats to her well-being.

The old lady was shell-shocked. How could such a thing be possible? Hasina's presence in the house was in itself an irritant—except when she came face-to-face with the girl and couldn't help brimming with sympathy for her. But that didn't mean Gojen needed to marry her! She rose, a hand on her hip, and said, 'How could you think of such a thing? It's bad enough that you bring a Muslim girl into the house, and now you want to marry her? Oh, god! This house has become a hell-hole. God, why don't you kill me first?'

She moved away into the alcove with the hearth and spent a long time teasing the embers with a half-burnt piece of firewood until they died out altogether. She was lost in thought—what was her grandson planning to do? She was startled out of her reverie by Gojen saying, 'Aai, I'm off to bed.' Pouring a little water onto the ashes out of habit, she entered the dining area of the kitchen and found Gojen's dishes on the floor, the plate covering a bowl. Lifting it, she saw that he had left half of the banana-milk rice for her as usual.

The old lady felt nauseous at the sight. She had lost her appetite and decided to retire for the night. The dishes could be put away tomorrow morning, before her bath. She turned out the lamp and got into bed. 'Oh Krishna, my benevolent Lord,' she prayed. But she found herself wondering—was the lord really benevolent? Sleep eluded her and she was haunted by two faces—one Gojen's, the other, Hasina's.

♦

Feeling wide awake a little before dawn, Gojen was struck by another thought. The medicine man had said that he would need to convert to Islam if he wanted to marry a Muslim girl. But the reverse could also be possible! The girl could convert to Hinduism and the wedding solemnized. It was the same thing! He eagerly awaited the morning to resolve this issue.

Immediately after breakfast, Gojen set off to see Bapudeu at the temple. The kabiraj, too, was reputedly a learned man, but Gojen could barely tolerate him. As he was leaving, his grandmother said, 'If Deu says the girl can be converted into a Hindu, I shall not object to the wedding.'

But after consulting both Bapudeu and the kabiraj, Gojen learnt that there was no provision in the scriptures or religious edicts of Hinduism to allow a person from another religion to enter its fold. A Hindu could convert to any religion; but the reverse was not possible.

Gojen carefully avoided telling either of the two men the reason for his quest. But however much he attributed it to mere curiosity, both men's suspicions were aroused.

Gojen was disappointed, but his resolve remained as strong as ever. In keeping with his stubborn nature, he made his momentous decision—if he couldn't make Hasina a Hindu, he would become a

Muslim and marry her, so that he could protect her from the brutes who were waiting to get at her.

He would take Hasina to the medicine man today and, after going through the conversion, would wed her right away.

◆

Gojen seemed detached and emotionless as he went through the act of conversion. Both that and the wedding needed preparation—but the medicine man declared that they would somehow make do with whatever was available. The wedding called for two witnesses—one from the bride's family and the other from the groom's—it was only when they heard the couple's acceptance of each other that the nikaah held good. The old man got a couple of his family members to do the needful, set the bride-price at eleven rupees, got Gojen to chant the kaalima—la ilaaha illallahu mohammadoor rasoolullah—and declared him converted. Then he gave Gojen one of his washed kurta-pyjamas to wear, a white cap to go with it. He also gave him a new name—Mohammad Abdul Ghani.

The medicine man then deputed himself guardian and conducted the wedding. Three times, he asked Hasina, 'Holodhor's son Mohammad Abdul Ghani has offered a bride-price of eleven rupees to marry you. Do you accept?' On the third round, Hasina replied, 'I do.' But before that, she stared long into Gojen's eyes and broke into sobs. Gojen too could feel a wetness in his eyes and a heaviness in his heart.

◆

Next to the kitchen was Aai's prayer room—a small space that housed an idol of Lord Krishna and, on a xorai beside it, a copy of the Bhagavad Gita wrapped in a patterned gamosa. The oil in the earthen lamp was burning low. Aai replenished it and knelt down to bow once again. This was something she normally never did.

'Aai!'

Even as she was bowed low, her heart skipped a beat when she heard Gojen's voice. He was back! So Hasina must have come too!

Although she had been waiting all day for this moment, she couldn't come to terms with the fact that a newlywed Muslim couple was now standing in the courtyard she tended so lovingly each day, and that the groom was none other than her own grandson! Her heart pounded in her chest. Hoping against hope, she wondered—what if Gojen had had a change of heart and the wedding hadn't happened after all?

'Aai—are you asleep already?' called Gojen. Night had barely fallen and it wasn't his grandmother's bedtime yet, he mused.

Carrying a lamp, its chimney half blackened with soot, Aai stepped out of the house and into the sparkling moonlight. Gojen was standing before her in a totally unrecognizable form, both his manner and outfit alien to her. Behind him stood Hasina, the end of her blue silk sari drawn to serve as a veil over her head—one of the medicine man's wives had taken the carefully saved new sari from her suitcase and draped it on Hasina for the nikaah.

Gojen turned to Hasina. 'Go. What are you waiting for?'

Hasina moved forward to touch Aai's feet. The old lady recoiled like she had seen a snake. 'Never mind. That's not necessary,' she said, her displeasure evident in her voice.

'Aai, I've married her. But I needed to become a Muslim first. There was no other way, you see,' said Gojen apologetically.

'There's nothing left to see. I've considered everything. I'm not about to let you into this house. For the moment, you can stay with her in the room by the loom-shed. You can eat there too—I'll send you the food until you make your own arrangements.'

'Do you really mean we can't enter this house, Aai?' asked Gojen. His voice was sad and it trembled as he spoke.

'No, you can't,' Aai replied, clear and determined. She placed the lamp on the ground and said, 'Hasina, take this lamp and go in—to your room. Baap, I'll get your belongings out and you can take them there,' Without leaving any scope for conversation, she slowly disappeared inside.

Gojen stood transfixed, as though turned to stone. Hasina, confused, stood by, staring pleadingly at him.

'Go—go to your room. And take the lamp with you. I am going out for a while. If Aai sends you any food, eat and go to bed. You must be tired. I won't be long. Make sure to shut the door carefully.' Gojen watched Hasina follow his instructions. As she was about to shut the door, he called, 'Don't be afraid. I'll be back soon.'

Gojen walked out of the compound and towards the river. To the people who passed him on the street, he looked familiar—like Gojen, to be precise—but his attire made them believe otherwise and they went on their way without hailing him.

Rupai and Konloura had been sitting on the bridge as usual and talking about him when he arrived. They were wondering why he hadn't come here even once in the week since his release from jail. They were hesitant to go to his house and find out for themselves— the fact that he had provided asylum to a Muslim girl had given rise to a host of stories. Some people in the village were also considering ostracizing him. But the old lady was a religious soul and the household was looked upon with a certain degree of respect thanks to her presence. So they had not been able to arrive at a decision yet. But it was enough to deter Rupai and Konloura from visiting. It was bad enough that they featured in the gossip, thanks to their guarding the homestead during Gojen's absence.

A man was approaching them and they hopped off the railing. They scanned the face of their visitor. The face was Gojen's. But the outfit?

'Rupai, Konloura!' The voice was Gojen's too! 'What are you staring like that for? It's me—Gojen. But from now on, I am Abdul Ghani—Ghani miyan.' He smiled as he tried to speak lightly.

His two friends continued to stare in amazement. Gojen hopped on to the railing. 'Rupai, haven't you brought your flute today?'

'No, replied Rupai mechanically. He was still in shock.

'Oh-oh! I was especially hoping to listen to your music today.'

'Well, you can listen to the music later. But what did you just say? What's this about you being Ghani-something from now on? What's the matter?' asked Konloura, his voice shaking with curiosity.

'What can the matter be? Can't you see? I've become a Muslim.'

'What?' Rupai and Konloura shouted in unison.

Gojen stared unblinkingly at the moonlight being reflected on the surface of the water. His two friends stood quietly, their heads hung low.

'Sit down. Listen...' And Gojen told them the entire story in detail, right up to the fact that his grandmother wouldn't let him into the house. He admitted that unavoidable circumstances had led him to this difficult decision, but now that it was made, he was ready to face the consequences. Whatever happened to him, at least he could now take care of Hasina without worrying about the repercussions. 'And that is how I am now Ghani miyan, do you understand?' Gojen concluded lightly.

For some time, the three of them stared wordlessly at the flowing river. Then Rupai said, 'Konloura, don't you think we should make a move? It's getting late.'

'Are you leaving already? Why—you haven't yet told me what you think of all this,' said Gojen, a little disturbed at the lack of response from his friends.

'What is there to say? You've already done what you've done,' said Rupai.

'Right—we can't seem to think of anything,' Konloura added.

'Come, Konloura. Let's get going. It's rather late,' said Rupai, ushering his friend along as he moved forward.

'Gojen, aren't you leaving too?' Konloura asked.

'I-I-I'll leave after a while. You carry on. I'll sit here for a bit,' said Gojen, feeling lost. He stared after his friends' receding backs until they were out of sight.

◆

Aai was sitting in the wooden chair on the veranda, a kerosene lamp lighting the doorway behind her.

A sound at the gate—and an unknown long, white animal was coming forward. Gojen!

From the courtyard, he called out, 'Aai, you aren't asleep yet?'

'She has fallen asleep. I asked her not to bolt the door from inside. Your meal is inside. She didn't eat—said she wasn't hungry. All the better if she doesn't eat today. I'm off to bed now.' She picked up the lamp and stepped inside, pulling the door shut behind her.

Gojen gingerly entered his room and barred it from inside. He looked around the room. Hasina was fast asleep on the bed. On a wooden chest was the lamp, its chimney now almost totally opaque with soot. On a patch of the floor lit by a small kerosene lamp were two meals on bronze plates, covered with two other plates. Next to them were Gojen's usual peera and another one. On a line strung up by the wall were Hasina's clothes, and along with them, a few of his. His bedclothes were on the bed she was sleeping in. While he was away, Aai had taken his things out to the veranda and Hasina had moved them here.

Gojen uncovered the meals and saw that apart from the rice and gravy, there was a bowl with banana-milk rice on each plate. It made him smile inwardly. On one side were a basin and a pot of water.

Gojen washed his face in the basin and took off his kurta. He covered the meals and moved the small kerosene lamp to the chest, where the other one gave almost no light. Sitting on the empty side of the bed, he looked at Hasina. She was fast asleep and the lamp lit up her hair, her neck, her bare arms, her heaving breasts—right down to her naked feet.

Suddenly, Gojen was overcome by waves of emotion. Was this the same Hasina whom he had carried in his arms to protect her from a raging storm? Or was she the child who had held his hand as she toured the Saturday market buying bangles and eating jalebis? Was this the girl whom he had carried piggyback when she had sprained her ankle—the girl who roasted corn and sliced cucumber for him at Mansoor bhai's home? Or was she the Hasina who had clung to his legs, burying her head in his knees when she managed to reach his home alive after the Kuroiguri holocaust?

This Hasina was now his wife—the girl he had married. He would now have to share her bed and hold her in his arms. This was a new Hasina.

Once again, he looked at the sleeping figure of his wife. Her sari had ridden up slightly, exposing her bare legs with their smooth calves. He noticed every curve of her body—her rounded breasts, her neck, her arms, her slender fingers and her soft face with its gentle features. Suddenly, it seemed as though she was aware that he was watching her. Even as she slept, her lips quivered, a soft smile playing on them.

He gently touched her lips with his fingers. Hasina woke up with a start and seeing Gojen sitting beside her, remembered that he would now sleep with her in the same bed. In the afternoon, the medicine man's wives had said things to her that had made her blush. They teased her and offered her advice. But she chose not to pay too much attention to them. These were such shameful things, they couldn't happen to her—at least not with Gojen. Of that she was sure.

Shocked and perplexed, her eyes filled with tears as they stared into Gojen's. He lay down beside her and wiped them away with his fingers.

'I'm afraid,' she quivered. Then, suddenly, she buried her head in his chest as her body melted into his arms. It was as though she had finally found a refuge—a safe haven where she was free of all danger.

The Hasina who had seemed a stranger to him just moments ago became intimately known to him. Unprecedented sensations assailed his body and mind and had him entranced. He drew her closer into his embrace.

Two totally inexperienced youngsters were overpowered by forces of nature and, in a supreme moment, their experience turned them into a man and woman.

◆

An early bird chirped to break the stillness of the sleepless night. Gojen and Hasina thought they should get some sleep. But then, Hasina said, 'I'm hungry.'

Gojen left the bed and picked up the bowls with the banana-milk rice. He emptied the second bowl into the first and carried it to the bed. Then he took turns in feeding Hasina and himself—Aai's concoction tasted like manna from heaven!

Their passionate encounter had left them in a state of delicious exhaustion and they both fell asleep instantly. It was almost morning.

◆

It was the day of the new moon, which meant a break from the crops. Gojen figured that most of his village folk would take their cows out for grazing, so he could catch up with them in the field and tell them about all that he had gone through. On the way back, he would pick up some material and stop by at the tailor's to get himself a few kurta-pyjama sets made. That was the outfit he would need to wear from now on. Then, if time permitted, he would drop in at Sarbai Pandit's home.

Having spent most of the night awake, his eyelids were heavy. Added to that was the heady feeling left by his intimate pursuits. Keeping to the side lanes so as to avoid prying eyes and questions, he made his way to the grazing fields. He'd wait and see which route to take on the way back.

From a distance, Gojen noticed that the village folk had turned up in larger numbers than he expected. They already seemed to be engaged in some discussion, sitting atop the anthills and under the shade tree.

A hush fell over the crowd as he approached. They looked him up and down, like they had never seen him before. Avoiding all eye contact, Gojen pulled out a coloured handkerchief from one of his kurta pockets and spread it carefully on the ground. On it, he placed a few whole tamul and five silver coins. He prostrated himself before the crowd and said, 'Folks, I bow before you for two reasons. One is that I have given up my religion and converted to Islam. I have wronged my village folk. I don't know what punishment you will mete out to me; I only wish to say that I had no other option. I apologize to all of you.

The second and more important issue which I would like to discuss with you is: who will now take over the fields abandoned by the Kuroiguri farmers?'

Suddenly, a young man who had been standing behind the crowd, spoke up. 'That is government land. Khargi mauzadar has already consulted the property lawyers and taken some steps. How does it concern us as to who gets the rights to that land?'

The people turned to look back. The speaker was Dino, son of one of the mauzadar's henchmen. Gojen looked at him and said, 'What else could one expect you to say? Gentlemen, that is exactly what I am trying to tell you. The Muslims made that land cultivable at the expense of their blood, sweat and tears. And now god knows who is pillaging the place. Since there is a police case on, nobody has dared to openly stake a claim. But we all know that a certain group has its eyes on that land.'

'But what can we do, now that Khargi mauzadar has already started working on it?' This time, the speaker was an elderly gentleman.

'I was thinking, let the totally landless people from our village and the Nepali settlement bordering Kuroiguri go settle there. The other half can be cultivated jointly by the two villages and can remain public property. Some day, if any of the Muslims happen to return…'

A middle-aged man suddenly stood up and interrupted loudly, 'Hey, Gojen. Forget your preamble. We all know you are here to plead the case of those Muslims. Earlier too, you had instigated us against the mauzadar on the pond issue and got us into his bad books. We aren't about to listen to you this time. Why do we need to worry about whose land it is, who made it cultivable, who took over or will take over? You have taken in one of those Muslims' daughters, haven't you? And you yourself have converted to Islam. So go settle on your father-in-law's land. Go take over all that land if you will.'

'Why don't you tell him what we were discussing earlier?' another man reminded the speaker.

'Yes, I will. Listen, Gojen. Before you arrived, we had a discussion and decided something. We, the village people have ostracized you. We shall have no dealings with you whatsoever. If you stay away from the house, Aai will still be allowed into the naam-ghar. But nobody will visit your home. Do you follow?' Then, turning to the assembly, he said, ;Come on, folks. Let's get home. We've already wasted too much time on these unnecessary issues.'

The people hurried to their respective homes. Gojen remained kneeling on the ground. It was the first time that he had appealed to people thus. In their rush to leave, the people inadvertently kicked at the handkerchief, tamul and coins and left them scattered all over. When they were some distance away, Gojen started screaming, 'You foxes, you monkeys, you cats! Of course I'll settle in Kuroiguri. I'll settle on my father-in-law's land. You don't need to order me to do so. If any of you steps into Kuroiguri, I'll hack you in two—I'll break your legs. I don't need the land like you do. My barns are always full. But I will go to my father-in-law's land. What can you get by ostracizing me? You can't do a thing to me—you can't touch a hair on my body…'

Suddenly, Gojen noticed that two young men at the tail end of the crowd kept turning back to look at him as he vented his anger. Then recognition dawned—they were Rupai and Konloura. They too had joined the crowd and were moving away!

After whiling away some time sitting on an anthill, Gojen realized that he was all alone in the grazing field. All was empty around him and he had no one around. He felt terribly lonely.

◆

Gojen sat alone on the railing of the wooden bridge over the river. It was the third day that he had failed to meet Rupai and Konloura. Each day, he had nursed a thin ray of hope that they would come; but he went back disappointed. He looked up at the cloudless late-autumn sky. It was studded with stars, their light reflecting off every gurgling ripple on the surface of the river.

In a flash, a matter on which he was undecided so far transformed into firm resolve. He would leave this village and move to Kuroiguri. He would build a house where Mansoor's once stood and start living there. Hasina had a right to that space. And, in the capacity of Hasina's husband, it was his duty to protect Mansoor's legacy.

Whenever he walked through the village in his kurta-pyjama, Gojen attracted curious looks from passers-by. They looked upon him as an alien creature until he himself started feeling unfamiliar with his surroundings. This morning, when he had gone to Sarbai Pandit's house to discuss the lawsuit, the teacher bade him sit all right, but spoke guardedly. He showed no interest in learning about Gojen marrying Hasina; neither was Gojen enthused enough to enlighten him. Pandit's wife, too, kept indoors, peeping surreptitiously through the curtains just once.

He decided that tomorrow, he would start making arrangements for his move to Kuroiguri.

21

Everything was ready in a week. In the place where Mansoor's hut once stood, Gojen had a nice, strong thatched house erected, and a bamboo fence put up around it. Bhodoram, a cousin from Nihali, was summoned to live with the old lady. He would also look after the fields and crops for her. It was also arranged that one of Kaila's nephews would live on the homestead. Gojen and Hasina's room was swabbed clean, holy basil water was sprinkled to purify it, and it became the room of the Nepali youth. Gojen would personally come by to check on his grandmother every couple of days. The arrangements were water-tight.

◆

The old lady's pain was unbearable, but she did not voice her torment. Somehow, she could never come to terms with her grandson's marriage with Hasina. It was true that ever since she had first come to the household with a sprained ankle, Aai had felt a strange affection for the girl; and it only got deeper after she was orphaned. Hasina's sweet face and even sweeter words filled the old lady's heart. But the thought of her darling grandson becoming Abdul Ghani and marrying the girl was totally unacceptable! Gojen, too, did not hope for any support or sympathy from his grandmother. He simply informed her of his decision, proceeded to make all arrangements and, one fine day, prepared to leave for his new home with his wife.

He had already sent a cartload of provisions—utensils, clothes, household goods and groceries to last the first few days. Aai watched the proceedings wordlessly. As they were leaving, she came out on the veranda, summoned Hasina, dropped a small paper packet into her hand and said, 'Open this packet and wear some of the vermilion in your parting. Also, wear a vermilion dot on your forehead. This is no religious ritual—it is only a social norm. It will do you no harm.'

Hasina, confused about what to do, turned to Gojen.

'Come on, do as Aai says,' he instructed her. Hasina opened the package.

'Wait—how will you do that without a mirror?' Aai turned to go inside to fetch one. Then, pausing for a moment, she turned around and walked towards the girl. 'Come, let me do it for you.' She picked out some vermilion from the pack Hasina held open in her palm and drew a streak along her parting. Then she drew a large dot on Hasina's forehead. Then Aai held out a small cloth bundle that she drew from her waist.

'This bundle contains a necklace, two pairs of earrings and a pair of bangles. You don't need to wear all of them. One pair of earrings—the keru—is thick-stemmed and you won't be able to wear them. Wear the other. Come, let me help you—you'll only fumble,' and Aai adorned Hasina with the earrings, necklace and bangles. Hasina wrapped up the remaining ornaments and handed the bundle to her husband.

Gojen was moved to tears at the sight of Aai putting the vermilion and jewellery on Hasina. Without any prompting, Hasina, pulled the veil over her head and touched the old lady's feet to seek her blessings. On the day of her wedding, Aai had allowed her to bow only from a distance; but now she allowed her to touch her feet. For a moment, Aai wondered if she should kiss the girl's cheeks. But no—that would be going too far. She tasted sacred prasad with her tongue, chanted the scriptures with her lips. These parts could not be sullied by kissing a Muslim girl, however sweet she was. No, that just wasn't possible.

Aai raised Hasina's hands and head from her feet and said, 'That's enough. Get up now. The sun is already pretty high. You need to get going.'

Gojen, about to leave, suddenly bent down and touched his grandmother's feet—something he had never done before. 'We'll take our leave, Aai. I'll keep coming by. Don't worry,' he said.

The thought of Gojen bowing to her brought a smile to the old lady's lips.

◆

Four months passed.

During the dry season, the monsoon whirlpools of the Brahmaputra left huge sand-pits in their trail. One winter afternoon, Gojen and Hasina frolicked in one such pit and, spent after a bout of lovemaking, soon fell asleep.

A tributary of the Brahmaputra flowed not too far away, but nothing was visible from inside the pit. Many boats passed through this waterway—boats loaded with milk, hay, fish or deer poachers going to the forests of Kaziranga. One such boat passed by, the boatman humming a Bihu song. When he neared the spot, he let out a shrill whistle. It woke Gojen, but he remained still, hidden in the pit.

Hasina was fast asleep and Gojen stared intently at her body. Then, slowly, on some impulse, he started pouring handfuls of sand on her until she looked like she was sleeping under a silver quilt. Only her head was visible and Gojen was mesmerized by her sweet face. He outlined her features with his finger—her eyes, nose, cheeks, lips, chin, earlobes and bare neck. Then he pressed his lips gently upon hers. Hasina slowly opened her eyes and tried to move. But Gojen's body pinned her down. 'Don't move,' he whispered. 'Let me watch you.'

He looked deep into her eyes and said, 'You know, Hasina, you are really beautiful. I wonder which god created you...'

'Your god or my Allah?' teased Hasina, giggling.

'My god created you and Allah created me. Don't you see? You got a Hindu husband and I got a Muslim wife!'

'I wasn't created by any divine power. It's you who made me what I am. You are my Allah. Come, let me worship you.' Hasina jumped up to a sitting position and only then realized that she had been covered with sand. But as the sand fell away, so did the end of her sari. The sight of her bare breasts embarrassed her and she hid herself in Gojen's arms, pummelling his chest playfully.

Gojen laughed out loud. A passing boatman called out, 'Who are you that laughs so loud? And who are you laughing with?'

Gojen stopped short. He and Hasina sat still, holding each other tight until the boatman's voice and the sound of the splashing oars faded away into the distance.

The early days passed in sheer bliss and contentment. The vast open skies, the Kuroi and the Brahmaputra, the silvery sands, soft grasslands and extensive fields yellow with mustard flowers, the winter sunshine, the soft moonlight, the first dew, the trees, creepers, leaves and flowers—they all set a rhythm that became the rhythm of Gojen and Hasina's life. And they blended in with their surroundings, discovering new pleasures, new gratification, each day.

◆

There was only one thorn in Gojen's flesh—the ill-will Jadob Bora and his gang had for him. Gojen followed Hasina like a shadow, but did not feel totally secure. He was always alert to face any eventuality. In fact, he had even asked his Nepali neighbours to come in, as a group, in case any danger befell him. A few of them found excuses to make occasional visits to Kuroiguri anyway to see if anybody had occupied the land. They hoped that once the case was closed, this land could be theirs.

Meanwhile, the dates for the hearing were announced. The first one would deal with Jadob Bora's complaint of a death threat from Gojen and Moti mistry's accusation that he had raped his wife. The second was to address Gojen's complaint of murder and arson against Bora and his men.

On the first appointed date, Gojen set off for the district headquarters, taking Hasina with him. Not wanting to travel by bus in case Bora and his men were also aboard to spoil his mood, he made inquiries and found an almost empty freighter that was leaving at a suitable time from a ghat not too far away.

◆

The cases against Gojen were pleaded and concluded, after much drama, in a single day. Modon had entrusted the cases to a very able senior of his, assisting him in every way possible.

Gojen followed Modon to the judge's chamber, stopping at the doorway while the latter carried the files in. As he was waiting, he saw Jadob Bora, Moti mistry and his wife enter the chamber with two of Bora's men.

The hearing started. The lawyers representing the plaintiff, and the defendant, had agreed to place both cases before the same judge. Jadob Bora's attempted murder and insubordination came up first under Section 307 of the IPC. Bora's lawyer tried to prove that it was a premeditated act. But Gojen's own confession—plus the defense lawyer's strongly worded narrative on how people can behave irresponsibly under tremendous emotional pressure—helped the judge see the truth. Gojen was freed of the murder charge; however a fine of twenty-five rupees was imposed for his disrespectful behaviour.

The second case followed immediately and with it came the drama. Modon and his senior had equipped themselves to disarm their opposition by all legal and crafty means although they did not rule out possible difficulties along the way. But Moti's wife did the unthinkable, and in the process, smoothened the course of the trial. Much as she was grilled, she stuck to two simple statements—that Gojen had never, even in the slightest, caused her any harm, forget rape. And that she hadn't met a more honourable man in her entire life.

Gojen was set totally free of the rape charges.

As she stood in the witness box making her statement, Moti's wife studiedly avoided looking at Gojen. He, however, stared unblinkingly at her as she spoke, unable to believe what was happening. His heart brimmed over with fond respect and he wished he could rush up to her and embrace her feet.

◆

Joba and Hasina were waiting at the gate. That morning, as soon as they landed at the ghat, Gojen and Hasina had gone directly to Modon's house. Modon's parents were away on a month-long pilgrimage, so there were no hurdles here. Leaving Hasina with Joba, Gojen accompanied Modon to the courthouse. He had already made plans regarding what he would do in the event that he was pronounced guilty and sent to prison, although he didn't tell anyone yet. In fact, he kept reassuring Hasina, 'Modon Kokaiti will help us win the case. There is no need to worry.'

From the moment they were left alone, Joba and Hasina bonded like sisters. Not only was Hasina awed by her first visit to an urban home, she was amazed at the warmth she received there. How could she feel so close to somebody she had never known—and that too in such a short span of time?

Modon and Joba had heard of Gojen's conversion to Islam. Yet, they decided, they would host him when he came to town for the hearing, and made all arrangements accordingly. They were even happier when they heard Hasina was coming too. It was really convenient that Modon's parents were away.

The moment Joba saw Hasina, she gathered her in an embrace and kissed her cheeks. This was the household of a Brahmin Sanskrit teacher, where various sacred idols and scriptures were housed with due sanctity, and all Hindu rituals conducted with due faith. Joba was the only daughter-in-law in that household, and the daughter of a temple priest at that. The fact that her kissing a Muslim girl could be a serious offence did not strike anyone at the time, least of all herself.

Gojen and Hasina would stay for two days. Modon and Joba decided that they could have free run of the house, except for the kitchen and prayer-room, which were sacred to his parents. However, they did not wish their guests to guess that they were kept away from these areas, and they took every precaution to ensure that.

While the men were away, Joba fussed over Hasina—combing her hair, draping one of her red saris on her, keeping her occupied while she did the cooking, having lunch at the same table, and napping in the same bed, her little daughter between them. And now they had spruced up for the evening as they awaited their husbands' return from court. Right through their waking hours, Joba had asked many questions of Hasina, which she answered in her accented Assamese. In between, they shared jokes and confidences, their giggles filling the house as the two of them abandoned themselves to their glee.

Tea was a happy occasion, especially so since the men had returned victorious. Then it was decided that Gojen and Hasina need not leave the following day as planned earlier. They could stay a couple more days. Joba could give Hasina a tour of the town; and a horse-carriage was arranged for the same.

The next day, as they moved around in the cart, Joba said, 'You know who showed me this town for the first time, Hasina? My husband. But I wasn't married to him then—I had another husband at the time.'

'I know. I've heard.'

'So Gojen has told you everything!'

'Yes, he has. He told me you were in love with Dada.'

'So how about you and Gojen? Have you fallen in love yet?'

Hasina simply blinked hard and smiled. She said nothing.

'Aha! This one looks like an innocent bud, but she's bloomed already! She's in love,' giggled Joba, playfully pinching Hasina's cheek. Hasina, embarrassed, covered her face with her hands and buried her head in Joba's lap.

◆

When Gojen and Hasina got off the bus at the crossroad on their way back home, he decided that they should first drop by at their old house and then hire a cart for their onward journey.

That way, they could also transport some more of their belongings. So without looking left or right, he walked resolutely ahead, Hasina following a couple of steps behind him.

Not too far from the crossroad, on the path to Gojen's old home, a government dispensary had come up about six months ago—the only such establishment for about twenty miles. It had initially started from one of the rooms in the house of the secretary of the local dispensary board, and recently moved to a temporary shelter in the current location. A middle-aged doctor named Nanda Sharma had been brought in from the headquarters and he single-handedly carried out the duties of doctor, compounder and nurse. He trained the watchman to assist him whenever necessary and worked tirelessly towards making the dispensary fully equipped and functional. For miles around, the people looked at the dispensary as an answer to their prayers.

As they approached it, from a distance, Gojen saw some men taking away a body on a bier. When they were closer, he asked someone at the dispensary gate, 'Who has passed away?'

'You know the dealer of local liquor, Moti mistry? His wife.'

'Moti's wife? What was her ailment?'

'It wasn't an ailment—it was a fire. The doctor couldn't save her.'

'Wha-a-a-t? A fire? How?' Gojen gasped. He felt his throat go dry.

'I don't know the details. I was just here to get some medicine,' said the man, holding up a bottle of red liquid on which the dosage was marked by a serrated strip of paper.

Gojen handed the suitcase he was carrying to Hasina. 'Here, hold this. Wait a moment—I'll be right back.' He walked briskly towards the doctor's chamber in the dispensary. This room, containing shelves filled with large bottles of medicines in various colours and dispensing tools, was out of bounds for visitors.

'Sir, this woman who just succumbed to burns—how did it happen, Sir?' he asked agitatedly.

The doctor, who had been wiping his hands on a towel hung on a wall, turned around and saw Gojen. 'Why have you come in? You know you shouldn't.'

'We can discuss that later. You can punish me later for having broken the rule. But first tell me, Sir, how did the woman catch fire? Why couldn't she be saved?'

'Wait—why are you getting so worked up? Come, sit down.' The doctor physically guided Gojen to a nearby stool. 'Who are you?' he asked.

'I am Gojen, Sir. Now I am Abdul Ghani. That woman…'

'Oh, so you are Gojen! I've heard about you.'

'The woman…'

'…was not in a state to be saved when she arrived here. This is only a dispensary and we don't have that many facilities. She was unconscious when she was brought in. I am told she ran out in flames and collapsed on the road. Two young men saw her and doused the flames with sand and leaves before carrying her here on their shoulders. We administered first aid through the night and she was gone by morning. Her husband showed up only after she was dead—said he was away to see a bhaona and she was alone at home. He had heard the news after returning from the show in the morning. A little later, the dispensary committee member Jadob Bora came by too.'

'Jadob Bora!'

'Right. That's what I'm unable to figure out. When I told him the case would go to the police, he personally went and fetched the in-charge of the beat office. They had a discussion, declared this a suicide case, and left. I suppose that's what will be eventually established. We don't have the infrastructure for a post mortem. But I have preserved the required sections and sent word to Nihali.'

Gojen was stunned by the doctor's story. As he listened in silence, he tried to piece together what had actually happened. 'But, Sir, were you able to figure out how she caught fire?' he asked again.

'There was kerosene on her. I could smell it—it will be confirmed later. The two youths said they smelt it too.'

'Who were the two, Sir?'

'They said their names were Konloura and Rupai.'

'Rupai! Konloura!'

'Yes. Apparently, they were sitting on a bridge and playing the flute not too far away. Suddenly, they saw something in flames moving onto the path and screaming. Hearing a woman's screams, they rushed forward and saw her.'

'But who poured the kerosene on her?'

'According to her husband, she was alone in the house. So it had to be her—she had committed suicide. Else, there was an accident and the kerosene spilled on to her and caught fire,' said the doctor with a sardonic smile.

Gojen jumped to his feet. 'No, Sir,' he shouted. 'They have killed her. They have poured the kerosene on her and set her ablaze. She had spoken the truth when she went to court for my lawsuit, and I was set free on her testimony. That's why they got even with her!'

He rushed out on the veranda and stood facing the street and screaming—'They have burnt her to death—they've killed her. These demons, the dogs Jadob Bora and his gang, they've burnt her alive. I won't spare them either—I'll settle the scores. I'll file another case against them—the curs, the crooks. If you are half the men you are, if you are the sons of your mothers, come admit it—that you have doused her with kerosene and burnt her to death. Will you dare do that, you curs, you lowly bastards...?'

Gojen's screaming brought the doctor out of the chamber and he stood behind him. Hasina, who was standing nearby, tried to lead her husband away by his arm. Gojen took one look at her face and broke down, sobbing. 'You know, Hasina, the woman died because of me. She refused to listen to those curs and dared to speak the truth just so that I didn't need to go to prison. It was because of me that she died—all because of me...'

When he finally stopped crying and looked up, he saw Rupai and Konloura standing in the distance and looking his way. But as soon as his eyes met theirs, they turned around and walked away.

Gojen opened his mouth to call out to them, but then realized why they were gone. He remained at the dispensary gate, and his mouth remained wordlessly open.

'Come, let's go,' said Hasina.

Gojen took the suitcase from Hasina and walked down the street, a few steps ahead of her.

22

Gojen was restless as he cheerlessly sat on a cot-like bamboo platform in the courtyard of his new house at dusk. During the course of the day, he had meandered through a series of unexpected situations. The full moon now rose like a bronze plate. He was tired—he had returned from the Saturday market only a little while ago. He had little reason to go to the market today. What he had really set out to do was meet up with the dispensary doctor and find out whether the police were taking any action on the information he had provided them on Moti's wife's death. The doctor informed him that they hadn't done anything yet, and it wasn't likely that they would.

'But why, Sir?'

The conversation took place on the doctor's rear veranda.

'I can't tell you. You are a volatile person and will raise hell.'

'I do raise hell at times, but only for the right reasons. I can't bear to see any injustice and stay quiet. I need to do something right away.'

'Which is why I can't tell you. You'll try to do something about it.'

'But would it be right for me to keep quiet when I see any injustice? Whether or not it yields any result, I do need to speak up, don't I?'

'If there are no results, what's the use of screaming in the wilderness?'

'I don't agree with you. This is no wilderness—we are talking about people. If anyone screams, someone is bound to hear. And once that happens, he realizes that his deplorable nature and his deeds have not gone unnoticed.'

'I had heard about you. The school teacher Sarbai Pandit had also told me about you one day. The first time I saw you, there was no chance of any conversation—you were so eaten up by your anger. I'm glad I met you today. Now I know that you are capable of balanced thought.'

'All that doesn't matter. I couldn't care less whether you liked me or not. I am a simple man who understands simple matters. So tell me now—why do the police want to let go of the case relating to the death of Moti's wife?'

'Look, please don't force me. I have left my family behind and come here at this point of my life just so that I can be of some service to the people. I don't want to entangle myself in any controversy. And I know that the moment you know, you will create some trouble that is bound to involve me too.'

'Sir, I promise I will not create any trouble. I swear on myself—and on my old grandmother—I will not react. But I absolutely must know.'

'You swear you will stay quiet?'

'Yes, Sir. I swear on my wife too—I will not allow any danger to befall you. If I choose to get myself into trouble, that should be no problem.'

The stately doctor with his close-cropped silver-streaked hair lit a cigarette. Then, looking at Gojen over the rim of his gold-framed spectacles, he spoke in his deep bass voice, 'The secrets of Khargi mauzadar's misdeeds and scandals were often discussed at Moti's den, and his wife had heard most of it. The mauzadar was aware of this. Besides'—the doctor lowered his tone—'Moti has been instrumental in many a murder, and has even been used by the mauzadar to further such ends.'

'Sir, how did you get to know all this?' asked Gojen in surprise.

'I am a doctor and I have my means of receiving information.'

'But, Sir, what does the woman's fiery death have to do with her husband being a murderer?'

'They had coached her as the witness to implicate you and then they saw that she could tell the truth if she chose. They started worrying that the next time around, she might spill the beans about Moti, Jadob Bora, the mauzadar...'

'Just because...' Gojen began to say something, but the doctor cut him short. Rising suddenly, he said, 'Gojen, you should leave now. Today being Sunday, the dispensary is filling up fast, and I am already late.'

The doctor walked in. Gojen felt the blood boiling inside his head. He waited until he got a grip on himself and walked slowly towards the street.

He did not spend much time at the market. As soon as he arrived, he bought a few things Hasina had asked for and a bundle of jalebis and handed them over to Kaila, who would deliver them to his house on their way back home. Then he walked over to the area where local brew was sold. The place hadn't changed at all since his school days. The same owner ran the stall, bidding for it year after year. Though much older than Gojen, he looked upon him with a degree of respect. He was excited to see Gojen after a long time, and engaged in a long conversation with him, carefully avoiding the topic of his conversion. Then he brought in some of his special brew in a glass.

Just as Gojen was picking up his second glassful, he noticed Moti mistry struggling with two bags full of liquor bottles. He had set them down and was wetting his throat from a half-bottle drawn from his pocket. Gojen drained his glass in a single gulp and walked towards him.

Seeing him, Moti smiled stupidly and said, 'Just look, Gojen— look at the plight the woman has left me in by dying.'

Gojen suddenly thrust out his left hand and grabbed the front of Moti's shirt. His right palm was tingling—should he box the teeth out of Moti's face? But no, he had, just a little while ago, sworn to the doctor—that too on Hasina and his grandmother—that he would brook no problem. The grip loosened on the shirt and his arm fell to his side. Clenching his teeth, he muttered, 'How cruel, how cruel!'

Gojen left the liquor den and made his way homewards. A short walk later, he saw a cloud of dust rising from the street in the distance—a car was approaching, a black car—Khargi mauzadar's Ford. Much before it reached him, he moved to the side and waited for it to pass. He saw that the mauzadar was wearing a Gandhi cap and the tricolour was fluttering on the car's bonnet.

The Ford passed by, masking Gojen in a cloud of dust. Then it stopped and reversed to where he was standing. As he was about to move away, the mauzadar called, 'What, eh, Gojen? I believe you have become a Muslim and married one of their daughters? And I hear you have settled in Kuroiguri and are lording it over more than a hundred bighas of land? Do you plan to become a landlord in Kuroiguri?'

'I would become the landlord of Kuroiguri if I could. And don't for a moment think it is because I need the land. You may have thrown him into jail, but the land my father left behind is enough to feed at least another couple of generations. I would be a zamindar just to protect the land from the clutches of the likes of you, and protect it for those who work for a living. Let's wait and watch which way the water flows. But remember one thing. As long as I am alive, Jadob Bora and his ilk dare not step into the Kuroiguri area.' Gojen finished speaking and, without waiting for a response, walked briskly away. With a rumble, the Ford moved away in the opposite direction.

The moment she saw him step into the courtyard, Hasina rushed out smiling. But the smile faded from her lips and she stopped short when she came near. Frowning at him, she said, 'You've swallowed that stuff again today. Never mind. But don't you move a step forward! You can sit outside and enter the house when the stench from your mouth is gone.' She stomped inside and pulled the door shut after her. Gojen stared after her. Her Assamese was still accented and sounded sweet to his ears. Slowly, he sat down on the bamboo platform in the courtyard.

Hasina came out with a small pot of water and a gamosa, plonked them down next to him and went back inside. Gojen washed up. A little later, she came out with tea in a brass tumbler, placed it on the ground near him and asked, 'What do you want in your puffed rice—milk, curd or oil and chilli?' She was still angry.

'Oil, chilli, onions, coriander leaves, some pepper, a squeeze of lemon…'

'Hah! You don't need to teach me how to make jhaal muri.' She entered the house once again, came out some time later carrying a bowl of the spicy puffed rice and placed the bowl on the platform where Gojen was sitting. Then she drew a cane stool and sat at the veranda.

'I'm not about to eat this alone,' said Gojen.

'Fine—don't if you won't. Just throw it away. The birds will eat it tomorrow.'

Gojen waited for a few moments. Then, slowly lifting the bowl, he asked Hasina, 'Hey, should I really throw it away?'

Hasina rose and moved slowly towards her husband. Sitting on one end of the platform, she took a handful of the mixture from the bowl, saying, 'Eat now.' The last traces of her displeasure echoed sweetly in her voice.

'Come on, come closer. Once I've eaten the raw onion and coriander in the mix, my mouth will stop reeking.' He drew her into his arms as he held the bowl in his free hand.

Both sat in silence in the bright light of the full moon, munching on their savoury snack. For Gojen, the peace all around was disrupted every now and then when he pictured Khargi mauzadar driving his Ford in a Gandhi cap, the tricolour flying on its bonnet— the same tricolour Gojen had hoisted in his courtyard on the 15th of August; the tricolour at the foot of which his grandmother had placed flowers and a lamp before bowing to it. When Khargi mauzadar's image got superimposed on the tricolour in Gojen's mind, he wondered where independent India was heading.

◆

Another Saturday, two weeks later. Gojen left the house, unsure of whether he would go as far as the market. He had two prime errands—one, to see his grandmother and the other, to consult with the doctor at the dispensary. Hasina hadn't been keeping too well lately. She could barely eat and spent the early part of the day retching. The kabiraj could help too, but now that there was a doctor at hand, it was better to consult him. However, he did need to drop in at the kabiraj's clinic; because as he was passing by, the man called out to him, 'Hey, Gojen! There's a letter for you. Come, take it.'

A letter? Who could have written to him? Gojen wondered.

As soon as he came up to the kabiraj, the man said, 'The postman handed it to me when I was at the post office a few days ago to receive a parcel. He said I could give it to you when you passed this way. He comes this way only once a week at the most, and that too when there is any mail to be delivered.' The kabiraj took out a letter from a drawer and held it out to Gojen. 'Yesterday, Jadob Bora offered to deliver it to you—said he was going to Kuroiguri anyway. But I refused to give it to him. He's busy with so many things, god knows where he'd forget it.'

Gojen was reading the letter and listening to the kabiraj at the same time, with the result that neither task got done thoroughly. But he did hear of Bora's offer to take the letter to him. 'So did Jadob Bora read the letter?' he asked the kabiraj.

'He may have. It was on the table before I put it in the drawer. Anyway, if it was some private matter, it wouldn't have been written on a postcard.'

'No, it's nothing private. It's just about the Kuroiguri lawsuit. The dates have been announced.'

After a casual conversation during which the kabiraj once again expressed his displeasure at Gojen's conversion, he suddenly said, 'Gojen, come with me to the other room. There's something important I need to tell you, and I'd rather speak in private.'

'Something important? A secret?' Gojen's mind was in turmoil as he followed the kabiraj into the medicine chamber and waited for him to speak.

'Isn't Kuroiguri the place you took me to once when one of the Muslim women was seriously ill?' asked the kabiraj as he ground some medicine in a mortar.

'Yes, it is. And now it is a stretch of lush crop-land.'

'That was where the Muslims lived?'

'Yes.'

'And they have now disappeared?'

'What do you mean, "disappeared"? They were slain and thrown into the river. The demons then burnt down the entire village.'

'Do you know who did it and why?'

'Isn't it obvious? It was their greed for the land. The poor Muslim farmers toiled day and night to convert the impenetrable jungles and dark grasslands into fields of mustard, lentils, potatoes and onions. They set up their own little village and learnt our language. But these vampires weren't about to tolerate them. They plotted to get them ousted and occupy the land. But they aren't aware that as long as I live, I'll not allow them to set foot on that stretch. Those fields will be owned by the landless—I have already made a list of people. And until the case is settled...'

'Wait—stop your lecture. You keep referring to "them". Who's "them"?' the kabiraj interrupted.

'You know that as well as I do. They assemble here and set off verbal sparks, and you...'

'Hey, don't involve me in all this. I simply buy the newspaper and they come here to read it. That's all. Now listen, let me give you some inside information.'

Gojen waited in eager silence for what was to come.

Continuing to grind the medicine, the kabiraj said, 'I know this is all to do with the land. But a more complicated noose is now being tightened from afar.'

'O Deu, please stop speaking in riddles. I have a lot to do and very little time. Don't beat around the bush. Please come to the point,' said Gojen impatiently.

'I, too, don't have all day. My patients will soon crowd this place and I need to grind some medicines before then.' The kabiraj suddenly walked up to the window, peered out, returned to his grinding and said, 'It is true that Jadob Bora and his lot have set their eyes on the land. But more importantly, they want to preserve its sanctity. Infidels cannot be allowed to breed here. There is one particular person who is more concerned about the purity of the land rather than about its ownership.'

'And the man who has no need for the land but feels he needs to protect it from infidels is Khargi mauzadar—right Dharmadeu? I get the drift. I, Abdul Ghani, am the one who has sullied the land. I am impious and immoral because, for want of a better option, I married a Muslim girl so that I could protect her from danger. I gave up my religion to adopt hers and became a pariah. But what about them? They hacked the people, had blood on their hands and yet retained their sanctity. Hah! They are worried that once they occupy the land, mine will be the one Muslim family in their neighbourhood. I'll be the odd one out and I'll spread my venom all around. That's their main concern.'

'Gojen, I'm telling you—the problem is not to do with the land alone. Its root lies much deeper, and it has to do with religion. You have guessed right. The main person in all this is Khargaram mauzadar. Now tell me—during the newspaper readings lately, have you heard of some lectures by people named Savarkar and Golwalkar?'

'Of course I have. Why, aren't they the ones who talk about some Rashtriya Swayamsevak Sangh or some such?'

'The mauzadar is very well versed with what they say.'

'How do you know that?' asked Gojen, bewildered.

'I go to the mauzadar's two to three times a month to conduct a routine check-up. He has a blood pressure problem and I need to keep medicating him for it. In his conversations, he has made his strong anti-Muslim feelings pretty clear to me. He keeps giving me leaflets by Savarkar and Golwalkar—in those, they state that ours should be a Hindu country. From the mauzadar's religious sentiments and Jadob Bora's discussions with his men, I have gathered that it is the mauzadar who was behind the Kuroiguri holocaust. He directed the entire operation from the background.'

Gojen listened intently to all that the kabiraj said. The seconds ticked by in silence. Then he asked, 'But Deu, why are you suddenly telling me all this today?'

'Look, Gojen. My father was a staunch Brahmin Sanskrit scholar, the royal priest. I too am a devout Brahmin—I say my prayers thrice a day. I have been deeply pained by your decision to become a Muslim. But I have no enmity with you. I am angry, yes. But although I am in the habit of berating you, I am truly fond of you. I'd like to tell you just one thing—be careful. Don't go gallivanting around all over the place. Be alert. Go now—my patients are waiting outside.' The kabiraj finished speaking and put away the medicine he was grinding into a small china jar.

'No one can touch Gojen. Remember that, Dharmadeu. And don't worry. Nothing is about to happen to me. I'm off now—there's a lot to do.'

'I know, Gojen. But there's no harm in exercising some caution. Go now.'

◆

Gojen left the clinic and stood at the gate reading Modon's postcard once again. It was only now that he realized that the date for the hearing was just three days away. Actually, the letter had reached him rather late. It had lain in the kabiraj's clinic for too long. The trial was in the sessions court, which made things even more serious. But the main thing was that, being the complainant, Gojen should be present in court at all costs, else the case could be dismissed.

There were many things he needed to discuss with his grandmother. As soon as she saw him, she asked, 'What, eh, Baap—how's Hasina?'

'That's what I've come to tell you, Aai. Don't know what's up with that one. She's losing weight, won't eat anything and keeps retching in the morning.'

The old lady smiled and said, 'Sounds like trouble.'

'What trouble, Aai?' asked Gojen impatiently.

'You're about to become a father. Good! Bring her over tomorrow or so and I will explain everything to her.'

'Oh, so that's it, is it?' A smile lit up Gojen's face. 'But wait, the case is going to be heard on Wednesday and I'll have to go. I will need to take Hasina along.'

'All that travel in this state…'

'Oh, that won't do. The trial is in the sessions court. I just got Modon Kokaiti's letter from the kabiraj. The police should have informed me—wonder why they haven't. Since it's in the sessions court, chances are that the verdict will be pronounced immediately. Once those creatures are in jail, our area will be nice and clean.'

'But wait, in your obstinacy, the girl…'

'No, Aai. She is the prime witness. I will definitely have to take her along. I'll get going. By the way, I thought she was ill and had planned to consult the doctor at the dispensary. But now that you have figured what it is, what do you suggest I do? Should I…?'

'You could consult a doctor. But that can wait for a few days.'

'Okay, then. I'm leaving now. I'll drop in on my way back. By the way, Aai, the vermilion you gave Hasina is almost over. She has asked me to get her some more. Goodbye, Aai.'

As he reached the gate, he heard Aai call from behind, 'When you buy the vermilion, also get a small box to put it in.'

'I will, Aai,' said Gojen, without looking back.

Once at the market, Gojen simply went overboard. He bought saris, blouses, a pair of slippers and various trinkets for Hasina. Then he went to the gambling den and by evening, earned himself a neat packet. Over drinks at the liquor den, he informed the owner that he was going to be a father. And they both drank a 'special' to that.

Suddenly, Gojen noticed that Ramchandra and Dino were watching him from a distance. He had caught them eyeing him at various times during the day, but they had slipped away every time. Now the market was almost deserted, except for the larger traders and the men drinking in the den. What were these two doing here so late? Were they hesitating to come in for a drink because he was there? He was about to move forward and call out to them when they slunk away. Gojen decided to forget all about it. He was slightly tipsy and not at all keen on worrying about deeper issues. He set off for home, a liquor bottle in his bag.

He entered his village and came to the deserted narrow by-lane that led past Moti mistry's house and the wooden bridge over the river. A little further down, he saw a small group of men discussing something in suppressed tones. It was a new-moon night and cloudy too, so visibility was low. As he passed the men, he craned his neck out and asked, 'Who may you all be?'

Seeing that it was Ramchandra's group, he said, 'Oh, it's just you guys. What's this serious conference about? Are you off to save the world? Isn't that you, Ramchandra and Dino? I saw you peeping around at the market today. If you wanted a drink, why did you run away when you saw me there?'

Wordlessly, the group dispersed one by one. Gojen decided that it wasn't worth engaging them in a war of words to lighten his mind. Today was a singularly happy day. He was going to be a father!

Gojen moved on. At one point, he thought Ramchandra and his gang were following him. So be it. Why did he need to know where they were off to as a group? It was just a whim. There was no need to turn around and check. He took a long draught from the bottle in his bag. By the time he reached his grandmother's, he was totally drunk. He told her that he had been in a celebratory mood all day ever since she told him about his impending fatherhood—he had even had a few drinks.

Gojen did not stay long. He told his grandmother about all that he had bought for Hasina, including the vermilion and the box. He also told her he would bring Hasina over tomorrow morning, because after that they would have to go to the district headquarters for the hearing. He left his grandmother's house. Kaila was guarding Hasina and it was getting late. The weather too was getting worse. There were strong winds in addition to the looming dark clouds.

Gojen clutched his large bag of purchases and rushed along, singing and muttering to himself in his intoxicated state. The clouds grew thicker and blacker, the wind, stronger. There was pitch darkness all around and no trace of life. Gojen walked faster. He was breaking into a sweat when the first of the raindrops fell. It'll be nice to get drenched, he thought.

Just then, he heard someone whistling a familiar tune behind him. From the movement of the torchlight beam and the speed of the approaching sound, Gojen figured that whoever it was was coming on a bicycle. Yes, he knew the tune—*Luitor paarore aami...* He squatted by the roadside to relieve himself and let out a burp just as the cycle was passing him. The whistling stopped and the person continued on his way.

Suddenly, Gojen recalled all that the kabiraj had told him in the morning. According to him, Jadob Bora and his gang hated him more for his religion than for his occupation of the land. Khargi mauzadar was not about to let these impure souls breed in his territory. Gojen had become an infidel by marrying a Muslim girl and now an infidel's son was going to be born here in Kuroiguri, on the banks of the Brahmaputra—a Hindu river by virtue of being the putra, the son, of Brahma, the Creator. A Muslim seed was about to sprout here, to the chagrin of the mauzadar, who had masterminded the devious deeds carried out by Jadob Bora and his men.

Gojen began shouting, 'Wait a few more days. The moment my son is born, I will dip him in the Brahmaputra. Let Brahma's son and Abdul Ghani's son embrace each other in the water. I'll wash his mother Hasina's blood in the waters of the Brahmaputra. Let's see if Brahma comes and tells me, "You can't bathe him in these waters; these are the waters of a Hindu river." Let's see how Brahma chooses to punish me—and whether Allah comes to my rescue. Brahma-Allah, Brahma-Allah, Brahma-Allah...' Gojen chanted in rhythm.

The storm broke and the rain poured down to the accompaniment of wind, thunder and lightning. Gojen was drenched through. Pouring the remaining contents of the bottle into his throat, he tossed it away and started singing at the top of his voice.

Two weeks ago, he had returned from the market along the same path. It was a full moon day. The night was bright and the sky, clear. But his mind was cloudy and agitated, his heart heavy. Tonight was a new moon. The darkness had swallowed everything in sight and the storm was tearing at the trees all around. Yet his mind was bright and his heart overflowing with happiness. He was going to be a father! He and Hasina loved each other to distraction and now that love had taken the form of a child in her womb.

Gojen wondered how the miracle had happened. He was a Hindu and Hasina a Muslim. Had his blood changed because of his nikaah? No way—it was a bunch of lies. He was what he was—a human being, just like Hasina. Mansoor bhai and his kin were humans too, but they were weak because they had been uprooted. Yes, they were weak and deprived and far from able to defend their rights. But he and Hasina would change things. There would be one more Gojen in the Kuroiguri area to raise his voice against injustice. All these years, he had done that alone; now he would have a companion. There would be two voices instead of one. Hasina was about to provide him with that companion—sweet Hasina, his darling Hasina...

He held the bag with gifts for her—saris, blouses, slippers, trinkets and cosmetics—closer to his chest. It was drenched like the rest of him. The box of vermilion, wrapped in a handkerchief, was in his pyjama pocket and he tried to shield it with his other hand. Holding tight to all that he carried, he felt goaded into running. As he ran, he screamed—Hasina, Hasina....

In one of the flashes of lightning, Gojen saw that he was at the entrance to the temple of the goddess. There it was—the huge banyan tree, under which was more darkness. Rays from a lamp or two filtered through the peeling plaster of the reed walls of Bapudeu's house. As he stood at the temple gate, Gojen remembered the sacrificial machete. Then the thought of Joba flashed through his mind.

He was looking towards the temple and walking past its entrance when he was suddenly blinded by the beams of several torch-lights being shone upon him. Another flash of lightning lit up the red reflector above the mud-guard of a cycle resting against the banyan tree. As he made to turn towards the temple once again, he felt something like an iron rod landing heavily on his head. A clap of thunder followed. 'Help! I'm dying!' he shouted as he ran towards the temple grounds, collapsing at the entrance. 'Bapudeu!' he screamed as he writhed.

Far away, he thought he saw Bapudeu open a door and step out to the veranda, a lamp in his hand. Then he felt two or three axes hacking at him. He opened his mouth to scream once again, but his voice failed him. He gurgled and his hand fell away from the bag he had filled with gifts for his wife. He had fallen facing the temple and his last memory was of the wind blowing out the lamp in Bapudeu's hand. And then all was darkness.

23

Aai had been busy since morning. She bustled around, instructing Bhodoram and Chaila about various chores. First thing in the morning, she made narikolor laru—candied coconut balls—rice pudding and Gojen's favourite pithas. Hasina loved them too. They could have these with their tea as soon as they arrived, though the rice pudding could wait until evening. Before long, lunch was also ready—joha rice, dal, ash-gourd cooked with lots of pepper, some fish from Pandit's pond and elephant apple from the garden. Hasina would relish its sour taste, especially at this time, though she couldn't be given bamboo shoots even if she craved them. The fish could be cooked with sesame paste—a little fancy cooking might whet her appetite. They could sit—and eat—in the living room, and it was duly cleaned and readied to receive them.

In the midst of all the preparations, Aai kept stepping out to look at the street. Why were they late? He had said they would come as early in the morning as possible—it was almost noon now!

Aai finished all her cooking and other chores and came to stand at the gate. The sun rose higher and higher and reached its peak. Her knees ached. What was all this? Why weren't they here yet? Suddenly, she saw Kaila walking towards the house.

'What, eh, Kaila? How come you are here? Aren't those two coming? Is all well with her?'

'Aai, Gojen hasn't come home since yesterday.'

'What? He dropped by and saw me last evening! Maybe he spent the night somewhere on the way because of the thunderstorm.'

'But in that case he should have come home in the morning, right?'

'That's right.'

Aai had a lengthy discussion with Kaila and Bhodoram and decided that Kaila and his family should take care of Hasina. She could sleep at their house in the night. They would tell her that Gojen had to suddenly leave for the headquarters because of the lawsuit so that she was not unduly worried. She had to be kept tension-free in her present state. Aai packed the snacks and sent them to Hasina.

•

Six days later. Aai sent Bhodoram out on a few errands, the chief being to check if Sarbai Pandit had received any news of Gojen. He had been missing these last six days. Each day, Kaila brought the news that Gojen had not showed up at home either, and that his wife was worried.

Aai too heard various bits of gossip from various sources. But her grandson was no ordinary man. Every morning, he hewed firewood and hoed the earth until the muscles in his arms and chest were a sight to behold. No one could touch him—of that she was sure. Anyway, Sarbai Pandit was checking out all avenues. He had also written to Modon. So Bhodoram should go find out if he had heard from any of his sources, and pick up a few digestive pills from Dharmadeu kabiraj on his way back.

Bhodoram returned with the news that the Pandit had no information yet. The police had also been informed. But unless they were given definite clues, they were not about to proceed in their investigation.

However, Bhodoram had picked up some news at the kabiraj's clinic. The first was that Jadob Bora and his men had won the case. They had enlisted the help of a reputed barrister from Guwahati who dismissed the case within moments of its being presented. He apparently said that nobody could be proved guilty on suspicion alone, in the absence of an eyewitness. So they had gone scot-free. Also, how could anyone prove that the gun mentioned in the report was Khargi mauzadar's? Another piece of information was that as of yesterday, Bora's goons were fencing the Kuroiguri fields to stake their rights.

But the most shocking news was that a sack with a man's body had been caught in a fisherman's net and the fishing baron had deposited it at the district police station. There was barely anything left of the body, except for a small box tied in a red-stained handkerchief in the pocket of its torn pyjamas.

'What did you say?' screamed Aai, gripping her head with both her hands as she collapsed against the wall. She was unable to speak and Bhodoram saw that she was staring unblinkingly at him, a glazed look in her eyes.

The following morning, at daybreak, Aai boarded a bullock cart for Kuroiguri. About two hours later, she got off a little away from Gojen's courtyard, stepping in just as Hasina emerged from her bath. At that particular moment, she sat at the veranda holding a mirror in front of her. With her finger, she scraped out the remaining vermilion from a glass bowl, drew a dot on her forehead and wiped the rest on her parting. Then, hearing a sound in the courtyard, she turned around and saw her grandmother-in-law.

'Oh, Aai!' exclaimed Hasina. She put down her mirror and rushed forward to touch the old lady's feet. Aai gave her a warm hug and looked deep into her eyes. Then, without a trace of hesitation, she affectionately kissed her on both her cheeks. Hasina was not wearing a blouse. Aai could feel the gentle pressure of her slightly swollen breasts as she embraced her, and was loath to let her go.

'When is your grandson coming, Aai?' asked Hasina.

Aai was speechless. Her lips trembled as a sharp pain seared her heart. She stared at Hasina's full body and stretched a wizened, trembling hand towards her slightly taut belly. Her hands trembled even more when her warm fingers touched the freshly bathed, cold skin. She looked into the young woman's face again. She saw that the gold earrings she had given her were sparkling on her lobes— the same earrings she had worn as a young bride.

Her eyes then moved to the dot on Hasina's forehead—the last of the vermilion seemed to glow on her forehead, a Muslim girl's forehead. Aai had put the vermilion dot when she had first blessed her. It was a symbol of her blessing. What should she do now? Would her blessing continue to glow bright and red? Aai couldn't get herself to think straight. She simply embraced Hasina and pressed her trembling lips to her forehead.

EPILOGUE

What could have become of Hasina after that? Let's not go into those details and move a few years ahead.

It was about twenty-four years since Gojen had died and meticulously planned communal riots had broken out in certain pockets of the district. One community's violence in one place triggered violent repercussions from another community in another. Vengeful emotions were sparked; arson and bloodshed followed. The administration let loose its remedial measures—Section 144, curfews, security forces, the army, peace corps, relief camps, food supplies and social service groups were pressed into service on a war footing.

One evening, while all this was going on, Justice Modon Sharma wound up his duties in the courtroom of the Guwahati High Court and was relaxing in his chamber over a cup of tea and the English newspaper just arrived from Kolkata. He was greying slightly at the temples, but Justice Modon Sharma was still a handsome man. If at all, the signs of ageing only added to his personality. From his modest beginnings as a small-time lawyer in his hometown, the one-time freedom fighter was now a senior district judge who lived happily with his wife Joba and their three grown-up children.

'Namaskar,' said Advocate Dutta as he entered the judge's chamber.

'Namaskar. Any issues?' asked Sharma, raising his eyes from his newspaper.

'There was this bail petition.'

'Is it complicated?'

'It's a case of IPC 352 and 506.'

'What's it all about?'

'It has to do with last week's riots. A team of junior doctors from the medical college had gone to assist with a relief camp in one of the riot-affected areas when they started fighting amongst themselves—a group clash.'

'Why?'

'It started with a difference of opinion regarding assistance to a camp of a particular community. Most of them decided to return without visiting it, saying it had been too long already, but three or four of them opposed the suggestion. Then the clashes started. A group of local youths sided with the majority. There was one rebellious doctor among the juniors, and he single-handedly challenged the rest. The clashes turned physical and quite a few people were injured. The security police from the camp intervened and brought the situation under control, although the atmosphere remained tense.

Anyway, they left the injured, protesting youth behind and came back in their vehicle. On the way, they filed an FIR that the youth had used his communal feelings to instigate the locals, and that he had assaulted them when they tried to stop him. The police immediately arrested him—he had hurt his head and was only semi-conscious when they arrived. The local government doctor advised that he should be brought to Guwahati, which is why the case has been transferred here.

This is the case history as I have gathered from the police report and the statements of two of the youth's companions. There is bound to be a later case to deal with the allegations about communal conspiracy and incitement. But there has been a plea for bailing him out now. The young man's mother has arrived in town with a letter from an advocate friend of mine.'

Dutta finished his monologue and placed the file before Justice Sharma.

'See if you can settle this case out of court, Dutta. Whatever it is, the complainants are his contemporaries. Besides, you say he is a junior doctor, right? He will get suspended.'

'Yes, those implications are there.'

'Are the formalities over?' asked Sharma as he opened the file.

'Yes Sir.'

Modon Sharma glanced cursorily through the file before signing in the assigned spot. Then, suddenly, he became animated. Almost shouting in his excitement, he asked, 'Dutta, where did you say the boy was now?'

'In police custody, at the medical college hospital.'

In a rush, Justice Sharma signed the file, held it out to Dutta and hastily rose from his seat. 'I would like to see this young man right now. Come with me, Dutta, take me to him.'

◆

Modon filled Dutta in on the youth's background on the drive to the hospital.

The young man, Abdul Rahim Keunt, was the son of Abdul Ghani aka Gojen Keunt. The father had been brutally murdered even before he was born in his great-grandmother's outhouse. Later, the doctor Nanda Sharma had trained his mother Hasina to be a midwife and given her a job at the dispensary. When the doctor was transferred to the district headquarters, he had got Hasina and her two-year-old son to move with him and got her a nurse's job at the hospital. He ensured that she was allotted staff quarters. The boy was extremely sharp and excelled in his studies. In fact, it was again the doctor who had attached the surname Keunt to the boy's Muslim name.

Modon had kept in touch with Hasina and her son for quite some time. But after accepting the judge's post, he had been transferred many times in the last twelve years, and had lost track of them. Today, all of a sudden, he saw the names of the young man and his parents in a file and realized it had to be the same boy. Gojen's son—the same blood running in his veins...

◆

Modon arrived at the ward with Dutta and, standing in the doorway, looked around. At the far end, a security staffer became alert and that caught his eye. Beside the security man, on the bed he saw a hefty young man with a bandage around his head, a drip in his arm and a lady sitting on a stool by his side. The lady raised her head to look towards the doorway and jumped to her feet.

'Hasina!' Modon's voice trembled with emotion. Through the rows of hospital beds, he rushed towards Hasina and Rahim Keunt, followed by a startled Dutta.

◆

Life had come full circle. Hasina had become a nurse; and she had trained her son Rahim to become a doctor. In his voice and in his ideals, she had unfailingly discerned an innate courage—and the strength—to stand up to injustice of any sort, all by himself if need be. And she knew that Gojen may be no more, but they had not succeeded in eliminating him.

He wasn't dead—he had become Rahim Keunt.

◆

9 788129 123954